# WE WHO REMAIN

by

Darryl M. Bloodworth

# Copyright

# Dedication

To the lawyers and staff at Dean Mead:  You have inspired me.

# Chapter 1

David Jordan pulled into the parking lot behind the Jordan & McKenzie's law offices earlier than usual for a Monday morning. He had a conference call scheduled with his opposing counsel in a routine breach of contract case and needed the extra twenty minutes to properly prepare.

He felt upbeat, despite having to navigate a treacherous commute on I-4—what with never ending construction coupled with rush hour traffic—and mused on his good fortunes of late as he walked briskly into his Orlando law office.

His good spirits, however, weren't solely based on surviving I-4 once again. He had won a jury verdict of $7.8 million for a fire suppression company in a breach of contract case, followed three weeks later by a defense verdict for a church whose senior pastor had been accused of sexual harassment of the church secretary. And within the last week, David got a $1.5 million settlement for the franchisee of a convenience store company when the franchisor wrongfully took back half of the exclusive territory the franchisee was supposed to have.

The early February weather contributed to his elevated mood. The morning chill at 58 degrees would gradually disappear as the temperature headed toward a perfect 72 under blue sky by early afternoon. The only things resembling clouds were the usual contrails from commercial airliners headed to all points north from south Florida. David snickered. His best friend from law school would be enduring snow and sleet in New York with temperatures forecasted to remain in the low teens.

*Thank God I didn't succumb to the temptation to go to work for a big law firm in New York.* Besides the better weather, he had tried many more cases than his friend in New York and was able to form his own firm much earlier in his career than would have been possible there. *I have much to be thankful for.*

"Hello, Karen," he said and smiled. He rather enjoyed exchanging smiles with the attractive and fit young receptionist whose smile could light up a room. But before she could return his greeting, the phone rang.

"Good Morning, Jordan & McKenzie," Karen announced. "How may I help you?"

Karen's smile quickly turned into a frown, as she moved the telephone away from her ear to distance herself from the loud, demanding voice on the other end. After listening for a moment, Karen asked, "May I tell Mr. Jordan who's calling?" Another short pause, and then, "One moment, please, Mr. Foster."

Karen glanced toward David—who paused in the reception room when Karen reacted so visibly to the caller—and said, "I have a very agitated gentleman on the phone who says it's urgent that he speak to you. His name is Max Foster. He's *really* upset, and he's demanding to meet with you today."

"Tell him I'll be with him in a minute," David said, bounding up the stairs two at a time as he headed for his second story office. His calendar was already full for the day, and he didn't know how he could squeeze in another meeting. But he was not about to turn down a potential new client without at least hearing what the case was about.

He shouldn't keep his new client waiting. However, David took the time to drink in the ambiance of his spacious office and the rich mahogany walls. He sat at his traditional executive desk. Two large client chairs faced him on an antique Persian, hand-knotted rug. A large picture window was above a credenza that matched his desk. He took another few seconds to gaze at what was formerly the back yard of this renovated home, tastefully converted into a parking area for the attorneys, staff and clients. Each time he looked out, he was grateful the construction workers preserved the three large old oak trees that provided an abundant canopy and a good source of food for the squirrels and birds that made their home there. As he picked up the phone, David noticed that the two bird baths in the parking area were full of robins this morning.

David breathed in a sigh of appreciation, then turned his attention toward matters at hand. "David Jordan here. How may I help you, Mr. Foster?"

"You can help me by meeting with me today," Foster snarled, obviously peeved that he had to wait more than 30 seconds to speak to David. "I've just been sued by my deceased wife's adult children, and they've made some outlandish allegations against me. I want to counter sue them for defamation."

"Well, before we talk about a counter suit, why did they sue you?"

"They've alleged I exercised undue influence over my wife and convinced her to prepare a new will and trust shortly before she died. They want me removed as personal representative of the estate, and also removed as trustee of the trust that holds all of her assets.  Mr. Jordan, that would be a disaster, not only for me, but also for my wife's estate and trust.  These kids don't know what they're doing."

David paused briefly before asking, "Give me some idea of the size of the estate we're talking about, Mr. Foster."

"Twenty million, more or less, depending on how some of the assets are valued."

The large number focused David's attention and resolved the issue of whether he would meet with Mr. Foster that day.

"Have you been served with a summons and complaint?"

"Yes, I was served at home by a process server early yesterday evening. It says our response to the complaint is due in twenty days. I immediately called my business attorney who told me I should call you as soon as possible.  He said you were the best attorney in Orlando to handle a contested will. I can't afford to lose this case, Mr. Jordan, for reasons I'll explain to you when we meet.  Can you take my case?"

Intrigued, David responded, "Well, we'll have to run a conflict check, and I can't make a final determination until I have a better understanding of the facts.  But absent a conflict, I don't see why not."

David glanced at his calendar. With a few adjustments, he could squeeze in an appointment with this new client. "I'm busy this morning, and we have our weekly attorney meeting at noon. But I can meet with you at two o'clock here in our offices."

Max agreed, and David inked the appointment in his calendar.

*     *     *

This Monday, like every other Monday, the four lawyers of Jordan & McKenzie met at noon in the firm 's conference room to go over new cases, discuss any new developments in the law possibly affecting their practice, and address any office issues.  David arrived a few minutes early to review his agenda. He always led the meeting, but any of the four lawyers could add items needing discussion.

As he sat, his thoughts wandered back to how the firm was established and had progressed since its formation. To him, the firm was his extended family. He felt a fatherly pride over the reputation they had earned in the legal community as well as in the central Florida business community.

David wondered whether the journey to this point was perhaps part of a larger plan. As if reliving parts of a whole, he thought about the steps that had led him to the decision to become a lawyer, then form his own firm.

As with the other lawyers in the firm, David's roots in Florida ran deep.  He grew up in Deland, a town northeast of Orlando. To his pleasant surprise, he won a full scholarship to Rollins College, a prestigious liberal arts college located in Winter Park, a northern suburb of Orlando well known for its beautiful chain of lakes, brick streets lined with oak trees, and its charming downtown featuring an urban park across the street from quaint stores and restaurants.  Many Rollins students were from wealthy northeastern families in which several generations had decided to forego an Ivy League education for Rollins and the joys of Florida winters in a beautiful setting on the Winter Park chain of lakes.

The students at Rollins were a cultural shock to him. His middle-class upbringing in Deland, like most of his childhood friends, had centered around family, church, school, and sports. Few had travelled far outside of Florida, and none of them had travelled abroad.  His new classmates, on the other hand, had travelled extensively.  Many were international students whose families could easily afford the cost of a private education in the United States.  Some of the American students had graduated from the best prep schools in the country, and all came well prepared for what David quickly learned was a challenging curriculum.  In short, his classmates were a heady mix of people from backgrounds familiar to David only from books and movies, and whose aspirations in life appeared to have no limits—or at least far fewer limits than David had anticipated for himself.

David smiled with the recollections.

Despite initially being intimidated by his classmates, he loved the Rollins environment. He liked how these serious students were interested in learning for its own sake—not merely to prepare for a job, as had been his focus previously.

Perhaps because of their privileged background, his classmates didn't see the challenges they would face in life as limitations on what they could achieve, either personally or professionally. Rather they viewed these obstacles as merely hurdles to be overcome.

He recognized how great wealth does make more things possible in life, but he gradually learned he need not be limited by his lack of advantages compared to his classmates. He would overcome any disadvantage through discipline and hard work.

Recalling this, David straightened with pride.

By the last semester of his senior year he had worked his way up to being ranked second academically in a class of over 400.

As graduation approached, David decided to meet with his Rollins guidance counsellor to help him assess his options following graduation. He remembered the scene as if it were yesterday.

"So, David, given your academic success here at Rollins, I assume you're considering graduate school or law school?"

"I don't know, Mr. McGregor. I've had to take out substantial loans to supplement my scholarship, and I'm not interested in finishing grad school with a mountain of debt. My parents have harped on avoiding borrowing my whole life, and I can't get their voices out of my head when I consider the cost of grad school. Besides, I'm not sure what I would study anyway."

"What about law school?"

"I don't know … I've never thought about being a lawyer, and I can't see devoting three more years of study for a career I'm not sure I want."

"Well, what do you want—or at least think you want?"

"Don't laugh, but what I've been thinking about is something entirely different—something rooted in the stories my father told me."

"What would those stories be?" asked Mr. McGregor, as hints of skepticism passed over his face.

"As you know, my father is the principal of Deland High School. But what you may not know is that right out of college he joined the Air Force and became a fighter pilot. He flew forty-one combat missions in Korea in the F-86 Sabre during the early 1950s. After leaving the Air Force, he got a master's degree in Education and eventually became a high school principal. The interesting thing, though, is that all the stories he told me were about his adventures as a pilot rather than his experiences as a high school principal."

"That's interesting, but what does that have to do with you and your graduate school plans?" Mr. McGregor's face tensed with impatience and even more skepticism.

"I think what I want to do is join the Air Force and become a pilot."

"Why in the world would you want to do that when you have so many good graduate school options available to you?" The expression on McGregor's face had transitioned from skepticism to antipathy.

"Well, there are several reasons. First, according to my father, no other experience in life better prepares one to be self-reliant than being the pilot of an airplane, especially if it's a single seat aircraft. Second, it's exciting. My father often told me that flying — especially in the F-86— was the most exciting thing he had done in his entire life. And, finally, as an Air Force pilot, I would be serving my country in a meaningful way while doing something I think I will enjoy."

"I see. Obviously, you've given this decision considerable thought. Although it's certainly not a choice I would make, if that's what you really want, go for it. Please just assure me you won't totally give up on going to grad school or law school someday."

"No, I haven't given up on the idea; I just don't think I'm ready. Besides, if I join the Air Force now, I'll be eligible for the G.I. Bill after my service—a financial resource should I later decide to attend graduate school or law school."

The meeting with McGregor solidified David's decision and led him to visit an Air Force recruiting office shortly before he graduated from Rollins. After attending Officer Training School at Lackland Air Force

Base, he was assigned to Moody Air Force Base in south Georgia for pilot training. There he quickly fell in love with flying.

The first six months of pilot training were in the Cessna T-37, a small twin engine jet having side-by-side seating for the student and instructor pilot. His first solo in the T-37, after only fifteen hours of flight time, confirmed his father's opinion that nothing prepared you to be self-reliant quite like flying an airplane—especially with no one else in it.

David leaned back in his chair as he recalled the second half of pilot training, turning and twisting as if he still lived in the moment.

How could he ever forget his first flight in the T-38? It was an afterburner climb to 40,000 feet which took only three and a half minutes. He felt like he was going all the way into orbit, and at that moment in his life he felt that he would never do anything more thrilling than fly a high performance aircraft. He had performed so well in the T-38 that he earned a coveted assignment as a T-38 instructor pilot. Following four months of instructor pilot training at Randolph Air Force Base in Texas, he returned to Moody Air Force Base to train student pilots.

David glanced at his wedding ring.

Within two years of returning to Moody, he encountered another turning point in his life. He and his bachelor buddies often went to Tallahassee for weekend dates with women attending Florida State University. He had never seen so many beautiful women on one campus, and all those he'd met seemed to be quite impressed with Air Force pilots—until his best friend and his girlfriend introduced him to Carol Blanchard. Although his friends thought David and Carol would be perfect for each other, Carol was initially unimpressed. She was getting her master's degree in English literature and education, and she was more interested in a man deeply vested in reflective thought and faith, rather than becoming a man of action. His father's theory that becoming a pilot makes one more self-reliant fell flat with Carol.

After four dates, David was discouraged; he was smitten with Carol, but she gave no indication she was seriously interested in him. Finally, an off-chance comment how he'd enjoyed tutoring his younger sister in English, aroused tentative hints of interest from Carol. From that meager beginning, their relationship blossomed; within less than a year they were engaged.

*Priorities do change*, he mused … and his did soon after he and Carol were married. As he told Carol, "Before I met you, I looked forward to the excitement of flying assignments all over the world in the hottest aircraft the Air Force had to offer. Now, those thoughts are being challenged by the appeal of putting down roots and raising a family. The simple life I left behind in Deland no longer seems boring and dull, but rather solid and prudent."

As always, Carol posed the critical question: "What will you do if you get out of the Air Force?"

To that he'd shrugged and said, "I don't know, but I want some of the same challenges and excitement flying has offered."

Perhaps that had been the stimulus needed to recall his discussion with Mr. McGregor. Whereas he wasn't interested in law school then, law school now sounded exciting, as well as solid and prudent. After several months of investigating every conceivable aspect of a legal career, and with Carol's blessing, David reached his decision: he would become a trial lawyer.

Once that decision was made, everything seemed to fall into place.

As soon as his military commitment was over, he separated from the Air Force, entered the University of Florida Law School and went straight through without taking off a single semester.  By attending both summer semesters he was able to graduate in less than two and a half years.  His sterling performance in law school, including being the managing editor of the law review, led to his being recruited by Smith & Bridges, a national law firm having fifty lawyers in their Orlando office and over 2,000 lawyers throughout the country.

Over the next eight years David worked on some of the most newsworthy cases in Florida.  He was the second-chair attorney on a highly contentious election recall case involving the mayor of Tampa.  He also was the lead attorney on several of the state's largest will contests involving several of Florida's richest families.  He gained a reputation as one of Florida's finest young trial lawyers, but as appreciative as he was of the work the big national firm brought him, he gradually came to realize his ultimate goal was to have his own firm — a boutique law firm of four to eight lawyers who would handle a variety of civil cases.

As David scoped the conference room once more, his gaze landed on the group photo of the firm's attorneys on the wall. He was proud of every one of them.  Each had been instrumental in developing the law firm of Jordan & McKenzie—especially Jessica McKenzie.  She had been one of the people who helped convince David to abandon the big law firm and form his own firm.

Jesse, as she was called, was David's first cousin, once removed— her grandfather and David's mother were brother and sister.  Jesse had grown up in Winter Park in an upper middle class family.  Valedictorian of her senior class, she achieved all that any one woman could possibly accomplish at Florida State University—homecoming queen, president of her sorority, captain of the women's tennis team, and an honors graduate with a double major in business and economics.  After college, she obtained a law degree and an MBA with an emphasis on business management at Emory University in Atlanta.

David saw himself more like an older brother to Jesse than a distant cousin. Naturally, when she approached graduation at Emory, he strongly encouraged her to apply to Smith & Bridges.  His sales pitch:  she would have the opportunity to practice at one of the largest and finest law firms, not only in Florida, but in the United States. And they would be able to work together.  David's arguments must have been convincing.  Despite an offer of an even bigger starting salary from a large Atlanta firm, she chose Smith & Bridges' Orlando office.

From the beginning, Jesse and David were a team, although occasionally each of them worked with other lawyers in the firm. David recalled how Jesse often said, "I prefer working with you more than any of the other lawyers, and not just because we're family. We aren't sidetracked by the persistent back-biting and petty jealousies we see hindering some of the other teams."

Additionally, Jesse was stunningly beautiful. With long blond hair and a body toned from hard daily workouts, the attention she received from the male lawyers in the firm was not always professional.  This was not a new problem for Jesse; she had been hit on by fellow students in college and in law school.  Back then, she had viewed their actions as mere annoyances. "They have no power over me," she'd say. "The advances will stop once I'm a lawyer."

But the behavior didn't stop as she'd hoped.

Some of the partners she had to work with, including those who evaluated her performance, were the most blatant—asking her out for drinks and endless flirting. Jesse had been savvy enough to politely let them know she was interested only in a professional relationship. Even so, it rankled her that she had to deal with these issues while handling stressful cases which required all of her energy and attention.

Jesse's disappointment had not been limited to warding off unwanted advances. She grew weary of the fierce competition among associates. The partnership track for associates took eight years, and the firm would only make one of every four associates a partner after eight years of long hours and frequent weekend work. Those who didn't make partner were usually given three to six months to find a job elsewhere. Associates were expected to log at least 2,000 billable hours each year, and there was intense competition to work with the busiest partners on the most high profile cases in order to increase their chances of becoming a partner.

Of course, Jesse didn't mind competition or hard work; she had thrived on both throughout college and law school. At Smith & Bridges, however, the excessive competition proved to be counterproductive, violating many management principles she had learned in her MBA studies.

Despite these problems, Jesse loved the complex cases she worked on. Her writing skills were superb, and all the litigation partners wanted her to draft the briefs for their appeals. Then they'd make minor changes … without crediting her contribution … and impress their clients with the high quality of their written product.

But Jesse's biggest strength was with juries.  She understood jurors typically are less than excited about being selected to sit on a jury for several days to a week or more.  However, when she was introduced as counsel, with her movie-star beauty and her down-to-earth personality, the jurors were suddenly delighted to be there—even the women.  Within three years of arriving at the firm, Jesse was usually asked to conduct *voir dire*.  Most experienced lawyers believe the jury selection process to be a critical part of any trial, and with Jesse's ability to connect with the jurors before the first piece of evidence is presented, Smith & Bridges' clients had an advantage that few other firms could match.  Allowing a young associate to conduct *voir dire* or cross- examine important witnesses was highly unusual at Smith & Bridges, but Jesse was not the average associate.

David recalled the day he treated Jesse to a celebratory lunch on the fifth anniversary of her employment at Smith & Bridges. She had just completed a six-day jury trial assisting one of the senior partners who was notoriously difficult to deal with. She had developed the winning legal theory, found the case law to support their theory, and uncovered the key facts during depositions, turning the case in their favor. It was a significant victory for the firm, as well as for her personally. Yet, she wasn't in much of a celebratory mood.

David was surprised she was in low spirits. "You know, Jesse, victories like this don't come along every day.  Savor the win and celebrate."

"Yeah, I know.  The client's pleased … and I'm proud of the work we did … but does a victory have to be so painful?  Working on this case with James Jacobs proved to be a miserable experience.  I can't imagine what I would feel like if we had lost the case."

Jesse told David she'd been relieved to have someone to talk to about the work environment at Smith & Bridges and how he was the only person she felt comfortable confiding in. "I can be sure what I say to you will remain confidential."

"Well, you won't have to work with Jacobs much longer," David said. "He plans to retire next year."

"I know … but, candidly, Jacobs isn't the only difficult partner to work with.  Most of the other litigation partners are just as miserable to work with, especially when they're stressed.  The thought of going to trial or handling an appeal with most of them over the next thirty years or so is a little depressing."

"I know you've been unhappy with some of the partners you have to work with, Jesse.  Is the problem bigger than just this one case?"

David's question opened the door for Jesse to bring out her entire list of grievances:  excessive competition rather than collaboration, more emphasis on money collected than quality of work, the paucity of women in senior management roles, lack of emphasis on community involvement, and the unprofessional treatment she endured from male lawyers in the firm.

"I didn't know things were quite so dire for you, Jesse, but I understand your concerns."  David hesitated, debating with himself whether to ask the question, then asked, "Have you ever given any thought to practicing in a boutique litigation firm?"

"Not really.  I mean, the idea sounds wonderful, but I don't believe I can get the same quality of cases I have at Smith & Bridges at a two or three lawyer office in Orlando."  She paused, suddenly realizing what he was suggesting.  "David, are you thinking about joining a boutique firm?  God knows, if you leave the firm, I don't know how long I would stay at Smith & Bridges."

He hesitated once more before responding.  He couldn't remember a day for the past several months he had not thought about forming his own firm.  Hearing Jesse identify some of the same issues he struggled with finally pushed David over the barrier in his mind that had allowed him to dream about forming his own firm but had prevented him from doing anything about it.

He nodded. "In fact, I have been thinking about it,"

Over the next hour David outlined his vision of the firm he wanted to form with her. They would start out with just the two of them, and perhaps add a young associate in a few years.  They would charge less than the big firms like Smith & Bridges but offer the same high quality of work of larger firms.  He explained how technology now allowed smaller firms to compete on a more equal basis with larger firms. As a new firm with lower overhead, they would soon be able to earn close to what the big firms pay without the associated issues they faced at Smith & Bridges.  Additionally, they would have the flexibility to take on less lucrative cases that involved important community issues.

"To summarize, Jesse, I want a firm that feels like family."

Jesse's broad smile let David know she was sold. In fact, she seemed more convinced than he that the risks of starting their own firm were worth taking.  Realizing they were on the same page; they then identified a list of issues they would investigate before making a final decision to take the plunge.

Over the next three months they came up with a business plan, identified current clients who would probably want to retain them, and found potential office space to rent—available in ninety days. David was amazed how valuable Jesse's MBA education had been during the planning process. They decided she would be the firm's chief financial partner, and David would be the managing partner and have the primary responsibility of getting new clients for the firm.

At the end of their ninety-day feasibility study, they were in agreement to form their new firm. On June 1, exactly six months after their initial discussion, Jordan & McKenzie opened their doors. His doubts were quickly put to rest when all of David's current clients and half of Jesse's, chose to retain their services. Amazing, since Jesse had only been practicing law a little over five years.

David thought back on the whirlwind of those first two years. Initially, the firm consisted of just the two of them, one secretary, a receptionist/backup secretary and an office manager/paralegal. The administrative duties of creating new office policies and procedures while simultaneously handling all of their cases kept David and Jesse working six days most weeks. At times they would even go to the office on Sunday night just to prepare for the breakneck pace of the coming week. Word of their successes quickly spread, and new clients wanted to use Orlando's hottest young firm to represent them in their cases likely to go to trial. Accordingly, their workload quickly mounted.

After little over a year, they both realized a plan was needed to prevent the firm from collapsing from its own success. David and Jesse would need to create the necessary infrastructure to keep their time available primarily for client work and business development. Two weeks later, they hired an experienced office manager, Sarah Garcia, who could also ably function as the HR Director and get the office efficiently staffed.  In short order, Sarah replaced the current receptionist with Karen Overton, found two experienced secretaries to work for David and Jesse, and convinced David to hire the paralegal he had worked with at Smith & Bridges — Rodrigo Alvarez. This decision pleased David since he and Rodrigo shared a passion for detective mysteries.

David would not have traded those formative years for anything. As if pieces of a puzzle coming together, their organization took shape as demand increased. With the addition of Rodrigo, David and Jesse felt they now had the infrastructure and personnel to take on additional work.  For several months, they had been forced to turn down some appealing new cases because they were unable to handle those cases with the high quality of work the cases deserved. Sure, they could take on new clients if they cut corners. But this was not the way he and Jesse wanted to practice law.  Having learned the importance of thoroughness and preparation at Smith & Bridges, they refused to compromise quality, even if their commitment meant taking on fewer cases and making less money.

Despite the addition of these excellent new people, David and Jesse foresaw the need to bring on a new associate to handle most of the legal research and primary writing duties. While debating whether or not to hire such a team member, a professor at the University of Florida Law School wrote David to inquire whether he would be interested in hiring an outstanding law student as a summer associate.

Steve Cutler was a twenty-seven-year-old Jewish man who had immersed himself in liberal politics while an undergraduate at the University of Miami. His work in both campus politics and congressional campaigns, however, resulted in mediocre grades for someone so gifted intellectually.  After graduating, he worked one year with an NGO in Israel.

When Steve decided to become a lawyer, he aced the Law School Admission Test and gained entry to the University of Florida Law School. The young man later confessed how, for the first time in his life, he devoted all of his energies and attention to his studies. The hard work resulted in his being ranked third in his class of 450 at the end of his freshman year.

David and Jesse welcomed the opportunity to evaluate Steve over the course of the summer. They knew they needed an associate, and they knew Steve had outstanding grades in law school. But they weren't just hiring a new associate—they were hiring someone with whom they would share the rest of their working lives. They determined to only hire someone who was intelligent, highly ethical, and would fit into the family culture they were building at Jordan & McKenzie.

As David considered the qualities they were seeking in a new associate, he thought about his Air Force experiences. What he missed most about those days was the relationships he had with the other pilots in his squadron. They were like brothers and sisters, and he realized he missed those relationships even more than the flying. This was the missing ingredient during his years with Smith & Bridges, and David was determined to have this kind of family environment at Jordan & McKenzie.

Jesse was equally determined. Though she didn't have military experience, she often compared the culture they were developing to the one-for-all team atmosphere she had with the FSU women's tennis team. "I'll approve hiring Steve permanently only if he fits in with the firm culture we want to develop," she'd said.

After only three weeks into Steve's clerkship, David and Jesse chuckled over any concerns they held previously. Steve fit in better than they had hoped, challenging their thinking and helping to improve their work product.  He saw things differently; his perspective was not antagonistic to theirs, but subtly different.  They didn't always agree with Steve's viewpoint, but he helped them analyze the critical legal issues they faced, offering innovative suggestions about how to present their arguments in the best light.

By the end of the summer, they viewed Steve as essential and asked him to join their small firm following his graduation, offering a salary and benefits comparable to what big firms paid. After hearing the terms, he accepted immediately.

*And you fulfilled your promise admirably, Steve.*

David and Jesse were amazed at how quickly Steve matured as a lawyer.  His research, writing, and analytical skills were superb, and they soon came to trust his judgment.  With his addition, the firm's ability to handle more cases expanded.

When Steve was hired, David and Jesse thought they would have four years before hiring an additional attorney.  Yet only two years later, they needed another associate.  This time, it was Jesse who found the new lawyer.

One of the organizations to which Jesse devoted significant time was the Orange County Bar Association Legal Aid Society. Orlando Lawyers were proud of the fact their bar association had been the first in the country to require its members to handle legal aid cases as a condition of membership.  That requirement of membership arose in the late 1960s when the Orange County Bar decided that it would be the primary provider of legal services to the poor in Orange County rather than federally funded legal assistance programs.  Jesse found it ironic that it was the very conservative leaders of the Orange County Bar at the time who had led the charge for legal aid for the poor, resulting in a legal aid society that had repeatedly won national awards from the American Bar Association for outstanding legal assistance to the poor. Jesse considered the legal aid society one of her two most important community based commitments, and she was elected to serve on the Legal Aid Society board of directors shortly after Jordan & McKenzie was formed.

David smiled as he recalled how the Legal Aid Society brought Maggie and Jesse together.

She had met Maggie Price while handling one of her legal aid cases.  Maggie was a senior at the Florida A & M University (FAMU) Law School, which opened in Orlando in 2002.  A predominantly black public university located in Tallahassee, FAMU had a law school in Tallahassee from 1951 until 1968. But in one of the worst chapters of higher education in Florida—not to mention legislative malfeasance—the Florida legislature voted to close FAMU's law school. All of its funding and assets, including the entire law library, were eventually transferred to the newly created Florida State University Law School, opened in 1966.

This historical injustice was not corrected until the Florida legislature finally voted in 2000 to re-establish a law school at FAMU, with the new law school to be located in Orlando. The campus opened its doors in 2002. By the time Maggie entered FAMU in 2011, the school was located in its modern new building close to the U.S. District Court for the Middle District of Florida, in downtown Orlando.

Maggie was a twenty-five-year-old black woman who had grown up on the west side of Orlando and had graduated from Jones High School, a predominantly black high school best known for its outstanding band.  The work ethic passed on to Maggie by her single mother clearly showed in Maggie's grades.  Valedictorian of her class, she earned a state-sponsored Bright Futures scholarship to attend the University of Florida, graduating with high honors and majoring in English literature.

When law school beckoned, Maggie realized she wouldn't be able to acquire enough scholarship money to cover all of her law school expenses.  Her choices were to take out a loan or to work part time while also being a full time law student.  The latter choice, she knew, would be grueling, but she chose not to take on a boatload of debt to get through law school.  As Maggie later told David and Jesse, "My mamma didn't make all of her sacrifices for me only to see me bogged down in debt for the rest of my life."  She quickly found a job working twenty hours per week during her first year of law school.  In the second and third years of law school, she worked part time as a research assistant for two different law professors.  In addition to those challenges, she was on the Moot Court team.  During her last year of law school, she handled cases through the Legal Aid Society, where she met Jesse.

Jesse and Maggie were assigned to defend a single mother who had been evicted from her apartment, along with her two-year-old son. When she complained about the air conditioning malfunctioning, a refrigerator that only worked intermittently, and roach infestation, the landlord took what he thought would be an easier, and cheaper, solution.  He filed suit to evict the woman and her son.  This turned out to be the worst possible decision.

At Maggie's suggestion, she and Jesse filed a class action counterclaim with the single mother as the class representative.  Suddenly, the landlord's lawsuit against a single mother over $5,000 of needed repairs had turned into defending a lawsuit by fifty-five residents over hundreds of thousands of dollars of needed repairs.  When Maggie served requests for production of documents asking for all complaints by residents and all the landlord's maintenance records regarding those complaints, the landlord saw the writing on the wall.  He promptly found a qualified buyer willing to invest the necessary funds to bring the apartment complex up to code.

This was a total victory for Jesse and Maggie's client, as well as the other residents of the apartment complex.  Plus, they now had a landlord who was responsive to their maintenance requests.

Jesse could not have been more impressed with Maggie's performance.  She was now on Jesse's radar as a potential associate for Jordan & McKenzie, and David was curious to meet her.  When she came to their office for her interview, however, she had an announcement of her own.  She had been offered a two-year clerkship with U.S. District Judge Amy Johnson and had decided the offer was just too good to pass up.  Maggie told David and Jesse she decided to go ahead with the interview with them because she was already looking forward to the day her judicial clerkship would end, and she wanted to know more about the firm.

Over the next two hours they learned even more about Maggie's background.  All of her achievements were laid out on her resume, but only when they prodded her with the right questions did they learn she had accomplished all these things while working long hours at outside jobs in addition to her academic load.  David and Jesse had both performed well in law school, but they had the luxury of devoting their entire attention to their course work.  Maggie was in the top ten percent of her class while always working at least twenty hours per week.

When the interview was over, David confided to Jesse, "I couldn't be more impressed if she had graduated first in her law school class at Harvard."

They made no job offer to Maggie then because that would prevent them from appearing before Judge Johnson while Maggie worked for her. But they agreed to talk further when Maggie's clerkship was over.

Fortunately for Jordan & McKenzie, Maggie's clerkship ended about the time they were desperate for a second associate. David and Jesse agreed; there was no need to even consider another candidate. They contacted Maggie for another interview, made a very competitive offer, and she accepted on the spot.

Over the next two years, she exceeded even David and Jesse's high expectations. Her research was thorough; her writing, while not quite as good as Steve's, was still excellent. But her greatest strength was in the discovery phase of litigation, especially electronic discovery. Modern lawsuits often turn on information found in documents stored electronically, such as e-mails, texts or memos. Large corporations frequently respond to a request for production of documents in a lawsuit by dumping hundreds of thousands, if not millions, of pages of electronic documents on the opposing side. Unless the lawyer who reviews the documents is both adept and efficient at finding the nuggets of helpful information buried in a forest of obfuscating data, the cost to the client of pursuing or defending the case may lead to a demoralizing but economically necessary settlement.

More than once, Maggie offered a silent prayer of thanks for the electronic discovery course she took in law school. With her basic background in electronic discovery, her instincts quickly enabled her to become a formidable weapon Jordan & McKenzie was able to use effectively in lawsuits against much larger firms.

David warmed with the pleasant memories.  Yes, indeed; Jordan & McKenzie was a firm of which he was justifiably proud.

*      *      *

David began the meeting by covering routine issues such as revising office procedures, finding a new coffee vendor, and a seemingly endless discussion about new software and computers.  Finally, David directed the discussion toward their current cases.

"Jesse, bring us up to date on the status of the Faulk case," David said.

David did a quick mental review of what he knew thus far.  James Faulk was an orthopedic surgeon who had joined a well-established practice begun by doctors Dawn Edwards and William Simpson called Orange Orthopedic Surgeons.  The word "Orange" was included in the name because they were located in Orange County, which includes Orlando, Winter Park, Maitland, and other municipalities.  After five years, they hired Dr. Faulk, promising to make him a full partner within two years at a buy-in price of $100,000.  They also had Dr. Faulk sign a non-competition agreement in which he agreed if he should leave the practice, he would not compete with Orange Orthopedic Surgeons within an area of thirty miles of their office in south Orlando for a period of two years. In addition, he would agree not to solicit any of their patients.  Doctors Edwards and Simpson had no such non-compete for themselves but insisted Dr. Faulk sign one.

When Orange Orthopedic Surgeons had not made him a partner after three years, Dr. Faulk left the practice and opened his own office in

25

Sanford, Florida, in Seminole County, immediately to the north of Orange County. On the day he opened his new practice, he was sued by Orange Orthopedic Surgeons for violation of the non-compete agreement. Orange Orthopedic Surgeons sought damages and also an injunction prohibiting Dr. Faulk from practicing orthopedic surgery within thirty miles of the Orange Orthopedic office for two years, as was agreed upon in his employment contract. He hired Jordan & McKenzie to represent him, with Jesse as the lead lawyer on the case, assisted by Steve.

"Our answer to the complaint is due this Friday," Jesse said. "We anticipate plaintiff's counsel will file a motion for an injunction prohibiting Dr. Faulk from practicing medicine within thirty miles as soon as we file our answer."

"What defenses do we have?" David asked.

"We have several," Jesse responded. "Here's our plan. To enforce a non-compete agreement, a plaintiff has to prove it has a legitimate business interest and the non-compete agreement is reasonably necessary to protect that legitimate business interest. We hope to show the medical market in Sanford for orthopedic surgery is an entirely different market than the south Orlando market. Dr. Faulk's office is 28.9 miles from Orange Orthopedic Surgeons' office, and we think this is too far to be part of a single market. We'll ask the court to find that I'm the radius of the non-compete area shouldn't exceed ten miles. Of course, we need to find an expert witness who will back up our arguments about the two separate markets.

"We also intend to file a counterclaim for breach of the promise to make Dr. Faulk a partner within two years and argue the plaintiff's first breach of contract voids the non-compete agreement altogether."

"Those sound like pretty good defenses," Maggie said. "Am I missing something?"

"Well, the plaintiff will argue a contract is a contract," Jesse replied, "and when the parties agreed on thirty miles for the non-compete area, they meant thirty. Dr. Faulk is scared to death he might lose. He's already invested $250,000 in his new office. If he has to move his office, he will lose much of that investment—not to mention he would then be sued by his landlord for breach of his lease. If this case goes badly, Dr. Faulk could wind up in bankruptcy court."

"I wish Dr. Faulk had conferred with us before choosing his new office location," David said. "What's going on with your Women's Crisis Center project, Jesse?"

David was familiar with the organization. The Women's Crisis Center---WCC as it was called---was a non-profit entity providing a safe sanctuary for battered women and children as well as for women dealing with drug addiction. To his knowledge, few facilities addressed both of these conditions. WCC did because the charity had been repeatedly presented with both sets of issues, sometimes involving the same women. Also, David's wife, Carol, had introduced Jesse to the organization. WCC was near and dear to Carol who was its founder and served as its president. Jesse said she was amazed at how much good WCC had accomplished with only limited resources. Two years previously she had been appointed to the board of directors upon Carol's recommendation. The demand for WCC's services always exceeded their capacity, however. Unless WCC could find new donors and raise at least $3.5 million for a new facility, Jesse wasn't sure how long WCC would be able continue its mission.

"We're trying desperately to find new donors, especially for the new facility." Jesse met David's gaze of concern. "Two foundations have told us if we can raise enough money for a more modern facility that shows we have staying power; we'll get funding from them. We've even received some positive feedback from Orange County Commissioners about possible funding from Orange County if we can get the new building. So, everything rides on getting the new building. It's a daunting task. Every board member has been asked to personally raise $40,000. But even if every board member raises that amount, there is still a deficit of over $3 million."

Perhaps frustrated by the difficult task ahead, Jesse changed the subject. "Who's the new client you're meeting with this afternoon, David? And what's that about?"

David shrugged. "All I know at this point is that our client has been sued by his deceased wife's two adult children to set aside the will and trust she signed shortly before her death. The children are alleging undue influence by our client. Some of you may have heard of him. His name is Max Foster."

At the mention of Max Foster, Steve let out a groan, quickly followed by, "David, do you know who this guy is?"

When David admitted he didn't, Steve continued, "He's a real estate developer who probably has been sued more than any other real estate developer north of Miami Beach … and that's saying something. Did he also mention to you his deceased wife was his third wife? The first two divorced him, with wife two alleging adultery. I have a good friend at another law firm who has represented Mr. Foster on several matters in the past.  He said Max Foster is the most difficult client he has ever dealt with."

"Thanks for the heads up," said David.  "Now that I know who I'm dealing with, I'll reserve making a final decision on whether to take the case until after I meet with him today.  Remember, though, even difficult or unscrupulous clients are entitled to a good defense. If we take on his case, he deserves to have us represent him zealously."

*I hope I don't come to regret taking on this client.*  With that thought, David directed the discussion to other cases.

# Chapter 2

Max Foster was still in a sour mood that afternoon when he approached the Jordan & McKenzie office on Hillcrest Street, located on the outskirts of Orlando's downtown district. The office was in a former residential area which had been converted to professional and business offices as the heart of downtown Orlando exploded in an orgy of high rise construction. Max's corporate lawyer was in one of the newer downtown office towers. If Jordan & McKenzie were such hotshots, as he'd heard, why weren't they in a similar fancy office in the heart of downtown?

From his view in the car, the Jordan & McKenzie office appeared to be a well-kept Southern Craftsman Restoration house painted a pale yellow. Max guessed the house had been built in the early-to-mid 1930s. The wrap-around porch provided a stately but welcoming exterior, and the lush landscaping gave the property a warmth no high rise could offer. This spoke well of the firm's attention to detail. He followed the directions on the small sign leading clients around the side of the house to the parking in back. After parking by one of the bird baths, he walked along the brick path to the front of the house.

Max's mood improved briefly when he was greeted by the attractive and fit young receptionist.

"Good afternoon, Mr. Foster. I'm Karen Overton. Mr. Jordan is expecting you and will be with you in a few minutes. Let me show you into the conference room."

Max followed the pretty young receptionist to the conference room located on the opposite side of the entrance foyer from her desk and waiting area. Karen offered Max coffee or water, which he declined, and then she returned to her desk. His mood soured again as he realized he would have to wait on his lawyer to show up for this appointment, one of the more important appointments of his life. His entire financial future was threatened by the lawsuit, and he felt the bile rise in his stomach as he thought about the possibility of some judge or jury passing judgment on him.

At last, his new lawyer entered, and offered a handshake. "Good afternoon, Mr. Foster. I'm David Jordan, and this is Maggie Price. Maggie is my associate who will be working with me on your case."

Max was taken aback with both David and Maggie. After what he'd heard about David Jordan, Max expected a big man at least six feet two inches or more, with a commanding presence that could immediately take charge of any room he entered. Instead, Max, who was six feet tall himself, was looking down two or three inches at a boyish-looking lawyer who appeared to be in his mid-30s rather than his late 40s—David's actual age, as Max knew from reviewing David's bio on his firm's website. The thought flashed through Max's mind that if this were a movie, David Jordan was not who would have been chosen from central casting.

Although Max was not sure why Maggie Price was attending the meeting, she looked very much like the woman lawyers he saw so often on television programs these days. Maggie was of average height, even in her three-inch heels, professionally dressed in a charcoal gray suit, a white blouse and red silk scarf. She looked Max straight in the eye as she offered a firm handshake. She was one of the most attractive women he had ever seen, but the combination of a boyish-looking lawyer who would be his lead counsel and a beautiful black woman attorney whom he didn't expect left Max confused and uncharacteristically silent. *Are these the lawyers I want to represent me in this case?*

Max's confusion eased somewhat as David quickly addressed Max's unspoken question. "Based upon what you told me on the phone, this is going to be a complex case requiring us to address many legal and factual issues. Since Maggie will be working closely with me on the case, I thought she should meet you and get the facts of the case directly from you rather than second hand from me."

David's tone told Max the question of whether Maggie would work with him on the case was not open to debate. He quickly decided to accept David's judgment—at least for now. "That's fine," Max stated. "I want you to bring all the people on board you think you need, Mr. Jordan. As I told you, I can't afford to lose this case."

"We understand, Mr. Foster. This is why Maggie's on the team for your case; she increases our chances of winning," David replied firmly.

"We're going to be working closely until the case is resolved, so I would prefer to be on a first name basis. Please call us David and Maggie."

Max paused for slightly longer than he intended, looked at David, then to Maggie, back to David, and then finally said, "That's fine with me. Call me Max."

"Good," David said as they sat down around the conference room table. "Did you bring a copy of the complaint with you?"

*           *           *

Max had brought along a copy of the complaint, and David quickly had two copies made for Maggie and him to review.

"Give us a few moments to look over the complaint; okay, Max?"

"Sure." Max leaned back in his chair; his nervousness still evident as his gaze darted from picture to picture on the walls while he fondled a pen.

David first looked to see who represented the plaintiff. He groaned silently within as he saw the name Larry Montgomery. Montgomery was a capable but extremely aggressive lawyer who was not above skating along the edges of unethical behavior to win a case. He usually handled his cases on a contingency fee basis in which he would keep one-third of any recovery he obtained for his client. This sort of self-interest in his cases seemed to blur the line between what he considered ethical or unethical. Montgomery had been charged with unethical conduct on two separate occasions, as David recalled from unconfirmed rumors. But the Florida Bar grievance committees that reviewed the charges were unable to find enough evidence for probable cause for the Florida Bar to pursue disciplinary proceedings against him. Although never found guilty of an ethical violation, Montgomery's reputation stood as an unprofessional but capable street brawler who would make opposing counsel's job doubly difficult.

David next looked to see which judge was appointed to the case. The Circuit Court for Orange County, Florida was divided into divisions, so David knew the judge appointed would be one of the eight judges in the Circuit Civil division, assigned through a blind draw system. He was relieved to learn the judge for this case was Sally Long.

34

David considered what he knew about Judge Long.  She had been two years ahead of him in law school.  Although he was only distantly acquainted with her then, he had handled several cases in which she was counsel once they were both practicing law in Orlando.  In fact, they had been on the same side in two of those cases.  She was competent, thorough, and had good instincts in identifying the key issues on which a case would turn, especially with a jury.  After practicing law for nearly twelve years, she was appointed to the circuit court bench by the governor six years ago.

As David recalled his cases with Judge Long, he remembered something else about her.  She was as morally straight as any judge he had ever known.  In a case like this one, he realized, evidence that both of Max's previous wives had divorced him—especially with the most recent divorce including allegations of adultery—would not play well with this particular judge.  Even before learning all of the key facts about the case, David realized that convincing Judge Long of Max's credibility would be one of his biggest challenges.  Credibility of the parties is a key issue in most cases, but in an "undue influence" case credibility is paramount.  *On second thought, Judge Long may not be the ideal judge for this case—given Max's history.*

David next turned to the factual allegations of the complaint.  Florida law requires fact-based pleadings, and in colorful prose Montgomery had laid out the allegations against Max in detail.

*　　　　　　*　　　　　　*

The complaint alleged that twice-divorced Max had married Martha Langley eighteen months ago.  Martha was a widow whose only previous husband, Charles Langley, had died suddenly of a heart attack at age fifty-eight, leaving Martha as the sole heir of an estate of over $20 million. Martha's husband had made his fortune in the computer software business, and he had sold his company only ten months before his heart attack. After the sale, he invested the proceeds in relatively safe stocks and bonds through an investment advisor. Martha had no business or investment background, but she had confidence in the advisor her husband had chosen. By following his recommendations, she believed there would be plenty of money for her to live in upper middle-class comfort for the remainder of her life, with sufficient assets remaining for a healthy bequest to each of their two children, now adults, upon her death. Following her husband's death, Martha had her husband's business attorney prepare a simple will leaving everything to the children.

Only a year after becoming a widow, Martha was introduced to Max through a mutual friend who made the introduction at Max's request. He had been divorced by his second wife a year earlier amid claims of adultery and mental cruelty by both parties, as well as the usual allegations of irreconcilable differences. The divorce had come at a critical time for Max because his mixed-use development of apartments, offices and stores known as Gateway Orlando had been stalled because his divorce had drained him of sufficient capital to continue the project. Without an infusion of capital, he could lose his entire investment and possibly face bankruptcy.

Despite his reputation, Martha found Max to be charming and helpful to her. He gained her confidence by pointing out the simple will that Martha's lawyer prepared included no tax planning for her estate, and she had taken no steps to legally protect her assets. Max down-played his financial issues with Gateway Orlando, and he told Martha he was interested in her—not her money. To reassure Martha he was not after her money, Max suggested they sign a prenuptial agreement which would provide that neither of them would be entitled to inherit from the other.  Their assets would be left to whomever they designated in their wills or trusts, and they waived the right to a "spousal share" of 30 percent to which every spouse is entitled under Florida law.  Within only ten months after their introduction, Max and Martha signed a prenuptial agreement and then flew to Las Vegas to be married, without any notice to family or friends.

Once they were married, Max made additional financial recommendations to Martha.  He suggested she place all of her assets, including the family home where Max was living with her, in a revocable trust with Max and Martha being co-trustees.  He told her she would be protected because any significant decision would require the consent of both of them, and Martha would retain the power to remove Max as a trustee at any time.  He also recommended her will state that, upon her death, all of her assets would pour over into the trust, with her children being the primary beneficiaries of the trust.  If he were still alive upon her death, Max would not inherit from Martha.  But he would be the personal representative of her estate and sole trustee of her trust until his death or inability to serve, whereupon a bank having a trust department would become the trustee.  Without seeking advice from any other sources, Martha agreed to Max's suggestions, including the lawyer he recommended to prepare the trust document and the new will.

Once the assets had been transferred into the new revocable trust, Max offered recommendations for how the trust assets should be invested.  Due to stock market reverses during the previous two years, Martha's portfolio of investments had returns of negative 2.7 percent and negative 3.6 percent, respectively.  He pointed out that although stock market returns had exceeded 7.5 percent over the three years prior to the last two years, her returns were unpredictable.  Therefore, she was at risk of a serious market downturn.  She could minimize her risks and obtain a stable return on her investments by lending his company $10 million at a fixed eight percent annual interest rate to complete his Gateway Orlando project.  He would minimize her risks by granting her a first mortgage on two of the smaller parcels in the project which were being reserved for future development. Once the remainder of the property was developed, those two parcels would have a value well in excess of $10 million.  Based on Max's representations and Martha's desire for a stable return on her portfolio, she consented to the loan.

Four months after she made the loan to Max, Martha was diagnosed with metastatic uterine cancer.  Her oncologist immediately put her on a regime of chemotherapy that left her weak, bereft of energy, and mentally confused.  Between bouts of chemotherapy, Martha would regain some of her energy and mental acuity, but with each new treatment her energy and mental acuity declined further.

After three months of chemotherapy, Martha had shown little progress.  Her cancer continued to grow, and she was weak mentally and physically.  With Max's project still in a critical state of development, he suggested to Martha that she amend the trust to make him the sole trustee of the trust while also promising her he would take no action without her consent. Max further suggested that he should receive one-third of the assets of the trust so he could ensure the Gateway Orlando project would be completed.  He verbally promised her that if he received one-third of the assets from the trust, he would include her children in his own estate plan since he had no children of his own. He told her the project would be so profitable that her children would receive more from him than they would as the only two beneficiaries of her current will and trust.

In her weakened state, Martha agreed without even asking any questions or suggesting bad new she should discuss his proposal with her children first. Max then scheduled an appointment with the lawyer he had originally suggested—the one who had prepared the existing will and trust. As soon as Martha was strong enough, Max took her to the lawyer's office to have her execute the amended will and trust.

Two weeks later, Martha died. Only then did her children learn of the amended will and trust. When Max refused the children's demand that he immediately resign as trustee of the trust and personal representative of Martha's estate, the children sued.

Based upon these allegations, the complaint alleged in count one that Martha lacked testamentary capacity when she executed the amended will and trust; therefore, they should be declared null and void. In count two, the complaint alleged that Max had exercised undue influence on Martha to get her to sign the amended will and trust. Finally, the complaint demanded that Max be removed as personal representative of the estate and as trustee of the trust, and additionally Max should be ordered to pay the children's attorney's fees and costs.

*       *       *

As David and Maggie simultaneously finished reading the complaint, they glanced at each other. From Maggie's expression, David assumed she had as many doubts as he did concerning the client whom they would represent in this case. If all of these allegations were true, Max had a long and difficult fight ahead that might not end well for him. But these were only allegations, David reminded himself, and the case would be decided on the facts actually proved, not on allegations.

"The complaint says you recommended the lawyer to prepare the will and trusts. Is this true, Max?" David asked.

Max raised an eyebrow as if surprised by the question. "Yes, at Martha's request."

"Did you also make arrangement for the meetings with the lawyer and take her there?"

"Yes, again at Martha's request. For the last meeting with the lawyer, Martha was too sick to travel there by herself, David. I had to take her. What would you expect me to do?"

"I'll get to that in just a minute. First, though, why didn't you or Martha inform her children about the will and trust amendment to make you a beneficiary, as well as the sole trustee and personal representative?"

"Martha didn't want to. She loved her children, but she had been somewhat estranged from them since we got married. They didn't approve of me, and she didn't want to have a confrontation with them during what she recognized were probably the last days of her life."

Max ping-ponged his gaze between David and Maggie in response to their glances between each other. "Why is this important? Do you really think they can prove I exercised undue influence—or whatever it's called—to take advantage of my wife?"

David leaned forward. "The reason we're asking these questions, Max, is because these are some of the same questions the judge will have to address in determining whether there has been undue influence."

"I've always thought the plaintiff has the burden of proof—at least that's what all my other attorneys have told me. Are you saying I have the burden of proof?"

"No, we're not telling you that, but undue influence cases are different. I thought this issue might come up today, so I've asked Maggie to explain how the burden of proof works in an undue influence case." Though David had dealt with this issue in many cases, and he fully understood how the burden of proof worked, Max acted as though he didn't have confidence in Maggie. David wanted Max to see how capable Maggie was and how David trusted her to explain such a key issue to an important client, which Max clearly viewed himself as being.

David leaned back as Maggie looked Max squarely in the eye and began her explanation. "The burden of proof in undue influence cases is controlled by 'In Re Estate of Carpenter,' a Florida Supreme Court case from 1971. The court held that the proponent of the will—that's you, Max—has the initial burden of proving the formal execution and attestation of the will, after which the burden of proof shifts to the party attempting to prove undue influence."

"That's what I thought," said Max. "So, how is this case any different from any other case regarding the burden of proof?"

"Here's the difference. Because of the difficulty of obtaining direct proof in cases where undue influence is alleged, Florida, like most states, permits the plaintiff to satisfy the burden of proof initially by submitting sufficient facts to raise a *presumption* of undue influence. If the plaintiff can prove both that a confidential relationship existed between the deceased and the defendant and the defendant actively procured the will or trust, then a presumption of undue influence arises. Fortunately, however, this presumption doesn't arise where the parties involved are husband and wife."

Max shrugged his shoulders and raised his hands as if puzzled before responding.

"Well, if no presumption of undue influence arises because Martha and I were married, what difference does it make whether I actively procured the will or trust?"

"Here's why," Maggie continued. "The factors a court must examine to determine whether a presumption of undue influence arises are the same factors a judge must consider when deciding whether undue influence, in fact, occurred."

Max's puzzled expression revealed he still wasn't sure why this was important. He asked, "What does 'actively procured' mean?"

"Actively procured means such things as suggesting the terms of the will or trust, recommending the lawyer, being present when the will or trust is executed, or taking the person to the lawyer to have the will signed," Maggie responded.

"Wait, are you saying that even though there's no presumption of undue influence because Martha and I were married, the judge is still going to look at the factors you just mentioned to decide whether I unduly influenced my wife?" Max turned away from Maggie and stared at David. "Is that really the law?"

"I'm afraid it is, Max," said David. "But this doesn't mean the judge will automatically rule in favor of the children even if the answers to these questions aren't helpful. They are just factors to consider, as Maggie will explain."

As David anticipated, Maggie quickly jumped in.  "That's right. The judge is ultimately going to decide this case on the greater weight of *all* of the evidence in this case, not just the evidence regarding active procurement.  But we'll have to present a reasonable explanation for your role in procuring the amended will and trust.  If you provide a reasonable explanation why Martha decided to amend her will and trust, even though there was a prenuptial agreement in place, then the children will be hard pressed to prove there was undue influence."

With a concerned expression, Max paused, and then asked, "Well, what if the judge just doesn't like my explanation or thinks the children should get all of Martha's estate, especially in view of the prenuptial agreement we signed before getting married?"

"Judge Long is a good judge," Maggie replied, "and fully understands the law which says that Martha's estate was her property to leave to whomever she wanted so long as there was no undue influence and she had the mental capacity to understand what she was doing.  This case, like any case, depends on the evidence presented. The children will have to convince the judge by the greater weight of the evidence that the amended will and trust are the result of your undue influence rather than Martha's independent decision.  Even more than in most cases, the credibility of the witnesses will be extremely important when the judge makes her decision."

Max sighed and became more sullen.  David assumed Maggie's comments were beginning to sink in.

"What you've told me is disturbing.  I was trying to help Martha, and myself.  But I gather some of the things I did to help my wife may turn out to be evidence used against me. That doesn't seem right."

*Yes, Montgomery will definitely use Max's efforts to procure the amended will and trust against him. And an unbiased person like Judge Long might well conclude Max was acting more in his own interest than in Martha's.* But David was not yet ready to address these issues with Max in greater detail. Instead, David replied, "That's why we need to have a reasonable explanation for why Martha signed the amended will and trust. Maybe it would be helpful for you to tell us more about the Gateway Orlando project."

Max straightened in his chair and his tension seemed to ease somewhat. His lips parted into a thin smile, and his mood seemed to brighten as he began to discuss his project.

"This is the largest private development project currently underway in central Florida. It's also the largest project by half that I've ever developed. Once it's finished, it will transform the north side of Orlando. As you know, high rise downtown office towers have been the rage in Orlando over the last decade. But this mixed-use plan of offices, residential apartments, restaurants and stores will be unlike any other project in central Florida. If I can just bring this project to completion, it will be one of Central Florida's most successful ones in a long time."

"What stands in your way of completing it?" David asked.

"The primary problem is construction financing. We have construction financing on most of the project, but there's a critical portion where most of the restaurants and stores will be located that doesn't yet have construction financing. I'm in negotiations now with a lender who's interested in providing the loan but wants more capital invested by me before extending the construction loan. I have the money available from the $10 million loan Martha made to me, but if the will and trust are thrown out and I'm removed as personal representative and trustee, the children will call the loan, leaving me without financing.  At this point in the project, I'll be at a loss to find additional investors."

*Now I understand Max's predicament.  He can't raise additional capital while the lawsuit is pending.  And if he loses the case, Martha's children will call the loan and he will likely lose the project—maybe even face bankruptcy.*

"Go on," David said.

"The second issue I'm facing is permanent financing for the portions of the project my company will keep.  That issue isn't critical now, but it will become critical if we can't get the remainder of the project completed."

"I see," said David.  "Obviously, time is very important to you in the project; and therefore, time is important in this case as well."

"It is," replied Max.  "What's the next step, David?"

"Maggie and I will draft an answer to the complaint and go over it with you.  In the meantime, you need to preserve all letters, emails, text messages and any other electronic or paper records even remotely relevant to this lawsuit—including all records regarding Gateway Orlando.  Any of those records could become relevant in the case, and if any of the records are destroyed, even inadvertently, it could have a devastating impact on your case. We'll send you a preservation letter confirming this."

When Max appeared to understand the importance of preserving all records, David continued.  "Once we've filed the answer, we'll begin the discovery process. We'll submit interrogatories, which are written questions, to the other side to get more information regarding their allegations.  We'll also submit written requests to the children to produce relevant documents.  Once we have their documents, we'll begin scheduling depositions.  Keep in mind, the other side will do the same."

Max scowled. "Yeah, I'm familiar with the discovery process. How long before this case will be set for trial?"

"Given the court's docket, we would normally be set for trial about twelve months from now," David replied.  "But given your time constraints, we'll ask the judge for an accelerated discovery period and ask that the case be set for trial on a date certain six months from now."

"That's about as far out as I can go without this case seriously interfering with my project," Max said.

David felt he had covered about as much ground with Max as he could in an initial meeting, so he presented his client with an engagement letter authorizing Jordan & McKenzie to represent Max in the case and outlining the fee agreement. Max asked a few questions, then signed the engagement letter. Once Max appeared satisfied, David concluded the meeting.

As Max left, David suspected his client's mood might not be any better than when he had arrived. In fact, from the window, David thought he saw Max pop two Tums as he walked to his car. *Max is in for a tough fight. I hope he is prepared for what lies ahead.*

David turned his attention toward Maggie. "So, what do you think of Max?

"He's not a particularly likeable person," Maggie stated candidly.

"Agreed," responded David.  "There are some clients whom you tell just to be themselves and tell the truth.  There are other clients you instruct to tell the truth, but the last thing you want is for them to be themselves. They need training on how to be more credible and more likeable. Max clearly falls into the latter category."

# Chapter 3

Depending on traffic, David's commute home to Maitland in the evening via I-4 usually took about twenty minutes. Today, however, an accident had tied up traffic as far as David could see. The construction on I-4 was in the fourth year of a scheduled six-year project, and days with accidents on it seemed more prevalent than days without. It was probably going to take forty minutes or more to get home to his family.

David loved his home, a two-story Spanish mission house on a small lake in Maitland, a peaceful respite from the increasing congestion of a growing suburban area. Central Florida had mostly been small towns, orange groves and unspoiled lakes before Walt Disney World opened in 1971. Since then, the area had become urbanized and now sprawled over four counties with a population of over 2.6 million people. Despite the government building roads at a furious pace, the combination of rapid population growth and 75 million tourists a year had overwhelmed central Florida roads. The fact that so many roads were under construction in an attempt to catch up with demand only made the traffic worse.

David normally used the commute home to transition from work mode to husband and father mode, and today was no exception. He treasured the evenings and weekends with Carol and Jenna. Hard to believe his daughter was twelve already. He took great pride in her. Jenna was at an awkward age, with braces, legs that seemed far too long for her height, and glasses that made her already large blue eyes seem enormous. Her awkward appearance was belied, however, by an unusually deep voice that often startled people meeting her for the first time. Had they not seen her before hearing her voice, strangers would swear they were speaking to a woman in her early twenties or beyond. The mature voice was reinforced by a quick mind and expansive vocabulary that kept her at the top of her class in all her subjects at Maitland Middle School. David smiled with pride. In short, Jenna had a maturity beyond her age, and far beyond her physical appearance.

David welcomed Jenna's hug after his 45-minute commute. "How was your day, Dad?" Jenna asked.

Bubbly as always, she excitedly reviewed her day before David could answer. "Mine was outstanding. I aced the algebra exam, and our soccer coach told me I will be on the starting team for our match on Friday."

"That's great news, Jenna," David exclaimed, surprised but pleased Jenna made the starting team. "When the season began you weren't sure you would even make the team. I'm proud of how hard you've worked and how much you've improved."

David had almost ceased being amazed by Jenna. She clearly had the intelligence to do well in school without overly exerting herself but making the soccer team was the result of grit and determination rather than natural talent. Carol had commented more than once that Jenna was her father's daughter in that respect.

As Jenna headed upstairs to her room to finish her homework, Carol greeted David with a kiss, but with a faraway, weary look in her eyes. "You look like you've had a long day," David said. "How did your meeting of the board of directors of the Women's Crisis Center go today? I saw Jesse leaving for the meeting about 3:30."

Carol sighed as she sat on the couch. "Unfortunately, it didn't go well. Although all the board members are working hard to collect $40,000 each for the new building, we've made no progress at all finding major new donors. Jesse reported that she spoke to one of the senior staff members with the Orange County Mayor's office, and she was flatly told that Orange County is highly unlikely to provide financial support unless we can get the new building out of the ground. Everyone says we have a wonderful mission and that we're accomplishing amazing things with our limited resources, but no one is willing to make a major commitment to WCC until we show we have staying power by completing the building.

"It's frustrating, David. We can't get the financial commitments we need unless we complete the building, but we can't complete the building unless we get the financial commitments we need. Unless we have additional donors within the next four to six months, we're going to run out of money, and the women we're helping have nowhere else to go."

"That *is* frustrating," David responded as he slid onto the couch next to Carol and gave her an understanding hug. "Is there anything I can do to help?"

"Not unless you have a few million dollars to spare that I'm not aware of."

"Is there anything *else* I can do to help?" responded David with a smile.

"I'm afraid not, but there *is* something else I need to discuss with you," said Carol, as her eyebrows furrowed, revealing that WCC was not her only concern of the day.

"What is it?" asked David, suddenly wary from the tone of her voice. Carol seemed as concerned about this new issue as she was about getting the building built for WCC, which had consumed her over the past months.

"Well, I told you I had an appointment for my annual physical today with Dr. Marsha Goldberg."

"Yes. I remember."

Carol's sigh jarred David. "And …

"And … she found a lump in my left breast."

"Oh, no. What's the plan?"

"She has scheduled a battery of tests for Tuesday of next week, with a consultation with an oncologist to follow later in the week. She made no diagnosis today—but … David, she has concerns that this could be cancer."

As Carol uttered the word "cancer," David had the sensation of being lost in a bad dream from which he could neither extricate himself nor understand what was going on. He was stunned into silence, unable to fully grasp what Carol had just told him. *Carol is only forty-six years old and one of the healthiest women I know. This must be a mistake; she couldn't possibly have cancer.*

All David could say was, "Oh, my God, Carol. Is she sure?"

"No, of course not—at least not without more tests, particularly since Dr. Goldberg isn't an oncologist. I've also had some nausea …"

"Some?"

"Well . . . a lot."

"And you've been so tired."

"True.  But I figured my exhaustion was due to working such long hours on the WCC building project."

Carol hesitated before continuing.  "And I've had some swelling in my hands and feet."

David hated to be so ignorant where his wife's health was concerned.  "What does that have to do with the lump in your breast?"

"Dr. Goldberg is concerned about these symptoms because they possibly indicate that if the lump in my breast is malignant the cancer may have already spread to my liver."

With this comment from Carol, David felt himself slip further into the bad dream, which was quickly becoming a nightmare.  His head began to spin, and he grabbed the arm of the couch to steady himself in order to gather his thoughts.

His mind quickly leapt to all sorts of possible outcomes, from Carol dying soon, to his trying to comfort Jenna who would be left without a mother, to how he could go forward in life after losing the only woman he had ever loved.  Then, the lawyer in him rose, and with great effort he forced himself to focus only on the facts they currently had: Carol had a lump in her breast and some other possible related symptoms, and no physician had yet made a definitive diagnosis.  He couldn't allow his mind to run wild with speculations about what might occur.

David said nothing immediately as the ramifications of what Carol told him continued to sink in.  Instead, he took her in his arms and held her tightly, telling her over and over that he loved her.

How could she stay so calm, when he secretly was shaking inside? Carol seemed to be taking the news more calmly than he was, but he sensed she needed his comfort and support—and he needed to be strong if he was going to comfort her.

Finally, while still holding her tight, he said, "Let's don't assume the worst, Carol. These symptoms may result in nothing. And in any event—good or bad—we'll get through this together. Have you said anything to Jenna yet?"

"No, and I don't intend to unless and until I get a definitive diagnosis. Do you agree with that?"

"Yes, I totally agree. We shouldn't lay this on her until we know something definite. Hopefully, we'll never have to have that conversation with her."

*      *      *

Jenna finished her homework and joined her parents for dinner. Though they tried to act as normal as possible during dinner, she could sense something was not quite right. Twice she asked, "Is everything okay?" and twice they said, "Yes, we're both just tired from having a stressful day."

*What's going on here? Are they hiding something from me?*

Over dessert, Jenna asked, "By the way, Mom, how did your physical exam go today?"

As nonchalantly as her mother could, she said, "It went fine; nothing to worry about. I may have a follow up appointment in a week or so, but nothing significant."

Jenna didn't follow up with more questions, but she had the distinct impression that everything was not okay—Mom and Dad were keeping something from her. She decided to ask Dad later. She was usually able to get whatever information she sought from Dad.

*     *     *

Jenna went to bed at her usual time—10 o'clock.  Carol and David seldom went to bed before eleven, so they could have some private time to talk.  The several hours since Carol had told David about her physical exam gave him time to deal with the startling and unsettling news. The question that continued to rattle his brain was—*Why?  Why would God allow a good woman like Carol to be stricken with a disease like cancer in the prime of her life and while running WCC, which clearly was a ministry of which God would approve?  If serving battered and drug-addicted women and their children didn't qualify as doing the Lord's work, what would?*

David knew the answers to his "why" questions weren't easy to find.  Though he and Carol usually attended the adult Sunday School class at the small Episcopal church where they were members, he hadn't given much thought to why bad things happen to good people until now—when the possibility struck home.

David remembered last year's Bible study of Job.  Most of the book was a debate over why all of the bad things happened to Job, who steadfastly declared his innocence to his friends—who, in turn, repeatedly told him that he must have sinned to have such terrible things happen to him.  David's main recollection from the study was that even when God showed up, spoke to Job, and rebuked his friends before restoring Job to health, he never answered their "why" questions.

As they began to get ready for bed, David asked Carol, "Do you ever wonder why terrible things like cancer happen to good people?  Why would God let something like this happen to you?"

Carol looked at David with loving and understanding eyes for a long moment before responding with humor, "Would you feel better about this if I weren't such a good person?"

Her retort had the odd effect of calming him, and they both chuckled.

Then Carol continued, "David, I don't see myself as good—and I believe I'm no better than the battered, drug-addicted women whom I serve at WCC.  I've just never been thrown into a horrible situation like they have.  I don't know why bad things happen to some people and not to others.  But of this, I'm certain.  God loves the women who come to us at WCC every bit as much as he loves our family or anyone else we might consider good.

"We shouldn't think I got cancer because God is unhappy with us any more than we should think God is punishing those poor women.  We just have to have faith and pray that I don't have cancer, and fight it if I do.  There are some things we aren't going to understand fully in this life, and my possibly having cancer is one of them."

David agreed with Carol's explanation.  Yet, the fact this was his wife who may have cancer left him feeling vulnerable and not in control, a feeling he detested.  He wished his faith was as strong as Carol's; she had accepted the news better than he had.  He realized he needed a faith as strong as hers in order to be supportive in the ordeal they may soon be facing.

For the first time in a long, long time, Carol and David prayed together before going to sleep.

# Chapter 4

David felt as if he were in a daze the remainder of that week. He and Carol decided they would tell no one about the possibility of her having cancer until they had a diagnosis from an oncologist. Carol, however, would not see an oncologist until shortly after the results of the tests she was to have the following week. They both felt like the sword of Damocles loomed over them—at least until they had some concrete answers—and each of them silently feared the result if the sword they dreaded actually fell. By mutual but unspoken consent, they avoided talking about the consequences should cancer be diagnosed. Yet, by not discussing the possibility, David felt the tension mount day by day while they waited for answers.

It was a miserable and painful situation, especially since they were trying their best to conceal their angst from Jenna. Despite their best efforts, she seemed to sense something was wrong. The more David and Carol reassured Jenna everything was okay, the more questions she asked. David and Carol had always been honest and forthcoming with Jenna. Perhaps their denying that anything was wrong wasn't in her best interest, after all, because Jenna obviously sensed something was badly wrong. Finally, she put her fear to them directly, "Are you two getting a divorce, or something?"

At this, David and Carol realized their trying to hide the truth from Jenna had created more problems than being forthcoming with her.  After a momentary stunned silence, Carol pulled Jenna to her, hugged her tightly and said, "No, darling; your dad and I love each other more than we ever have.  And we love you as much as any parents have ever loved their child."

"The reason we're uptight right now," Carol continued, "is because I have to have some medical tests run next week."

"Medical tests? Mom, what's going on?"

Carol took Jenna's hand. "Please don't worry.  We don't think the tests will result in any problem that can't be dealt with medically, but it's never fun to face a bunch of unpleasant medical tests."

"So that's why you two have been acting all weird? And you're not getting a divorce?" Jenna responded as her face relaxed with relief.  "Thank goodness; I was afraid I might have to choose which one of you I wanted to live with, and I didn't know how I would ever be able to make that decision if I had to."

David and Carol both hugged Jenna once more to reassure her.  However, Jenna suddenly stiffened and her eyes clouded over with apprehension.  "What kind of tests are you getting, Mom? Is it something really serious?"

David and Carol looked at each other and nodded in silent agreement to let Jenna know as much as they knew.

"Honestly, Jenna, right now we're uncertain," Carol said.

"Why are you uncertain, Mom?  Tell me!"

"It's possible I have cancer, but no diagnosis has been made yet.  We won't know for sure until we get the results of the tests and my doctor has reviewed them. I'm sorry we left you in the dark, sweetheart. We just didn't want you to worry about this until we knew something definite. We realize now we weren't being fair to you."

Jenna scowled slightly as if to say, "Why didn't you think you could tell me?"

Carol squeezed Jenna's hand. "I promise you that once we have a diagnosis from my doctor, we will clue you in on everything—the diagnosis and the treatment."

"Thank you for being honest with me, Mom. I'm sure everything will work out, even if you have to be treated for cancer."

David gazed in amazement at his daughter who had just given a response far more mature than her age. But he also sensed Jenna might be masking her true emotions for her parent's sake. Although her response was optimistic, perhaps she feared she had not been told how serious things might be. Nevertheless, Jenna seemed braver and more determined than David had ever seen her before. *I just hope Carol's cancer—if it is cancer—doesn't throw our daughter into adulthood before her time.*

After a few more minutes of discussing when they might find out something more definitive about Carol's condition, they sent Jenna upstairs to finish her homework and go to bed. When they were alone, David said, "I don't know why we thought we couldn't be honest with Jenna. She's an observant and remarkable girl. Keeping her in the dark made her fears worse than telling her the truth. We won't repeat that mistake again."

"I agree," said Carol. "Whatever the diagnosis turns out to be, this family is going to go through this together. I need both of you."

As David embraced Carol, he offered a silent prayer that he would be as strong as his twelve-year-old daughter appeared to be.

David was especially grateful he was able to go to work for the remainder of the week. The only way he was temporarily able to think about anything other than Carol's condition was to immerse himself in his cases. He was better than most professionals at compartmentalizing his professional, home, and social life. He rarely discussed his cases with Carol or with Jenna. In fact, except when he was about to go to trial, he seldom even thought about his cases while he was at home. Likewise, he was usually able to concentrate solely on work while he was in the office. Though his family never left his mind completely, he was able to defer the enjoyment of thinking about them much as a connoisseur of fine wine might defer opening his finest bottle.

At least, usually he could.

Even with David's ability to compartmentalize, however, thoughts of Carol lurked in the recesses of his mind while he was discussing Max's case with Maggie on Wednesday—two days after they had initially met with Max. By force of will, he was able to focus on what he and Maggie needed to accomplish.

"Let's first go over our checklist of the items we need to accomplish for Max's case," David commented as he and Maggie settled into the conference room to review the cases they were working on together. "We told Max we would draft an answer to the complaint for his review as soon as possible. When do you think the draft will be ready?"

"I've already started on it. Based on what Max has told us so far, most of the factual allegations will ultimately have to be admitted; but because Montgomery did his usual job of arguing his case in his pleadings rather than simply providing a straight-forward statement of the relevant facts, we'll initially deny many of the allegations."

David nodded his approval.

"Where it's appropriate, I'm including some language in our response that explains why we're denying the allegations. But I must say, David, the more I go over these allegations, the more I'm convinced we're going to have to provide good, reasonable explanations for what Max did. If not, Judge Long will rule against us."

"I share your concern," responded David. "Let's hope Max has better explanations than he's given us so far. That brings me to the next item to address with Max—the preservation and review of all documents regarding his Gateway Orlando project. With all the litigation he's been involved in, he should know what the consequences would be if he even inadvertently destroys any documents relevant to this lawsuit. We need to follow up on the preservation letter we sent him and emphasize how important this is."

David was pleased Maggie was nodding in agreement.

"I've already contacted Max's office for an appointment to see how they maintain their electronic files," Maggie responded. "And I spoke to their IT director, James Moss. As it turns out, Mr. Moss has worked previously as the IT director of a law firm, and he understands the importance of preserving all electronic documents."

"That's good."

"He's put a litigation hold on all of their files. I'm meeting with Max and Mr. Moss this Friday morning at 11:00. I'll find out then how they maintain their files, and I'll make a copy of their hard drive to preserve their documents and allow me to begin reviewing them."

David smiled with appreciation for Maggie's efficiency. "That's excellent news, Maggie. But we also need to see any personal emails or texts Max may have had with Martha, especially any regarding Martha's estate planning and the loan she made to Max for the Gateway Orlando project."

"I already have that on my checklist to cover with them when we meet on Friday," confirmed Maggie.

*Maggie has certainly become thorough with the discovery process.*

"I'll also get an inventory of all computers, cell phones and other devices on which any messages or documents may be stored," she continued.

David glanced at the handwritten agenda he'd prepared for their meeting. "That brings me to the final item on *my* checklist: a request for production of documents to serve on Montgomery to see what communications may have been exchanged between the children and Martha regarding Max, the estate planning, or the administration of her estate. Max said the children and Martha didn't communicate much after they married, but she may have had more communications with them than he knows about."

"Good point." Maggie scribbled a few notes on her pad, then looked back at David. I'll draft requests for production of documents to serve on Montgomery for your review. We should be able to serve them by the middle of next week."

"Once we've reviewed the documents Max has to produce and the documents we get from the children, we should have a better handle on the facts of this case." David hesitated momentarily, then continued. "Often, the documents in the case tell the whole story, but I have a feeling that, in this case, the whole story *won't* be found in the documents."

With that comment, they moved on to discuss other cases.

*       *       *

Maggie arrived promptly for her appointment with Max and his IT manager, James Moss. The office was easily identified by the large *Max Foster Enterprises* sign in a new strip mall Max had developed that included offices, stores, and a deli on north Orange Avenue, not far from the border between Orlando and Winter Park.

Maggie quickly reviewed what she knew of Max's staff—relatively small considering the size of the Gateway Orlando project.  Besides himself as CEO and Moss as director of information technology, Max employed a director of operations, a chief financial officer, a marketing director, and support staff.

Max personally met Maggie upon her arrival and led her into the nicely appointed conference room able to accommodate up to twelve people around a large marble table. Maggie's attention was immediately drawn to the four wall paintings. "Are those original Highwaymen paintings?" she asked.

Max smiled.  "Yes, they are.  I'm impressed that you recognize them.  Are you interested in Florida art and artists?"

"I'm more interested in literature than art, but some of the novels set in Florida I studied in college mentioned the Highwaymen.  I know they were all black painters from the Ft. Pierce area, and the value of their paintings has soared in recent years.  Beyond that, I don't know much about them."

Clearly delighted to share his knowledge, Max walked over to the paintings. With an authoritative air, he said, "The Highwaymen were a group of young black artists—about twenty-five men and one woman. As you mentioned, they were from the Fort Pierce area and took up painting to try to work their way out of depressing jobs in the Florida citrus groves and fruit packing houses in the 1950s. They had a white mentor named A.E. "Bean" Backus who taught them to paint landscapes. He emphasized more classical ideals of landscapes, but they used his techniques to create their own unique style—sometimes referred to as 'motel art.' All of their paintings depict in some fashion a romanticized Florida that's both exotic and appealing, while capturing Florida's natural beauty."

"From what I read, the Highwaymen produced over 100,000 of these landscapes and often sold them to tourists out of the trunks of their cars."

"You're correct. Their works sold like boom-time Florida real estate in the 1950s and 60s, but then fell out of favor and often wound up in the buyers' attics. Then in the mid-1990s, they were rediscovered and recognized as American folk artists."

Maggie slowly scanned the paintings, appreciating the vivid colors the painters used to depict Florida's unique beauty. "Is that when they became known as the Highwaymen?"

"Yes. After their rediscovery, the price of their paintings, which were initially at rock bottom prices, have been going up rapidly. I was very fortunate to find these four Highwaymen paintings ten years ago. Similar paintings today go for three or four times what I paid."

Maggie was impressed with Max's knowledge about the Highwaymen, but more impressed that Max actually showed some warmth as he discussed the famous artists. *Maybe there's hope for Max to be a good witness after all*, Maggie mused, as James Moss walked into the room.

Moss introduced himself to Maggie, and they all sat around the conference room table. After a brief exchange of pleasantries, Maggie said, "I was delighted to learn you worked as an IT director in a law firm previously and understand the importance of a litigation hold on all electronic and paper documents during the course of the litigation. We'll need to get a copy of the hard drive on the company server to preserve the documents."

Moss nodded. "Yes, I do understand the importance of preserving documents, and I made this a priority when I joined Max Foster Enterprises. As you probably know, litigation is not uncommon in the real estate development business, and we've never had an instance of spoliation of evidence since I've been here. We'll get the server copied immediately."

Maggie noticed that Max made no comment about the amount of litigation the company was involved in, and added, "In this case we have to preserve not only the company records, but also Max's personal emails, texts, and other documents having anything to do with Martha or with the company business. This includes paper documents and electronic documents stored on computers or mobile phones."

"I have no mobile phone, other than the one I have through my company. I do have a personal laptop, but I seldom use it," explained Max. "I find it more convenient to handle all of my email through my office computer, so James should have almost all of my emails. Any personal correspondence will be with my office files."

"What about emails or texts regarding the $10 million loan Martha made to you?" Maggie asked.

"That was all verbal, as I recall, other than the promissory note I signed and the mortgage documents in which I gave her a first mortgage on two parcels of property. If there were any emails or texts regarding the loan, I don't recall them. If there are any such emails or texts, they will be on my iPhone or the email server."

"That simplifies things," Maggie said. "But James should investigate whether there are any such emails or texts." Moss nodded approvingly.

"Max, we're going to serve a request for production of documents on the children to see what communications they may have had with Martha related to the issues in this case," Maggie continued. "Where did Martha keep any emails or texts she may have sent or received?"

"Martha had an office in our house which, as you probably already know, was her house before we married. She called it her study. She had a computer in there, but I don't know how much she used it. I've never used her computer and have no idea what's on it."

"Is it still in your possession?" Maggie asked.

"Yes, it's still in the study. I haven't been in there since Martha passed away."

"What happened to Martha's mobile phone?"

"I believe it's in Martha's study. I haven't seen that either since Martha passed."

Speaking now to Moss, as well as Max, Maggie said, "David and I should take possession of Martha's computer and her mobile phone so we'll have a good chain of custody and be able to show that no one has altered any of the content on those devices."

Moss nodded in agreement and said he would deliver the computer and mobile phone to Maggie. She was pleased Max made no objection. If Max had been emailing or texting with Martha about the loan or the need for an amended will and trust, he might have objected to the firm taking possession of them—unless Max had already erased any such documents from those devices. Given all the litigation Max has been involved with, he should know by now a computer expert could readily determine whether any documents had been deleted; and, if so, when.

"Max, do you know of any letters, memos or other paper documents that might have been exchanged between Martha and the children?"

"None that I'm aware of," said Max, "but if any exist I suspect they would be somewhere within Martha's study."

Maggie gazed directly at Max to emphasize the importance of her next question. "Have the children had access to your house, particularly the study, since Martha died?"

"No, and they've shown no interest in looking for anything in the house," replied Max.

"We need to add another task to our to-do list," said Maggie. "James, would you please inventory what files are in Martha's study? Our firm will have a computer expert review Martha's computer and mobile phone. Max, you should also lock up Martha's study and give us the key so we can establish that Martha's study has been undisturbed since she died."

"I have no problem with that," added Max, to Maggie's relief. Max was being much more agreeable and cooperative than Maggie had expected. Now, she just needed to find some documents that would help David and her come up with good, reasonable explanations as to why Max requested the loan and why he suggested that Martha sign the amended will and trust. Those items would occupy her time the remainder of the day at Max Foster Enterprises.

"Max, David and I anticipate we'll receive requests for production of documents from Montgomery any day now. I want to get a head start on responding to their requests for production by going over with James how your records are kept and where we will find the documents we need to respond to Montgomery's requests. You're welcome to join us, but I suspect you have more important things to do during the remainder of the day."

"Yes, I do need to tend to some things." As Max started to leave the room, he turned toward Maggie, and to her surprise, said, "Thanks for coming today, Maggie. I appreciate what you're doing for me."

Maggie and James spent the rest of the day going over the organization of the company's files and conducting word searches for Maggie to get some idea of the size and content of the ocean of documents they would have to navigate through over the months ahead. By the end of the day, she was convinced of James' knowledge about the company's records and that he could be trusted to maintain the litigation hold on all of the documents in his possession. Although she felt somewhat better about Max, she still had a nagging suspicion she and David might encounter some surprises before the case was over.

# Chapter 5

As usual, the attorneys at Jordan & McKenzie met at noon in the conference room the following Monday.  After the house-keeping items were addressed, David asked Jesse and Steve for an update on the Faulk case

"We filed our answer on Friday, and … just as I anticipated … at 5:15 that evening we received plaintiff's motion for a temporary injunction; the hearing is scheduled for thirty days from now.  Additionally, plaintiff's counsel has scheduled Dr. Faulk for deposition in two weeks. We're going to take the depositions of Dr. Edwards and Dr. Simpson the following week."

"What about experts?" asked David.  "Do you think the plaintiff is going to call an expert witness at the hearing, and do you intend to call one?"

"We don't know yet whether Orange Orthopedic Surgeons will call an expert witness, but this case is assigned to Judge Marvin Cook."

"I'm familiar with Judge Cook," David said.

Jesse continued, "He usually requires a disclosure of all witnesses, including expert witnesses, at least 10 days before an evidentiary hearing.

"Steve and I assume the plaintiff will present an expert on the issue of whether there is, in fact, competition between Dr. Faulk and Orange

Orthopedic Surgeons, given Dr. Faulk's location in Sanford. We're in the process of retaining our own expert. Steve had a preliminary meeting on Friday with Dr. Timothy Markham, a tenured professor in the Economics Department at the University of Central Florida." Jesse turned to face Steve and asked, "Please give us an update on that meeting."

"Sure," he began. "As you know, a plaintiff seeking to enforce a non-compete agreement must establish he has a legitimate business interest to protect and the non-compete agreement is reasonably necessary to protect this interest. That's why we're asking Dr. Markham to address whether the market for orthopedic surgeries in Sanford is part of the same market as the one in south Orlando where the plaintiff is located. If the two offices are in two different markets for orthopedic surgeries, then arguably there is no legitimate business interest to enforce."

"Good point," David said.

Steve nodded. "Even if there is a legitimate business interest, the question is how large is the area in which that interest can reasonably be protected. A non-compete having a thirty-mile radius is probably too large. For example, if Dr. Faulk had moved to Tampa, no court is going to enforce a non-compete agreement for orthopedic surgeons that far away, even if the agreement had specified a 200-mile radius. Tampa and Orlando are clearly two different markets. Hopefully, Dr. Markham will be able to testify that Orlando and Sanford are also two different markets."

"Did Dr. Markham agree to testify on Dr. Faulk's behalf?" asked David.

"Not yet," responded Steve. "His initial reaction was that they are, in fact, two different markets, but he has to research the issue further before he can confirm his initial opinion. One of Dr. Markham's areas of expertise is medical economics, and he has performed more research on the topic of medical markets than any other expert we've been able to identify. He wants to review his own research and the research of others on the relationship between a patient's home and the location of the surgeon's office and any hospitals at which the surgeon performs surgeries."

"So, Dr. Markham believes that where an orthopedic surgeon's patients come from helps define the market area?" David asked.

"Yes, it is an important—although not exclusive—factor. Dr. Markham wants us to ask Dr. Edwards and Dr. Simpson what percentage of their patients reside in Seminole County. Jesse and I suspect this will be a small number since neither Dr. Edwards nor Dr. Simpson has admitting privileges at any hospitals in Seminole County. All of their surgeries are performed at hospitals in Orange County. Likewise, Dr. Faulk didn't have privileges at any hospitals in Seminole County while he was with Orange Orthopedic Surgeons. Now, he has privileges *only* at hospitals in Seminole County."

"What testimony do you anticipate from the other side on this issue?" asked Maggie.

"We're not sure, but we suspect one argument Michael Preston— Orange Orthopedics' attorney—will make is that the federal government designates certain areas as Metropolitan Statistical Areas, or MSAs. The Orlando MSA includes all of Orange and Seminole Counties, as well as all of Osceola and Lake Counties. We suspect Preston will argue that since both offices are in the same MSA and the parties agreed to the thirty-mile restrictive area, the court should enforce what the parties have agreed to— especially since the federal government seems to indicate this is all one big market."

"What does Dr. Markham say about Preston's argument?" asked David.

"From an economist's viewpoint, it's nonsense," responded Steve. "He said he would have no difficulty showing actual economic markets are not directly related to MSAs. We're concerned that Preston will, nevertheless, make the argument even if he can't find an expert to support his position. And Judge Cook may just buy his argument."

"I see why you're concerned," David said. "Judge Cook is a good judge, but economics isn't his strong suit. And he tends to give deference to what the parties have agreed to in their contracts, even when what they have agreed to is questionable under the law."

Turning to Jesse, David said, "Let us know if Maggie or I can assist you and Steve in any way on this case."

He took a sip of much needed coffee, pushing back thoughts of home, and asked Jesse, "How is your WCC project coming along?"

"Unfortunately, I have nothing positive to report," she replied. "We have no new donors, other than a few small ones. Even the board members are having difficulty raising $40,000 each, and we have no prospective major donors who will get us to the $3.5 million we need to build the new facility. You know better than I do how hard Carol has worked on raising money to build the new facility, but we've hit a stone wall everywhere we turn."

Jesse paused, and then continued, directing her gaze at David. "I'm worried about Carol; when I saw her this past weekend she seemed more down emotionally than I've ever seen her. This project seems to be getting to her."

David started to say that Carol's demeanor wasn't entirely due to the fundraising issues with WCC, but caught himself, and said, "If you know of any potential donors, please let Jesse know.  We can't let WCC go under.  The women and children the organization serves have nowhere else to go."

Turning to Maggie, David said, "Please bring Jesse and Steve up to date on the Max Foster case."

"Sure," she responded, as she picked up the yellow pad that contained her to-do list. "David and I have a draft of our answer to the complaint ready to file.  We'll have a final review of the answer with Max on Wednesday before we file it.

Maggie glanced at her pad before continuing.  "I met with Max and his IT director on Friday.  The good news is that Max *has* an IT director— James Moss—who previously worked as an IT director in a law firm.  He understands the importance of preserving electronic documents through a litigation hold.  I asked Mr. Moss to gather all the hard documents, including the ones in Martha's study, and inventory them."

"What about Martha's computer?" asked Steve.

Maggie finished the last of her fruit-flavored water, then replied, "Glad you asked.  He's going to deliver Martha's computer and mobile phone to us so we can have our computer expert review and preserve the information on them.  Max claims not to have any computers or mobile phones other than the ones issued through his company, so we should have all such devices under our control.  Martha's study will be locked, and our office will have the key as soon as Mr. Moss completes his inventory."

"What discovery has taken place so far?" asked Jesse.

"We just received today the plaintiffs' initial document requests and interrogatories, so we have thirty days to respond and produce documents. I've drafted our document requests and interrogatories, and we'll serve them on opposing counsel this week when we serve our answer to the complaint. I spoke this morning to the associate working with Montgomery on this case, and he and I agreed that we should begin depositions in about forty-five days. Montgomery will take Max's deposition first, and we'll take the children's depositions the following week.

Maggie smiled. "More good news—Montgomery is not going to oppose our motion for expedited discovery and a trial date only six months from now. I can only assume that Montgomery is as anxious to get this case to trial as Max is."

"Maggie, do you think Max is turning over all relevant documents and electronic data to you?" Steve asked.

"I have no reason to believe otherwise … so far," Maggie said. "Mr. Moss seems to know what he's doing, and we discussed with Max the consequences if he tries to hide any documents. Max actually was quite cooperative during our meeting last Friday."

Steve raised a concerned eyebrow. "Well, I hope Max has learned his lesson."

"What do you mean?" David asked.

"A friend of mine told me Max was sanctioned by the judge in a case my friend handled because Max failed to disclose all documents he was required to produce. Max wound up having to pay over $30,000 for the opposing party's attorneys' fees."

"Really?" asked Maggie.

"All this is a matter of public record, so I'm not disclosing any confidential information," Steve replied.

"Thanks for letting us know. We'll be especially diligent with our discovery responses." As he said this, David reminded himself that both he and Maggie were concerned there would be surprises lurking in the case. Like any good trial lawyer, David hated surprises. Disliking them, however, didn't stop them from occurring. Most cases had a surprise or two; he just hoped he could discover the surprises in Max's case before they caused too much harm.

*       *       *

David navigated the rest of the week as if in a fog, uncertain of what was ahead.

On Tuesday, he accompanied Carol to the hospital where all the tests, including a biopsy, took place. Of course, no results would be available for a few days, and Dr. Goldberg wanted to go over the results of the tests, especially the biopsy, with Dr. Sidney Marks, the oncologist Dr. Goldberg recommended, before Carol met with him. The meeting with Dr. Marks was scheduled for the following Monday morning—conflicting with the weekly firm meeting.

David decided he would accompany Carol to her appointment, but his absence from the firm meeting would likely raise questions for the other lawyers, especially Jesse. David never missed a Monday meeting unless he was in court. He considered these weekly meetings a sacrosanct part of the firm culture, and insisted all lawyers attend, unless they were in court.

David regretted he couldn't let Jesse know the reason for his absence, but neither David nor Carol was ready to announce to anyone else the potential cancer diagnosis—not even Jesse. When David asked her to conduct Monday's meeting in his place, she looked at him inquisitively. Gratefully, she didn't press for a reason, but simply said, "Sure, I'll be happy to take over."

David rested in Jesse's knowledge that he occasionally clamed up if he were bothered by a personal matter and that she had always respected his privacy.

*       *       *

At home, after the hospital tests on Tuesday, an unspoken anxiousness descended on the Jordan household. Jenna was full of questions during dinner. "Mom, how did it go today? Did you get any more information about a diagnosis?"

David had no appetite, and Carol had barely touched her plate. Jenna played with her food, waiting for an answer.

"No, nothing yet, Jenna. Dad and I will visit Dr. Marks, an oncologist, on Monday . . ."

"Oncologist? What's that, Mom?"

"A cancer doctor. We'll discuss the results of the tests, and then we'll know what treatment is recommended ... if any treatment is needed."

"Okay," Jenna said with obvious feigned calm. "So, do you want to hear about my soccer game?"

David smiled, but the heaviness in his heart remained as Jenna described her team's victory on Friday—although with less enthusiasm than usual.

As Jenna talked, David considered how their family, like any family, had experienced disappointments from time to time. But his family had never faced the prospect of a catastrophic event like cancer— something that could fundamentally alter their lives—possibly even cause

Carol's death.  The uncertainty of what lay ahead was the worst part, robbing them of the simple joy of sharing a meal together until that uncertainty was removed, either for better or for worse.

# Chapter 6

The following Monday, David and Carol awoke to another beautiful late February morning which they greeted from the window of their upstairs master bedroom.  There was not a cloud in the sky, and the early morning sun reflected softly off the lake in front of their house. Tiny ripples formed as a mamma duck and her babies swam away from the shore.  Two joggers slowly trotted by their house on the narrow road between their house and the lake.

"I never get tired of looking at the lake in the morning, especially this time of year," Carol commented from the window.  "I'm always amazed at how peaceful it is, even though we're surrounded by a bustling suburban area with so much traffic."

David nodded in agreement from the edge of the bed, just a few feet away.  His attention, though, was not on the beautiful morning or the peaceful scene unfolding before them.  His mind was in turmoil over what lay before them this morning.  David had decided to skip work today to take Carol to her appointment with Dr. Marks at 10:00.  They would finally learn whether she had cancer—and, if so—how far it had progressed.  The stress from the uncertainty of what they might learn and what the ramifications might be had continued to build in David over the weekend.

Pressure in his temples and tightened muscles were nothing new; he had experienced them many times before, especially at the beginning of a trial. But this was different—and worse. His wife—the love of his life—was facing potentially life-threatening news, and he could do nothing to prevent what might happen. The loss of control both frightened and angered him.

Even more unsettling for David was Carol's reaction to the impending appointment. As the day of the appointment drew near, Carol became calmer—and outwardly at least—less frightened. She was the one who comforted him.

Jenna also seemed to approach the big day with far less fear than David anticipated. She was optimistic in all her comments to her mother about what the doctor might say, and she stubbornly refused to talk about worse case scenarios with David or Carol.

*Am I the only one with so little faith that this is scaring me to death?*

Carol and Jenna's equanimity only emphasized to David his own internal turmoil and left him feeling inadequate and empty. In all of his legal cases, he had been the strong one who encouraged and reassured his clients when they were stressed or nervous, especially as the trial date approached. David desperately wanted to be strong for Carol and Jenna, and to comfort them. But thus far he was the one needing comfort more than either of them.

David and Carol arrived at Dr. Marks' office located on the second floor of the professional building across the street from the largest hospital on the north side of Orlando shortly before 10:00. David noted the medicinal coldness of the "office modern" decor, providing little warmth or appeal, especially for patients waiting to receive news of what might be the biggest fight of their lives. The atmosphere did nothing to lift his spirits or diminish his stress level, but Carol appeared almost serene as the receptionist took her information and asked them to have a seat until the doctor was ready to see them.

Carol took David's hand, squeezed it, and said, "I'm ready for whatever comes. Thank you for being here with me."

Before David could respond, Dr. Marks' nurse appeared, and asked Carol and David to follow her to the examination room. She took Carol's vital signs, asked a few preliminary questions, and reviewed Carol's current medications. "Dr. Marks will be in very shortly," she said, then left.

True to the nurse's word, Dr. Marks entered almost as soon as the nurse had left. He smiled warmly and said, "Hello. I'm Dr. Marks."

Carol introduced David, and added, "I hope you don't mind my husband being in the room with me while we discuss my case."

"Not at all." Dr. Marks said as he offered a friendly handshake.

David estimated Dr. Marks to be in his early fifties. He had graying hair and a kind, weathered face that looked like he had taken on too many of his patients' cares and worries.

David had researched Dr. Marks on Google and confirmed he was one of the most highly qualified oncologists in Florida. Besides having an impeccable reputation among his peers, Dr. Marks had recently helped formulate a number of new therapies for treating cancer. David's fears eased somewhat as his personal assessment of Dr. Marks corroborated what David had learned from his research. *Regardless of the outcome, we have Carol with the best oncologist in central Florida*

After a few initial inquiries and a brief examination, Dr. Marks glanced briefly at a file, then addressed Carol. "I've reviewed the results of the tests Dr. Goldberg ordered. After analyzing them, I have some bad news and some good news."

"Might as well give me the bad news first," Carol said, her face serene.

"You definitely have a carcinoma in your left breast. Unfortunately, the cancer has already metastasized to your liver; that's most likely the cause of your recent nausea, extreme fatigue, and swelling in your hands and feet. As best we can tell, the cancer has not spread beyond your liver."

"Any questions at this point?" Dr. Marks asked.

David glanced toward Carol to see how she reacted to the depressing diagnosis that confirmed his worst fears. David was fighting to maintain his composure, but to his surprise, Carol was still serene, seemingly untroubled by what Dr. Marks had just announced—almost as if she actually expected his diagnosis. Carol's only question was, "Since the cancer has already spread to my liver, is it a stage 4 cancer diagnosis?"

"Yes," Dr. Marks responded simply.

Carol nodded her head as if to say, "That's what I thought."

"Doctor, you also said you have some good news," David said, his voice unsteady. "What news do you have?" At this point, he couldn't imagine what the good news could be, given what he had just heard.

"The good news," responded Dr. Marks, "is there have been some significant improvements in available therapies for breast cancer— especially stage 4 breast cancer—over the past ten years or so. We've found combinations of chemotherapy drugs that are more efficacious than single or paired drugs; therefore, we've been getting better results in recent years. These newer therapies are not a magic cure. However, survival rates with these treatments have improved significantly. And we are better able to manage the cancer, if not put it into remission."

This information lifted David's spirits, and he again glanced at Carol for her reaction. She remained serene, giving no visible reaction to Dr. Marks' encouraging words, just as she had not reacted to his earlier dire diagnosis. To David, Carol seemed detached, as if the conversation were about a third person whom she only knew casually.

"What type of treatment do you recommend for me, doctor?"

"Well, since the cancer has already spread, we can't perform surgery at this time. Over the next three months, we'll alternate one week of chemo with two weeks off to recover. We'll insert a temporary IV catheter for your infusions here at the hospital. During the week of chemo, we'll do a total of four infusions. At the end of the three months, we'll evaluate the results and decide on subsequent treatments. We may follow up with another three months on the same schedule, or we may decide surgery is appropriate at that time."

Dr. Marks paused again. "Questions?"

"I understand," Carol said flatly.

Dr. Marks continued. "My nurse will provide you with information about the possible side effects of the chemo treatments and how to minimize them. Fortunately, we now have drugs to mitigate some of the more unpleasant side effects."

After considering what Dr. Marks said for a long moment, Carol met her doctor's kindly gaze, and asked, "What is my prognosis, Dr. Marks?"

He hesitated before responding.  David assumed giving a prognosis might be difficult, especially with metastatic cancers.  After glancing at David, Dr. Marks looked directly at Carol, and said, "That's difficult to say at this point because it depends so much on how your body responds to treatment.  Statistically, twenty-seven percent of women in the United States live at least five years after the initial diagnosis of stage 4 breast cancer.  The median survival period following the initial diagnosis is three years."

David's shoulders slumped.  *I don't like those numbers.*

Dr. Marks continued, offering a smile of hope.  "However, you're in good health—other than the cancer—and you're young and strong enough to handle the chemo treatments.  I think you have a reasonably good chance of reaching the five-year threshold."

"And if I elect not to have the treatment you recommend but only receive palliative care, what is my prognosis?"

As Carol asked this question, David quickly diverted his gaze to his wife, unable to believe what he had just heard.  *You can't possibly be considering that*!  Despite David's stunned reaction, Carol's demeanor didn't change. She was still calm and unruffled by the information Dr. Marks had given them.

Although David was taken aback by Carol's question, Dr. Marks did not seem surprised. "Your question is not uncommon, Carol, though most young people choose to fight the cancer. But to answer your question, if you receive only palliative care, it's unlikely you'll live to celebrate Christmas."

*               *               *

As they walked from Dr. Marks' office to the car, David couldn't recall ever feeling so undone by unanticipated events beyond his control. Yet Carol, although quiet, didn't seem undone at all. She remained serene and gave no outward sign she feared the path before her.

On the way home, David asked, "You aren't seriously thinking of only receiving palliative care, are you?"

"No, at least, not at this time. I fully intend to receive the best treatment possible. But, David, there could come a time when treatment is ineffective, when the side effects of the chemo are robbing me of the enjoyment of whatever time I have remaining. If I ever reach that point, I will seriously consider receiving only palliative care." Her gaze pierced him. "Would you do anything differently?"

Stated that way, David had no defense against her logic. "No, I understand what you're saying."

"Good."

"Just promise me you will continue to fight the cancer as long as Dr. Marks believes further treatment could be effective. I can't imagine life without you, and Jenna needs you as much as I do."

"Of course I will," responded Carol. "But I needed to know how quickly the end might come if I'm no longer receiving treatment other than palliative care." With that, David and Carol retreated into their own thoughts for the rest of the way home.

*         *         *

When Jenna got home from school, her first question was, "How did it go today with Dr. Marks, Mom?"

Carol squeezed Jenna's hand as she quickly responded. "Not as well as we had hoped, Jenna. Dr. Marks' diagnosis is that I have stage 4 breast cancer, which means it has already progressed beyond the breast to my liver.  Next week I'll begin a regime of chemotherapy consisting of four treatments in seven days, followed by two weeks off to recover.  This cycle will continue for three months.  He will reassess my treatment at that time."

"Mom, I'm so sorry."

"On the positive side, Dr. Marks did say that the newer forms of chemotherapy are more effective than chemo has been previously, and they're now getting better results."

Tears formed in Jenna's eyes as she took in her mother's words, but her voice was strong and steady as she hugged her mother.  "We'll beat this. What can I do to help you?"

"I don't know yet, Jenna.  I suspect I'll need a little more help around the house and with preparing meals.  Between the chemo treatments and continuing with my duties at WCC, I may have a little less energy than normal."

David was taken aback by her comment. *What is she thinking?*  "Carol, how are you going to be able to continue your duties at WCC while going through your chemo treatments?" David asked, dumbfounded that she would even attempt it.

"Yeah, Mom, don't you need to conserve your energy to deal with the chemo treatments?" Jenna quickly added.

"Look, you two," Carol responded with the rawest emotion she had shown all day, looking first at David, then at Jenna and back to David.  "Please don't start putting restrictions on me or start treating me as an invalid.  You know how important WCC is to me; I started it, and I've been the president since it was founded."  We're in the middle of a campaign to raise $3.5 million for the new building, which is essential if WCC is to continue its mission. No one else can realistically step in now to head up that effort. If we don't reach our goal, the women we serve will likely be on the street with nowhere else to go."

David responded with his only defense. "But you are my wife and Jenna's mother. Our first concern is for you."

Carol sighed, then responded with conviction, "As much as I believe I was meant to be your wife and mother, I also believe I was meant to carry out this mission to the women we serve at WCC. You ask how am I going to continue working at WCC while getting chemo treatments? I'm just going to suck it up and give it everything I've got as long as I possibly can . . ."

"But . . ."

"No buts. I would greatly appreciate the two people I love most in this world also sucking it up and helping me do what I think you both know I have to do ..." As the emotional impact of what lay ahead appeared to catch up with her, Carol fell silent.

David and Jenna were both stunned, unable to speak for what seemed like minutes, although it was only a few seconds. Simultaneously they both embraced Carol, whispering to her how much they loved her and would support her in what lay ahead. Neither David nor Jenna was quite sure how Carol was going to be able to carry out her normal duties at WCC while undergoing chemo treatments, but if she was determined to attempt to work, they were going to do everything they could to support her—no matter what.

Despite his resolve to support Carol, though, David felt as low as he could ever remember feeling. Before going to bed that night, David went into his study and opened his Bible randomly, hoping to find words of comfort.  Instead, his eyes fell upon Psalm 6: 6-7, which described precisely how he felt:

> "I am weary with my moaning;
>
> Every night I flood my bed with tears;
>
> I drench my couch with my weeping.
>
> My eyes waste away because of grief."[1]

# Chapter 7

The following morning, David asked Jesse to join him in his office as soon as she arrived. Sensing something ominous, she closed the door upon entering David's office, and sat in one of the two client chairs facing his desk. David's usually cheerful face was drawn and pale with his blue eyes failing to hide the distress lurking behind them. Jesse had never seen such sadness on David's face before.

"I know you're wondering why I asked you to conduct the firm meeting yesterday," David began. "There are only a few reasons, other than being in court, that would cause me to miss a firm meeting, but this was one of them."

Jesse sensed David had bad news to share as he nearly choked on his words.

"When Carol had her annual physical a few weeks ago, her doctor found a lump in her breast. Her doctor then ordered more tests, and yesterday we met with Dr. Sidney Marks, an oncologist. Unfortunately, the news wasn't good. Carol has stage 4 breast cancer."

"Does that mean it's metastasized?"

"Yes, it's spread to her liver."

"Oh, my God, David," Jesse exclaimed. "I can't believe it. I'm so sorry. What can I do to help? You know I'll do anything I possibly can to help Carol or you or Jenna."

"I knew you'd be ready to help, Jesse. That's one of the reasons I wanted to speak to you first thing this morning."

"And the other reason?"

"Carol is insisting that she's going to continue her duties with WCC while undergoing chemo treatments. I don't see how she'll have the strength or energy to do both, especially in the middle of a campaign to raise $3.5 million for a new facility."

"Oh, my! Yes, that will be difficult. Do you want me to talk to her about the possibility of turning her WCC duties over to someone else?"

David leaned back against his chair; his usual firm jaw a little shaky. Jesse hated to see David so unsettled. "Frankly," he said, "I don't think Carol is amenable to stepping down—at least not yet. She's determined to see the capital campaign through to a successful conclusion. Without a successful campaign, she doesn't believe WCC will survive."

Jesse sighed. "Unfortunately, she's probably right. It's a discouraging situation."

David nodded. "What I hope you, and perhaps other WCC board members, will do is provide as much support as possible for Carol so she doesn't deplete all her energy at work. The chemo treatments are going to tax her strength, to say the least. If she gets run down, her metabolism might suffer, leaving her prone to infection. This could seriously affect her treatments."

Jesse offered a reassuring smile. "That's a good idea, David. There are two other board members besides me who should be able to assist Carol so she can focus primarily on the capital campaign."

"Of course, if at any point along the way you believe Carol may consider stepping down from being the president of WCC, Jenna and I would both be most appreciative if you would encourage her to do so."

"Yes, of course. Speaking of Jenna, does she know about her mother's cancer?"

"Yes, we've already told her. We tried keeping her in the dark before we met with Dr. Marks."

"I'm guessing she was on to you?"

"Spot on. Jenna could tell something was wrong, and she leapt to the conclusion Carol and I were getting a divorce. We're going to keep her fully informed so no further misunderstandings occur."

"Probably wise."

David chewed his lower lip for a few seconds, then continued. "But Jesse, you know how much Jenna admires and respects you. She may need someone other than Carol or me to help her get through this. Maybe you could let Jenna know you're available if she wants to talk? After all, you and Carol are almost like sisters. You'll be going through this with us, and Jenna will need another woman to talk to about her mom."

"I 'll be happy to speak to her. Knowing Jenna, she'll probably offer me as much comfort as I can offer her."

David fell silent, and Jesse honored his need for privacy, both thinking of the effect of Carol's illness on Jenna. After what seemed like a long moment, Jesse brought up a concern that crossed her mind. "David, how are you going to be able to carry the work load you have while helping Carol through this?  Your caseload is extremely heavy right now, and the Max Foster case is on an accelerated docket.  Do you want me to take over some of your cases for you?"

David shook his head emphatically.  "I appreciate the offer, Jesse, but your own caseload is as heavy as mine.  And you're going to be assisting Carol as much as possible at WCC."

"Yes . . ."

"So let's keep our respective cases but be ready to pinch hit for each other as necessary. We'll both probably have to rely even more than we currently do on Steve and Maggie.  Thank heaven they've matured as lawyers as quickly as they have."

"Speaking of Steve and Maggie, do you want me to speak to them, or do you intend to do so?" Jesse asked.

"I've thought about that, and I think it's better that I speak to them, as well as all other firm employees.  Unless you recommend otherwise, what I intend to do is call a meeting tomorrow morning of the entire firm and tell them briefly about Carol.  I think they would be disappointed if they heard about her illness from anyone other than me."

"Probably true."

"What I would like you to do after I speak to everyone is follow up with Steve and Maggie to see if they have any questions or suggestions as to how we can best help each other, especially since you and I will have heavier responsibilities outside the firm for the foreseeable future.  The other firm employees may have some questions or concerns too, so I hope you can speak to them as needed."

"I agree with your plan, David, but if at any time you feel you need to take a break from the office, we'll cover for you.  We'll get through all this somehow."

David was comforted by Jesse's pledge of support, and he felt his normal calm composure return.  "Thanks.  I knew I could count on you.  But I'm going to try to follow Carol's example.  She said she's just going to 'suck it up' and handle her WCC duties while receiving chemo treatments.  And she expects Jenna and me to suck it up and carry on with our work, school, and home duties while she continues to handle her WCC duties.  If Carol is going to carry on in this manner, I don't see how I can do anything less."

After they discussed a few other firm-related issues that could arise as they tried to cover for each other, David concluded the meeting with a prediction: "The days ahead will be challenging beyond anything we have previously experienced at Jordan & McKenzie."

Jesse nodded her head in agreement.

*      *      *

The meeting the following morning with all firm employees went about as well as David hoped it would.  Everyone was as shocked as David was initially.  Karen Overton and Maggie wept softly as the news sunk in, but all were obviously genuinely concerned and offered to do whatever they could to help.  When their offers were given, David realized once more how thankful he was for every person in the firm—his second family.

"I greatly appreciate your offers to help, and we will take you up on your offers as needed.  Understandably, I'll have less time available in the office because I need to give priority to Carol's needs.  Jesse will be assisting Carol with her duties at WCC as much as possible.  That means

93

Jesse will also be absent from the office more often as well. Maggie works with me on all my cases, and Steve works with Jesse on all of hers. So they'll be carrying heavier loads."

David hesitated slightly as the reality sunk in how his personal struggle would impact his second family. "The rest of you can best help by stepping up and offering your assistance whenever a need arises in the office, regardless of who asks for or needs help. I've often said we're a family here, and I've never been prouder of each of you than I am right now. Together, we'll get through this."

*        *        *

As the meeting ended and the attendees headed back to their desks, Maggie approached David, wiping tears from her eyes. "I hate to bring this up now, but I need to discuss some issues in the Max Foster case with you. Do you have time today to meet with me?"

"Sure. Now is as good a time as any. I'll meet you in the conference room in a few minutes."

Maggie nodded and left the meeting room, David not far behind. Once they settled into the conference room, Maggie handed a document to David, and said, "This is a draft of our response to Montgomery's first request for production of documents. Our response is due next Wednesday."

"Thanks for handling this so promptly."

"As you know, I've been going through the mountain of documents we will be producing. Most of these documents will have little or no effect on the outcome …"

"But?"

"There are at least three documents you need to know about. I'm struggling to come up with a good faith basis for asserting a privilege that would justify our not producing them; I can't imagine Judge Long sustaining any objection I've thought of. We don't want her looking at us askance, particularly this early in the case."

"What have you found?" David asked, worried Maggie may have found a proverbial smoking gun that could be used against Max at trial.

"Well, the first document of concern is an email Max sent to his friend Greg Oliver, asking him to introduce Max to Martha."

"What's concerning about that? There's nothing wrong with a divorced man wanting to meet an attractive widow."

"That's true," Maggie continued, her worry lines increasing. "But the email includes an extensive discussion about all of the financial challenges Max was facing at the time with his Gateway Orlando project. After discussing those challenges at length, Max asked his friend to introduce him to Martha."

"Okay. I'm beginning to understand why you're concerned. Go on."

"There's nothing expressly stated in the email to indicate Max was looking at Martha's money as the solution to his financial problems, but the implication is there. You know Montgomery will pounce on this email to argue Max planned from the beginning to use Martha as a piggy bank to enable him to complete his project."

"I see," David responded with disappointment. "We need to discuss this email in depth with Max because you're correct—Montgomery will question Max extensively about this email at his deposition."

"The second document that caught my attention is a lengthy memo Max wrote to Martha only three weeks after they were married.  Judging from the memo, he had already begun discussing his financial recommendations with her during their honeymoon in Las Vegas.  She apparently asked Max to put his recommendations to her in writing so she could better analyze and consider them in the context of the advice her financial advisor had given her.  Max had already spoken to an attorney—I suspect it was the same attorney who eventually prepared the will and trust for Martha—and laid out very specific recommendations in the memo."

David shook his head as he considered how these documents could upset their best efforts to defend Max.  "Go on."

"Max recommended that all of Martha's assets be put into a trust, with her as the primary beneficiary.  He didn't recommend he be included as a beneficiary of the trust, but he did recommend she appoint him as co-trustee with her during her lifetime.  Martha would retain the power to remove him as a co-trustee at any time, but upon her death, Max would be the sole trustee while her children would be the primary beneficiaries of the trust."

"So, Max didn't urge Martha to make him a beneficiary of the trust or of her estate?" David asked.

"No, not at that time. Of course, the request came later when the amended will and trust were prepared.

"This *is* troublesome,"

"Getting back to this memo … Max even told Martha he had an attorney in mind to explain the finer points of the estate plan.  He added he would arrange a meeting so Martha could meet this attorney.  So much for the issue of whether Max was the procuring cause of the estate plan."

"I see what you mean."

Maggie raised her eyebrows, an indicator she had more to say on the matter. "David, the paper trail makes it appear Max intended all along to get access to Martha's assets in order to insure he would be able to complete the Gateway Orlando project. At least, Montgomery will be able to plausibly make this argument to Judge Long."

"That's not good news at all," David agreed, shaking his head. "This memo also makes the attorney who prepared the estate plan an important witness. We need to find out what conversations he had with Max before Max introduced the attorney to Martha."

After pausing for a moment to consider what testimony the estate planning lawyer might give, David turned back to Maggie. "You said there were at least three documents you were worried about."

"Yes, the third document is another memo Max wrote to Martha. As I mentioned, Martha liked to see his recommendations in writing to help her think through the issues. This memo was written by Max within a week of the assets being transferred into the revocable trust. It shows that he was very familiar with the extent of Martha's assets and how her investments had performed over the previous five years. It further points out Martha's portfolio had a negative return over the past two years. Although the stock market had performed well during the three years before the last two, most market prognosticators were predicting a high level of risk and volatility over the coming years."

"Yes, I'm familiar with market predictions at the time."

She nodded. "All of what the memo points out about market volatility is true, but Max's proposed solution for Martha to avoid market volatility was to lend him $10 million to see his project through—in return for 8% annual interest and a first mortgage on portions of the Gateway Orlando project."

"I see the problem," David said with resignation.

"David, I'm not a financial advisor, but I'm pretty sure Montgomery will have no problem finding a highly qualified expert witness to opine that investing $10 million in Max's project was considerably riskier than Martha's stock market portfolio.  Further to Max's disadvantage, the stock market has been on a tear lately; Martha's portfolio has exceeded an annual return of 8% since the loan was made.  So, she has lost investment income by making the loan to Max."

"What about the two parcels of property on which Max gave Martha a first mortgage? Didn't those mortgages offer a higher degree of safety for Martha's loan?"

"Some safety, perhaps.  And Max addressed the mortgages at length in the memo, saying they made this a rock solid investment.  What he didn't say, though, is those properties would be worth considerably less if the Gateway Orlando project failed and Martha had to file suit to foreclose the mortgages.  Once again, it's safe to say Montgomery will enjoy going over this memo with Max at his deposition."

"You're full of good news today," David said dryly.  "Are there any other documents you think are problematic for us?"

"There are some other documents that could be construed against Max, but these three are the worst ones …"

"And?"

"And that in itself is a problem.  There are almost no emails, memos, or other documents discussing any of the financial issues once Martha was diagnosed with cancer.  Keep in mind that the amended will and trust appoint Max as the sole personal representative and the sole trustee respectively, giving Max total authority over Martha's assets. Unlike the original trust, the amended trust also includes Max as a beneficiary."

"Am I right in assuming you found no emails, memos, or other documents from Max or Martha discussing or questioning any of these issues?" David asked.

"Yes. Given that Martha liked to see Max's recommendations in writing, the silence in the documents on these issues after her cancer diagnosis is puzzling, to say the least."

"What about the fact neither Max nor Martha told the children about the amended will or the amended trust, or even that Martha had made a $10 million loan to Max? Did you find anything in the documents to indicate why the children were told about none of this?"

Maggie shook her head. "No, there is no mention about any of those issues in the documents I've reviewed. Remember, Max said Martha didn't want to tell her children because she feared Max's suggestions would further estrange her from her children. But I've found nothing to confirm Martha didn't want her children to know about the loan or the amended will and trust. Again, we should anticipate Montgomery will argue it was Max who wanted to keep this information from the children."

"Maggie, based upon what you've just told me, Montgomery should be able to prove most of the facts he has alleged in the complaint without having to rely on anything more than the documents we will be producing."

Maggie's deep sigh matched David's concern. "Yeah, it seems that way to me also. Max better have a very good explanation for all of this, or it won't end well for him.  Do you agree there's no legal privilege that would prevent us from having to produce these documents to Montgomery?"

"Unfortunately, I agree with you.  All of these documents will have to be produced.  I suspect Montgomery already has a copy of them anyway."

*        *        *

Over dinner, David told Carol and Jenna, with pride, about the unanimous offers of support he'd received from all law firm employees that morning.  "I was so encouraged. Everyone asked what they could do to help.  I told them to be ready to pitch in and help when Jesse and I are out of the office.  We are so fortunate to have two capable young lawyers who can cover for Jesse and me when needed."

Carol set her fork down and stared at David.  "Why will Jesse be dealing with other issues?  I understand why you may have to be absent from the office more often, but why Jesse?"

David cleared his throat, trying not to be defensive.  "I guess Jesse hasn't spoken to you yet.  She mentioned that she and the other board members are going to assist you as much as possible so you can devote yourself fully to the fundraising effort for WCC.  Given the importance of raising money for the new building and your critical role in this effort, the other board members want to free you up as much as possible to reach the fundraising goal."

"I see."  Carol's gaze seemed thoughtful, as she contemplated out loud how much additional time this would afford her fundraising activities.  After a few minutes she said, "That *will* be helpful.  Frankly, I've been worried about how I'm going to be able to reach the fundraising goal while also handling my administrative duties in the midst of the chemo treatments. This gives me hope that we may be able to get it all accomplished,"

"I thought so, too."

Carol met his gaze. "But, David, please don't ask me to give up my duties at WCC. This is something I have to see through. I can't explain why … I just know I have to."

David quickly glanced at Jenna before turning his attention back to Carol. "We understand your feelings on the matter, Carol; and we'll do all we can to help you achieve your goal at WCC. But please promise us you'll follow your doctor's advice if he ever recommends you suspend your work during your chemo treatments."

Carol turned her gaze to Jenna who was looking intently at her mom with a mixture of love, concern, and sadness. After nearly a minute of silence while she pondered her response, Carol said softly, "If Dr. Marks actually does make such a recommendation, I promise I will think seriously about it."

This wasn't the unreserved commitment David hoped for, but he realized this was most he would be able to get from Carol for now, and he turned the dinner conversation to happier topics.

# Chapter 8

The following Monday, David met with the attorneys for their usual weekly meeting. Since the staff would be transitioning to the latest version of Microsoft Office, Sarah Garcia brought the attorneys up to date on the installation expected within the next two weeks. She then went through the accounts receivable report in exhaustive detail, urging the lawyers to contact their clients on any invoices that were at least 60 days overdue. Finally, after forty-five minutes of such administrative discourse, David reached the end of his tolerance for administrative detail and asked Jesse to report on the Faulk case.

"Our opposing counsel, Michael Preston, is going to take Dr. Faulk's deposition on Wednesday of this week. We have an appointment with Dr. Faulk tomorrow to prepare him for his deposition. He's never given testimony under oath before, so he's understandably nervous about what's going to take place, particularly when he has so much at risk in this lawsuit. However, Dr. Faulk is normally quite personable. I expect he'll make a good witness *if* he follows our instructions to listen closely to the questions, testifies only to what he knows, and keeps his answers short and to the point."

"Always a big if, Jesse." David commented with a smile. He was glad Jesse was handling the case. Clients seemed to usually follow her instructions.

"I also plan to caution him against losing his composure during questioning," Jesse continued. "Preston doesn't intentionally berate or badger witnesses, but he's so darn repetitive and methodical when examining witnesses that they often get frustrated or angry, which never leads to anything good."

"How do you get a witness to avoid getting angry or frustrated in a deposition, Jesse?" Steve asked. "I've always warned witnesses about losing their cool in a deposition, but they often lose it anyway. Of course, they apologize later—even though it's their own case they've harmed—but by then the damage has been done."

Jesse nodded. "The technique I use is to first warn my witness how losing their composure or getting angry can damage their case. Then, I urge them to make a game out of it, if necessary,"

"A game?" Steve asked.

"Yes. I tell the client to make up their mind ahead of time that there is nothing the opposing attorney can possibly do to cause them to lose their cool. Even if the other attorney insults their ancestry or accuses them of something illegal or immoral, they are to pause and respond calmly and with confidence. If the witness does this well, it's often the opposing counsel who gets frustrated."

Jesse glanced at David, who had taught her this technique, and continued, "This technique has worked well with most of my witnesses, at least when they remember to respond this way."

After they batted this technique around for a few minutes, Maggie asked, "What about your expert witness, Dr. Markham? The last time we discussed the case Dr. Markham was still researching whether there is a relationship between the locations of patients' homes and the orthopedist's office and hospitals at which orthopedic surgeries are performed.  As I recall, Dr. Markham was trying to determine the size and extent of the markets for orthopedic services in central Florida."

Jesse smiled.  "Fortunately, Dr. Markham's research has confirmed his tentative opinion that Dr. Faulk's new office in Sanford is in an entirely different market for orthopedic surgeries than his former office with Orange Orthopedic Surgeons.  All of his surgeries with Orange Orthopedic were conducted in hospitals in Orange County, whereas now all of his surgeries are in hospitals in Seminole County.  Based upon Dr. Markham's research, the vast majority of patients seeking orthopedic services in Orange and Seminole Counties receive those services in the county where they live; only a small percentage go to the other county.  He has an outstanding resume and will make a strong witness for Dr. Faulk."

"What about an expert for Orange Orthopedic?" asked David.  "Have they disclosed an expert yet?"

"Indeed they have," responded Jesse.  "Just this morning we received a written disclosure from counsel for Orange Orthopedic identifying their expert witness as Marion Gonzales, an economist in Miami-Dade County who has a PhD in economics from the University of Miami."

"Interesting that Preston chose an expert from Miami," David commented.  "There are excellent—and probably far cheaper— economists in central Florida he could have hired."

"According to the disclosure," Jesse continued, "Dr. Gonzales will testify that for purposes of orthopedic services the Orlando Metropolitan Statistical Area is all one market and there are sound economic reasons—in other words, a legitimate business interest—for Orange Orthopedic requiring Dr. Faulk to sign a non-compete agreement when he joined Orange Orthopedic."

"So, you will have a battle of the experts at the temporary injunction hearing?" asked Maggie.

"It seems so," said Jesse with a shrug of her shoulders. "But I look forward to cross-examining Dr. Gonzales. I'm not sure she's familiar with central Florida geography and may not realize the Orlando MSA includes all of Seminole, Orange, Osceola and Lake Counties. The southern tip of Osceola County goes all the way down to Yee Haw Junction, about 100 miles from Sanford where Dr. Faulk's office is located. Even Judge Cook, who has a tendency to accept anything the parties have agreed to in their contract, will have difficulty agreeing that Sanford and Yee Haw Junction are all part of one big market for orthopedic surgeons."

"But isn't the actual question whether Dr. Faulk's office is in the same market as Orange Orthopedics' office in Orlando, not whether it's in the same market as Yee Haw Junction?" asked Maggie skeptically.

"Technically, no," came the prompt response from Jesse.

David smiled to himself, knowing how much Jesse enjoyed Maggie's challenging questions. He welcomed the banter in their meetings because these exchanges helped to sharpen their responses for similar questions, they anticipated from the judge at a hearing such as the temporary injunction hearing fast approaching in the Faulk case.

"The actual question is whether Orange Orthopedic had a legitimate business interest to protect, one that extended all the way to Dr. Faulk's office in Seminole County. They will argue the Orlando MSA is all one big market, and they have a legitimate business interest to protect by prohibiting Dr. Faulk from competing in the *entire* market."

"What is your counter argument?" Maggie asked.

"If we can convince the judge this argument is bogus because it purports to make all of the area from Lake County and Seminole County to Yee Haw Junction one big market for orthopedic surgeries, we should win the hearing."

Maggie looked puzzled—still not convinced.

Jesse continued. "For example, Dr. Markham points out that virtually every economist would agree the market area for convenience stores is quite small, perhaps three to four blocks. The market area for different types of businesses vary greatly.  He will testify there is no factual basis for concluding the geographic market for orthopedic services is somehow related to the MSA.  He has been unable to find a single article in economic literature asserting *any* relationship between geographic markets for orthopedic services—or any other medical services for that matter—and the MSA in question."

"Are depositions of the expert witnesses going to be taken before the temporary injunction hearing?" asked David.

"No," interjected Steve. "I spoke to opposing counsel just before this meeting and we've agreed just to exchange written reports by our expert witnesses before the hearing.  We think this will work to our advantage at the hearing.  As it turns out, Dr. Gonzales appears to be a professional witness.  She testified twenty-seven times last year alone, and she has derived more than eighty percent of her income over the past five years from giving expert testimony.  And, get this … she's charging $650 per hour for her services in this case."

"None of that will play well with Judge Cook," commented David. "Let us know if you need any help getting ready for your hearing."

Turning to Maggie, he asked her to bring everyone up to date on the Max Foster case.

"We've filed our answer, so the case is at issue. For the past several weeks I've been going through hundreds of thousands of documents to determine which ones are responsive to plaintiff's document requests."

Steve chuckled. "That many?"

"Yeah, that many," Maggie said with a weary smile. "This has been an interesting exercise because the requests have been so broad, they include almost every document having anything to do with Mr. Foster's Gateway Orlando project. We've found a few documents that are not at all helpful to our client, and none to exonerate him. What's unusual is there are virtually no documents that discuss the key events leading up to the execution of the amended will and amended trust. Whereas there are memos and emails discussing the original will and trust in detail, there are no memos or emails discussing the amended will and trust despite the fact very significant changes were made in the amendments. The absence of any emails or memos regarding these key documents is suspicious, and we anticipate Montgomery will attribute the absence of any such documents to skullduggery on Max's part."

"Are you sure you're getting all of the responsive documents from Max?" asked Steve. "As I've mentioned before, Max has a history of being less than forthcoming when it comes to producing all relevant documents."

"Max has been cooperative. He has turned over the responsibility of gathering all responsive documents to James Moss, the IT director for Max Foster Enterprises. Moss is both knowledgeable and professional, and he understands the consequences of hiding documents. So, yes, I believe we're getting all relevant documents from our client."

"Maggie, when will you get the document production from the plaintiffs in Max's case?" inquired Jesse. "They may have some documents that you haven't seen that could impact the case."

"We'll be producing Max's documents on Friday of this week; the plaintiff's documents will be produced Friday of next week. Of course, both sides are producing their documents electronically in a searchable format, so we'll be able to run word searches on any topic to quickly find the relevant documents to any particular issue in the case."

By now, the meeting had exceeded an hour and a half, and David brought the meeting to a conclusion by saying, "This will be a busy week: Dr. Faulk's deposition on Wednesday and Max Foster's document production on Friday. Since Carol begins her chemo treatments on Wednesday, I'll be out of the office. Hopefully I'll be back to work on Thursday and Friday."

*      *      *

The dreaded commencement of Carol's chemo treatments turned out better than either David or Carol had anticipated. After hearing so many stories of the patient being nauseated following chemo treatments, they both anticipated the worse. To their pleasant surprise, Carol was tired but otherwise feeling good following her treatment on Wednesday. David offered to stay at home with Carol for the rest of the day following the conclusion of her chemo infusion, but she preferred to have some time to herself and urged David to go the office.  Carol just wanted a nap before Jenna returned home from school and soccer practice.

More good news awaited David at the office.  Shortly after he arrived, Jesse stopped by to inquire about Carol and to report that Dr. Faulk had performed admirably during his deposition.  He had kept his answers short, his temper in check, and did his case no harm, which is about the most a lawyer can hope for when his or her own client is being deposed.

# Chapter 9

Jesse always enjoyed the drive to the Seminole County courthouse which was devoted only to civil cases.  It sat in the city of Sanford across East Seminole Boulevard from Lake Monroe, a fifteen-square-mile lake that was part of the St. Johns River system.

On the way, she recalled the courthouse's history.  Built in 1972 in a mid-century modern style, the building now seemed slightly antiquated and out of style, particularly compared to the new Seminole County Criminal Justice Center, located some five miles to the south, built in 2004.  As she drove along Lake Monroe from I-4 to the courthouse, she was reminded why she always looked forward to the trip.

The Interstate had been its usual congested mess.  But as soon as she and Steve took the exit to Sanford along Lake Monroe, traffic was light, the sun reflected peacefully off the ripples in the lake, and birds were skydiving into the lake in search of their breakfast, bringing a temporary sense of calm to what promised to be a tense morning.

As they approached the courthouse, Jesse turned her attention from the peaceful sights to their task at hand—the temporary injunction hearing that would determine whether Dr. Faulk could continue to practice medicine from his office at its present location in Sanford, barely within a thirty-mile radius from his former office with Orange Orthopedic

Surgeons.  Although the hearing this morning would not technically bring the case to a close, the issue to be decided by Judge Marvin Cook would resolve the major issue in the case and could have disastrous effects on Dr. Faulk if Orange Orthopedic prevailed.  He had sunk his life savings into his new office, and his landlord had already threatened to sue if Dr. Faulk broke the lease and moved out, whether court ordered or not.  Dr. Faulk had learned a bitter and costly lesson:  he should have a lawyer review a contract *before* signing, not afterwards.

Once she and Steve passed through security, they met Dr. Faulk outside the courtroom where Judge Cook would conduct the hearing.  After Dr. Faulk's deposition two weeks ago, Jesse and Steve had prepared him thoroughly for his testimony, especially as to what he could expect during cross-examination.  Since the judge only allocated three hours for the hearing, Jesse and Michael Preston—her opposing counsel—had stipulated to most of the undisputed facts so they could complete the hearing within the allotted time.

"All rise," announced the Bailiff once the parties and all counsel were in the courtroom. "The Honorable Judge Marvin Cook presiding."

Judge Cook took his seat at the bench, glanced briefly at the file folder before him, and began, "Please be seated. I've read the briefs filed by both sides in this matter, and I commend all counsel for so cogently laying out your respective positions and legal arguments.  Given the short time we have available for this hearing, I see no need for opening statements.  So, unless any counsel disagrees, we will proceed with testimony.  Mr. Preston, please call your first witness,"

As anticipated, the first witness called by Orange Orthopedic was Dr. Dawn Edwards.  In addition to being one of the two founders of Orange

Orthopedic, she was by far the better witness as compared to her co-founder, Dr. William Simpson.  During their depositions, Jesse had found Dr. Edwards to be a compelling witness, whereas Dr. Simpson was argumentative, arrogant, and neither likeable nor persuasive.  Preston had chosen his witness wisely.

Preston efficiently took Dr. Edwards through her background as a physician, had her relate how Orange Orthopedic came to be formed from the demise of a much larger group of orthopedic surgeons, and had her describe the nature and extent of the medical practice of Orange Orthopedic Surgeons.  She was well spoken, reasonably attractive, and perhaps most importantly, lacked any outward sign of arrogance or superiority that physicians and other professionals sometimes exhibit when testifying.  Jesse could sense that Judge Cook found her to be a credible witness.

Preston then had Dr. Edwards describe how Orange Orthopedic came to hire Dr. Faulk. She emphasized how virtually all of their patients were referrals from primary care physicians, hospital emergency rooms, or emergency clinics.  Therefore, their relationships with those medical providers were essential to the sustainability of their practice.  They simply could not afford to bring a new physician into their practice, introduce him to all of their referral sources, and then allow him to move nearby to compete with them.  She testified at length about the cost of hiring a new physician.

"It usually takes about two years for a practice to recoup the expense of bringing in a new physician, especially when the practice is generous with what they pay the new physician," Dr. Edwards explained.  "It also takes time for the new physician to build a practice."

Preston had Dr. Edwards identify the employment contract with Dr. Faulk and describe in detail how she had suggested he have an attorney review it before he signed.

"Did he, in fact, have a lawyer review the contract?" Preston asked.

"No.  He refused."

Preston continued, "I note that the radius of the non-compete area is thirty miles.  How was that number determined?"

Glancing at Dr. Faulk, Dr. Edwards said, "The first draft of the non-compete agreement had specified a fifty-mile radius within which Dr. Faulk could not compete if he ever left Orange Orthopedic.  He balked at the fifty-mile radius because that would include the coastal area in Brevard County, immediately to the east of Orange County, where Dr. Faulk said he might go if he ever left Orlando."

This testimony was a surprise to Jesse.  In none of her discussions with Dr. Faulk had he ever mentioned he had negotiated the area of the non-compete agreement; he merely told her his interview went well, he trusted Dr. Edwards, and when the agreement was presented to him, he signed it.  The fact he had balked at a fifty-mile radius, but not at a thirty-mile radius, might lead Judge Cook to conclude Dr. Faulk believed a thirty-mile radius was reasonable under the circumstances.  Furthermore, this issue indicated he was able to negotiate the area of the non-compete agreement rather than be faced with a take-it-or-leave-it offer for employment following his orthopedic residency.  Jesse immediately knew she would have to address this issue on cross-examination even though she had not prepared for this line of questioning beforehand.

Preston wrapped up Dr. Edwards' testimony by having her describe how she learned of Dr. Faulk's intended departure to set up his own office.  His final inquiry of Dr. Edwards was whether Sanford and Orlando were both part of the Orlando Metropolitan Statistical Area.

"Yes," she said confidently.

Preston had taken his lead witness through all the essentials of her testimony in a logical, efficient manner within twenty-five minutes.  Jesse's assessment was that Dr. Edwards was an effective witness to whom Judge Cook was listening closely and apparently found persuasive.  In short, Preston had done a good job with this witness. As Jesse rose to begin her cross-examination, her respect for Preston as an adversary had just gone up a notch or two.

"Good morning, Dr. Edwards.  I'm Jessica McKenzie, attorney for Dr. Faulk.  Please tell the court how long Dr. Faulk was employed by Orange Orthopedic Surgeons as a physician."

"He was with us just slightly over three years when he left."

"How long was Dr. Faulk required to be with you before he was to be made a partner in Orange Orthopedics?  You may refer to his employment agreement if you need to."

Without referring to the employment contract, Dr. Edwards replied, "Two years."

"So, despite the promise in the employment agreement that he would be made a partner after two years, he was still not a partner when he left after three years.  Do I have that right?"

"Well, the years are correct, but we weren't entirely happy with his performance.  And of course, the recession hit at about the same time he was eligible to become a partner."

"You do recall that your attorney has provided a copy of Dr. Faulk's personnel file to us in this case, don't you?"

"Yes . . ." Dr. Edwards responded warily.

"Part of that file is his annual written review prepared by you and Dr. Simpson?'

"Yes."

"Isn't it true there is not a single complaint from you or Dr. Simpson about the quality or amount of work performed by Dr. Faulk in his personnel file?"

"Yes, but we weren't good about filling out the paperwork."

"Isn't it also true that neither you nor Dr. Simpson ever gave a negative oral review of Dr. Faulk's performance, at least not until after he gave notice he was leaving you?"

Dr. Edwards shifted in her seat. "I don't recall the specific times of the negative oral reviews we gave him."

"Well, if Dr. Faulk testifies that he was never given a negative review until after giving you notice, you have no facts with which to refute his statement, do you?"

Jesse could sense Dr. Edward's discomfort—realizing she was backed into a corner. "No," she said softly.

"Do you recall the meeting you had with Dr. Faulk to inform him that he would not be made a partner in the practice?"

"Yes."

"That meeting took place about the time Dr. Faulk had been with you for two years?"

"Yes."

"During that meeting the only reason you gave Dr. Faulk for the decision not to make him a partner was the effect the recession was having on Orange Orthopedics' finances, correct?"

Dr. Edwards glanced at Preston before responding weakly, "I don't recall specifically."

"Well, you prepared a memo to his personnel file following that meeting, didn't you?"

"I believe I did . . ."

"There is no reason listed in that memo—other than the effects of the recession—for not making Dr. Faulk a partner at the time, is there?"

"Not to my recollection." Dr. Edwards was looking increasingly uncomfortable on the witness stand. Her initial air of confidence was evaporating, and she repeatedly glanced at her attorney for help that was not forthcoming.

"Isn't it true that the income earned by you and Dr. Simpson actually went up each of the three years Dr. Faulk was with the practice?"

"Yes, but we had to cut back on staff to keep up our income levels."

"Isn't it also true that Dr. Faulk was the one who initially suggested you had more staff than was necessary?"

"He may have made such a suggestion; I don't recall. But it was my decision and Dr. Simpson's to reduce staff."

"Do you recall the comment in Dr. Faulk's personnel file where you mentioned he had inquired why Orange Orthopedic Surgeons had so many non-professional staff employees?"

"I may have mentioned something to that effect," Dr. Edwards muttered, apparently realizing she hadn't been as thorough as she should have been in preparing for this hearing. She seemed uncertain and wary of what else might be in Dr. Faulk's personnel file.

At this point, Jesse went to a new topic. "Did you drive to this hearing from your office today, Dr. Edwards?"

"Yes."

"Did you use a navigation system or Google Maps to provide directions?"

"Yes, Google Maps," Dr. Edwards responded, her head slightly tilted as if wondering where this line of questions was going.

"Did you notice what the distance is from your office to the courthouse according to Google Maps?"

Dr. Edwards straightened. "It was about thirty-six miles."

"You know that Dr. Faulk's office is only one-half mile from the courthouse, right?"

Dr. Edwards just nodded her head affirmatively.

"So, you would agree that, by road, Dr. Faulk's office is more than thirty miles from Orange Orthopedics' office?"

"Maybe so, but the distance for non-compete purposes we agreed upon was as the crow flies, not by road."

"I know you have reviewed the language of the employment contract you had Dr. Faulk sign. It doesn't include the words 'as the crow flies,' prominent does it? The agreement simply mentions a thirty-mile radius?"

"Well, we all knew what that meant."

"Since you and your attorney drafted the employment contract, you could have easily said, 'thirty miles as the crow flies,' or 'a radius of thirty miles in a direct line,' to remove any ambiguity, couldn't you?"

"I just left the wording up to my lawyer," Dr. Edwards responded dismissively.

"Now, you testified that the first draft of the non-compete clause spoke about a fifty-mile radius, to which Dr. Faulk balked.  Isn't it true you were willing to reduce the radius of the non-compete area because you don't get any patients from Brevard County or other areas thirty to fifty miles away?"

"It's true we don't get patients from Brevard County, but we were also trying to accommodate Dr. Faulk."

"Dr. Edwards, you do not have admitting privileges at any hospital in Seminole County, nor does Dr. Simpson.  True?"

"That's true."

"And when Dr. Faulk was with you, he had no admitting privileges at hospitals in Seminole County, did he?"

"Also true."

"Now that his office is in Seminole County, Dr. Faulk has privileges *only* at hospitals in Seminole County and none in Orange County.  Isn't that true?"

Jesse met Dr. Edward's glare and noticed a slight twitch of her jaw before she responded, "Yes, that's my understanding."

"Over the last three years, you and Dr. Simpson have treated only one patient who lived in Seminole County, and that patient lived in Orange County when his treatment began, correct?"

"I believe that's correct."

"So, based upon the past three-year history, Orange Orthopedic Surgeons will suffer no loss of income or other competitive disadvantage if *all* of the orthopedic patients in Seminole County go to Dr. Faulk for treatment.  Isn't this true?"

"I don't know," said Dr. Edwards meekly.

Dr. Edwards slumped slightly in her chair, appearing to feel as if she were on a sinking ship.

Jesse almost felt sorry for the doctor. The language of the non-compete agreement Dr. Edwards thought was rock solid didn't look very solid anymore. However, the hearing was not won yet. Dr. Edwards had hired a very expensive expert witness from south Florida who might still save the day for Orange Orthopedic Surgeons.

Jesse took her seat.

After Preston tried with limited success to rehabilitate Dr. Edwards' testimony on re-direct, he called his expert witness, Dr. Marion Gonzales, to testify. She had no knowledge of the facts of the case—other than the facts relayed to her by Preston. But due to her education, training and experience, she was permitted by court rules to render opinion testimony with respect to key issues in the case.

"Dr. Gonzales," Preston said, "Please tell the court what your qualifications are to testify as an expert witness on economic issues."

"I earned a PhD in economics from the University of Miami. For the past 10 years, I have had my own consulting firm—providing business advice and testifying as an expert witness on economic or business issues. I have been accepted by courts in Florida to testify as an expert on economic issues over 400 times."

Preston continued, "In the present suit, a key issue is the size of the geographic area in which Orange Orthopedic Surgeons could reasonably claim to have a legitimate business interest to prevent an employee doctor, such as Dr. Faulk, from competing with Orange Orthopedic if he left the practice. In short, the issue is whether Orange and Seminole counties constitute one big market for orthopedic surgeries, or whether they are two separate markets. What have you done to form an opinion on this issue?"

After Dr. Gonzales told the judge what she had done to be able to render an opinion on this key issue, Preston presented the key question to her.

"Dr. Gonzales, have you formed an opinion, to a reasonable certainty, whether all of Orange and Seminole counties constitute a single market for orthopedic surgeries, or whether they are separate markets?"

"I have formed such an opinion."

"Then please tell the court what your opinion is and state the basis for that opinion," instructed Preston.

"In my opinion, the entire Orlando Metropolitan Statistical Area—which includes all of Orange, Seminole, Osceola and Lake counties—constitutes a single market for orthopedic surgeries. Therefore, a medical practice such as Orange Orthopedic Surgeons has a legitimate reason—what I believe the law calls a legitimate business interest—for insisting their physician employee not leave the practice and compete with them within that market for up to two years after leaving."

Dr. Gonzales paused and looked directly at the judge before continuing.

"The basis for my opinion is as follows: it is the U.S. Office of Management and Budget—the OMB—which defines the MSAs."

Preston nodded. "Will you explain what an MSA is?"

"Certainly. A MSA, or Metropolitan Statistical Area, consists of a core area, such as the City of Orlando, together with adjacent communities having a high degree of economic and social integration with the core community. In this case, the City of Orlando is surrounded by Orange

County, as well as Seminole, Lake and Osceola Counties, and together they form one big market as defined by the OMB.  Consistent with this market, the parties to Dr. Faulk's employment contract agreed upon a non-compete radius from Orange Orthopedic Surgeon's office in south Orlando that extended to the northern edge of the Orlando MSA."

As Dr. Gonzales finished her testimony, Preston smiled slightly at Jesse as if to say, "Let's see what you can do with this testimony," but said simply, "Your witness."

Jesse was on her feet immediately and took her position behind the lectern where Judge Cook required the lawyers to remain while questioning a witness.

"Dr. Gonzalez," Jesse began, "you have not performed any independent test or study with regard to the market for orthopedic surgeries in connection with your testimony here today, have you?"

"No, I have not."

"You have not reviewed any scholarly article in the field of economics that purports to show a correlation between the market area for orthopedic surgeries and a specific Metropolitan Statistical Area, have you?"

"No."

"In fact, you have never even *seen* an article written by an economist attempting to show a correlation between a market area for orthopedic surgeries and a MSA, have you?"

"No."

Jesse resisted the urge to smile.  "Well, within any given market area for a particular kind of services, would you expect those services to be available from most, if not all, providers throughout the market area?"

"Generally, yes, although most providers of services, including medical service providers, usually get more of their customers or patients from close by than they do from customers or patients toward more remote parts of the market."

Jesse sensed Dr. Gonzales had an idea where this line of questions was going and she would give ground grudgingly, only as she had to.

"So, given your testimony that Orange, Seminole, Lake and Osceola Counties are all one big market, you would expect Orange Orthopedic Surgeons to get at least some of their patients from Seminole, Lake and Osceola counties, right?"

"Yes, that is what I would expect, although I would expect them to get most of their patients from Orange County."

"Dr. Gonzales, according to their own records, your client has treated *no* patients from Lake or Osceola counties over the past three years, and only treated one patient from Seminole County, and that patient lived in Orange County when treatment began. That's not consistent with what you just testified you would expect to find in a single market for all four counties, is it?"

Dr. Gonzales blinked twice; a sign she was becoming uncomfortable. "Well, no, but over time, more patients may begin to come to Orange Orthopedic from the other three counties."

"As of this time, however, your client's records clearly show patients are *not* coming to Orange Orthopedic from the other three counties, correct?"

"That's … correct," Dr. Gonzales admitted grudgingly.

"And you can provide the Court with no assurance patients will *ever* come to Orange Orthopedic from the other three counties, can you?"

Dr. Gonzales gave a slight shake of her head. "Well, I can't provide any *guarantees*, but given that the OMB considers all four counties to be part of the Orlando MSA, I believe Orange Orthopedic can reasonably expect to get some patients for orthopedic surgeries from Seminole, Lake and Osceola counties."

With this testimony, Jesse decided to shift direction to make her point. "Dr. Gonzales, do you know where Yee Haw Junction, Florida is?"

Dr. Gonzales looked bewildered. "I don't believe I do, although I seem to remember seeing a sign for it on the Florida Turnpike."

"Will you accept my suggestion that Yee Haw Junction is at the southern tip of Osceola County?

Dr. Gonzales shrugged. "Okay."

"And will you also accept my suggestion that Yee Haw Junction is over 100 miles from Dr. Faulk's office in Sanford?"

"Okay."

"What evidence do you have that Yee Haw Junction and Sanford are in the same market for orthopedic surgeries, other than the fact they are both part of the same MSA?"

After pausing for a long moment, Dr. Gonzales said simply, "Being in the same MSA is my only basis."

"And what evidence do you have that the plaintiff's office in South Orlando and Dr. Faulk's office in Sanford are in the same market for orthopedic surgeries, other than the fact they are both part of the same MSA?"

After an even longer pause, Dr. Gonzales said, "Being in the same MSA is my only basis, and I think that is sufficient."

"So, it's your testimony that being in the same MSA is a sufficient reason for opining that Orlando and Sanford are in the same market for orthopedic surgeries, although there is no basis for this opinion in *any* business or economic literature you can identify?"

"Yes, that's my opinion."

Jesse paused for longer than normal to allow the significance of the last question and answer to sink in. She then posed her final questions for Dr. Gonzales.

"Testifying as an expert witness accounts for what portion of your income over the past five years?"

"About eighty percent."

"What hourly rate are you charging for your preparation and testimony here today?"

"Six hundred and fifty dollars per hour."

Jesse looked at Judge Cook, who was unable to hide his shocked expression, said, "No further questions," and sat down.

Rather than address any redirect questions to Dr. Gonzales, Preston announced, "Plaintiff rests, Your Honor."

Jesse peeked quickly at her watch. It was nearly noon, and Judge Cook would most likely declare a lunch break before asking Jesse to call her first witness. She wanted to stay on the offensive.

Before Judge Cook could announce a break, Jesse stood and said, "Your Honor, before we proceed, I have a motion to make. I move to strike Dr. Gonzales' entire testimony because her own testimony establishes there is no known economic or other specialized knowledge which establishes a correlation, much less a direct relationship, between a MSA and a market area for orthopedic surgeries. Her clear testimony was that the *only* basis upon which she opined Dr. Faulk and Orange Orthopedic were in the same market for orthopedic surgeries was because their offices are in the same MSA. Although Dr. Gonzales has a PhD in economics, this does not qualify her to opine to novel economic theories not supported elsewhere in economic literature. Her testimony should be stricken in its entirety."

Before Preston could respond, Judge Cook intervened. "I'll tell you what I am going to do," he began as he glanced at the wall clock. "I'm ready for a break. Over the lunch hour, I'm going to consider Ms. McKenzie's motion. If you want to argue against her motion, Mr. Preston, you will have ten minutes within which to do so when we return."

He glanced directly at Preston, who by this time appeared to have little doubt about the direction the hearing was taking. "My suggestion to both of you, however, is that your time could be spent more productively over the lunch hour by trying to find a reasonable settlement in this case. I will see both counsel at one o'clock."

Once the judge had left the courtroom, Jesse, Steve and Dr. Faulk went into the hall outside the courtroom to wait for Preston, who was engaged in an animated but hushed conversation with Dr. Edwards as Steve closed the door to the courtroom.

"Mr. Preston will have a tough job convincing Dr. Edwards to make a reasonable settlement offer," Dr. Faulk remarked ruefully. "She has great difficulty believing she could possibly be wrong about anything."

"Well, after Preston explains that if they lose this hearing, they are likely to lose the entire case and will have to pay your attorneys' fees, she may become a little more reasonable," Jesse responded. She fully believed what she was saying. But she also recognized that with someone like Dr.

Edwards, it would probably take most of the lunch hour for reality to sink in.

Nor did Jesse expect Dr. Edwards would make a reasonable offer just yet. She anticipated Orange Orthopedics' initial offer would be ridiculous and unacceptable, but she also had in mind how she would frame her counteroffer so Dr. Edwards would be under no illusions about what her options were.

As expected, after five minutes of agitated but muffled discussion from the courtroom, Preston came out the door and asked Jesse to join him. When they were off by themselves, Preston began, "Jesse, I've finally talked Dr. Edwards into being reasonable about resolving this matter. She will allow Dr. Faulk to buy out of his non-compete agreement for only $50,000. That will reimburse my client for some of the costs of Dr. Faulk leaving the practice and allow him to move forward with his practice in Sanford without the court requiring him to move outside the thirty-mile radius of the non-compete agreement."

He paused for effect, then asked, "Can we announce this settlement to Judge Cook when he returns from lunch?"

Jesse flashed a knowing smile at Preston and said, "Well, that's almost exactly what I expected from Dr. Edwards. No disrespect to you, Michael, but let's cut the crap. Here's the only offer we will agree to, and this offer only remains open until court reconvenes after lunch. We'll stipulate to a joint motion to dismiss the case, with prejudice, meaning the case can't be resurrected by either party, and each party will pay his or its own attorneys' fees. The only reason Dr. Faulk is willing to forego Orange Orthopedic being required to pay his attorneys' fees and damages for their failure to keep their promise to make him a partner is because he wants the case over today.  If Dr. Edwards doesn't agree by the time we reconvene, the offer is off the table, and there will be no further settlement offers from our side."

Her position clearly stated, Jesse turned back toward Steve and Dr. Faulk.  "Let's go to lunch."

Over lunch, Dr. Faulk listened closely as Jesse recounted her conversation with Preston.  "Okay," he said, "you told him exactly what I wanted you to tell him, but what makes you think Dr. Edwards will accept our proposal?"

Jesse smiled.  "Dr. Edwards is stubborn, but she isn't obtuse.  She saw how the hearing was going this morning.  If she failed to understand the hearing was not going her way, Preston surely has enlightened her by now.  She badly underestimated your willingness to fight this lawsuit, and she overestimated the strength of their case.  As soon as she realizes that nothing good is going to come of continuing the fight, she'll agree to our proposal."

Dr. Faulk's nod signaled his admiration and respect for his lawyer.  But Jesse could tell he was so nervous he couldn't enjoy his lunch—probably because he would soon be taking the stand if there was no settlement.

*   *   *

"All rise. The Honorable Judge Marvin Cook presiding," announced the Bailiff as Judge Cook entered the courtroom.  He took his seat at the bench, looked at the lawyers, and asked, "Counsel, where are we?"

Jesse looked over at Preston.  He was looking inquiringly at Dr. Edwards who appeared to be still in the midst of trying to decide how she

128

wanted to proceed.  After staring at Preston for a long moment, a look of resignation passed over Dr. Edwards' face, and she nodded her head at him in agreement.  Finally, Preston slowly arose, brought himself to his full height, and said to Judge Cook, "Your Honor, I believe we have a settlement."

# Chapter 10

At the Monday meeting the following week, the attorneys at Jordan & McKenzie were still in a festive mood from the hearing in the Faulk case. "I don't know when I've seen a more appreciative client," Steve commented. "Dr. Faulk was nervous about testifying and terrified the judge might rule against him. To get out of the hearing with the entire case being resolved, without his even having to testify, was almost more than he could believe. He's convinced Jesse is the world's best lawyer."

Jesse smiled. "I have to admit, he did seem appreciative. In fact, he called me late Friday to invite Steve and me to dinner next Saturday to celebrate the good result." Jesse glanced toward Steve. "I accepted on behalf of both of us. I hope you're available."

"I'll join you and Dr. Faulk for drinks, but I'll cut out before dinner. Dr. Faulk is much more interested in celebrating with you than he is with me, Jesse. I'm sure you won't mind having dinner alone with a handsome, single doctor who also happens to be an awfully nice guy."

Jesse blushed slightly but didn't object to Steve's plan. *It will be nice to have something resembling a social life.* Since she and David had formed Jordan & McKenzie, Jesse had been so consumed with work she had little time for a social life. She had been impressed with James Faulk from their first meeting but had kept their relationship strictly professional while representing him.  Now that the case was over, she looked forward to getting to know him personally.

Looking about the room at the sly smiles and inquiring looks from David, Steve, and Maggie, Jesse quickly decided to turn the conversation to another topic.  She asked David, "What's happening in the Max Foster case?"

"This week is going to be devoted to a final review of the key documents and to preparing Max for his deposition, which will take place Thursday of next week.  As you know, he needs a lot of preparation, so we're going to spend most of this Friday, as well as next Monday and Tuesday going over documents with him and generally getting him prepared for his deposition.  Max has been involved in a lot of litigation and has been deposed many times … but this case involves his personal life.  Given the allegations against him, it's critical that he be well prepared and not let Larry Montgomery get him rattled."

Steve and Maggie gave each other a knowing look.  "Well, good luck," Steve said.  "You have your work cut out for you."

*       *       *

When David arrived at home that night, Jenna met him at the door, concern plainly evident on her face.  "Hi, Dad.  Mom's taking a nap.  She said her chemo treatment went well this morning, but afterwards she met with a couple of potential donors for WCC.  Apparently, they weren't very encouraging about making a big donation.  I can't tell whether Mom is just worn down from the chemo or is discouraged about fundraising.  I don't ever recall seeing Mom so down, Dad.  What can we do?"

"We just need to keep loving her and encourage her all we can, Jenna.  The combination of chemo and a challenging fundraising campaign is enough to wear anyone down. I'll order her favorite dish—lasagna—from Antonio's tonight. That usually cheers her up."

Jenna set the table while David ordered and went to get the lasagna, Caesar salad, and Antonio's famous tiramisu for dessert. When David returned, Carol was up from her nap, but she still appeared worn out and discouraged. Her mood improved noticeably when she saw the lasagna and tiramisu, and they all sat down to dinner.

Since Carol had begun her chemo treatments, their dinners together had taken on deeper meaning than they had previously. Although no one ever mentioned it, and all three repressed the thought whenever it arose, they all recognized their time together could be limited. Dinners together became a precious event

"I'm sorry I'm not very cheerful tonight, guys," Carol commented as she took a bite of lasagna, "although I would be even less cheerful without the lasagna and tiramisu."

"Right on, Mom," Jenna said, then took a big bite.

"It's just so discouraging to me that so many potential major donors see the value of what we're doing at WCC but are still unwilling to make a major donation until we have the new building. Both donors that I met with today were willing to commit to only $10,000 each, but both said they will be willing to make a much larger donation if we get the new building. We're just going in circles with our contributors. I know I'm doing what I'm supposed to be doing, but why does doing the right thing have to be so hard?"

David squeezed Carol's hand. What could he say?

He had no clear answer why doing the right thing had to be so hard. In his own work, he had often asked the same question. Some lawyers seemed to skate by without giving much thought to whether what they were doing was the right thing and seldom paid a price for their indifference.  Judges and the Florida Bar would usually punish *flagrant* violations of the ethical rules.  But too often the less ethical lawyers would get by without adverse consequences when they took the easy road by overlooking ethical rules that were inconvenient to them at the time. David consoled himself with the knowledge most judges knew who the ethical lawyers were and who weren't.  David was determined he wouldn't sully his reputation by playing fast and loose with the rules, no matter how inconvenient or difficult.  *In the long run, nothing is more beneficial to a trial lawyer, and therefore for his clients, than a reputation for ethical behavior and professionalism.  Besides, for one concerned about maintaining high moral character, doing the right thing is its own reward.*

Carol's situation was different, however, and had nothing to do with someone acting in an unethical manner.  The potential donors were understandably concerned.  If WCC were unable to raise enough capital to sustain their ongoing operations in a building that met their needs, any donations made would be wasted, or at least would have no lasting effect.  The donors wanted to ensure their charitable donations would contribute to a *permanent* solution to benefit the women and their children served by WCC.

David wished he had concrete advice to give to Carol.  All seemed to recognize the benefit of an expanded operation for WCC in a new, larger building.  David understood the donors' caution, but their prudence seemed to be conspiring against bringing the fundraising campaign to a successful conclusion, which was essential if the WCC women were to continue to have the care they so desperately needed.  Indeed, as Carol asked, "Why does doing the right thing have to be so hard?"

"I don't know why doing the right thing is often so hard, Carol," David finally replied. "But I do know that achieving anything worthwhile is usually hard.  It's hard because if it were easy, it would have been achieved long ago."

He offered Carol a wide smile as he squeezed her hand one more time.  "We are so proud of you for creating WCC and taking on this mission to serve a group of people who were ignored or forgotten."

David glanced toward his daughter.  "Jenna and I agree that you're doing what you're supposed to be doing.  I wish I had an answer for how to raise the money needed, but Carol, I do believe you will get the money.  WCC will continue and will prosper."

"I believe that, too, Mom," Jenna quickly added.

Carol simply nodded. "Thanks for the encouragement, you two . . . ." She sighed.  "I'm still wondering how we're going to raise three and half million dollars.  Especially while having to deal with these damn chemo treatments!"

*          *          *

The preparation for Max's deposition was tedious.  There were literally hundreds of documents that Montgomery might ask him about, and David wanted to be sure Max had reviewed all of the documents recently.  There's nothing worse for a client's case than to have his testimony contradicted by a letter or memo he himself wrote months ago— the reason David always insisted on going through all of the key documents in detail with his clients before they were subject to examination by opposing counsel.

134

In addition to refreshing the client's recollection of the facts, going through the documents with the client helped David understand the client's thinking as the facts were unfolding.  Having this understanding usually enabled him to anticipate most of the areas of inquiry from opposing counsel.  It also helped him minimize on redirect examination any potentially harmful effects of admissions made by his client during direct examination.

Max, however, was pushing back on having to go through the tedious task of reviewing all of the documents Maggie had identified for him to review.  "I know what's in the documents about the Gateway Orlando project, and I certainly know what Martha and I discussed," Max had indignantly told David and Maggie.

David tried to remain calm at Max's obvious lack of insight.  "Max, you may know the facts contained in most of your emails, letters, and other documents but remembering *why* you said or acted the way you did is critically important in this case.  An action or statement you made innocently could appear to take on a sinister intent in retrospect, especially in view of your becoming the sole trustee of Martha's trust and the personal representative of her estate."

"I'm not sure I follow you," Max said, still indignant but genuinely puzzled

"Well, let's talk about your friend, Greg Oliver.  How close were you to him?"

"Greg has been a close friend since we were in college together.  He's a very capable businessman, and he and I have discussed our respective businesses many times over the years. Greg has helped me work through some significant problems affecting my company, and I've helped him from time to time."

"Would you say that he has been a confidant of yours—someone whom you would confide in when you might not confide in anyone else?"

"Yes, I think that would be a fair statement."

"Did you confide in Greg about the financial problems you were having with the Gateway Orlando project?"

"I believe I did."

David pointed to a printed email. "Max, look at this email you wrote to Greg two years ago. It lays out in precise detail the financial problems you were having with Gateway Orlando. You were having trouble getting all of the construction financing you needed. Some of your investors were late making the contributions to capital they promised to make, and the City of Orlando's requirements for the project were driving up the cost of construction."

"Yes, all of that was true … and not unusual for a project as complicated as this one."

"Max, you go on for nearly two pages about the financial problems the project is facing. Then, in the very next paragraph you ask Greg to introduce you to Martha."

"Yes, but my asking Greg to introduce me to Martha had nothing to do with the Gateway Orlando project. Martha and I had mutual friends, including Greg, who told me a lot about her and encouraged me to call her. After being divorced for a year, I was ready to meet someone. Based upon what my friends told me, Martha was the woman I wanted to meet."

*How can Max not connect the dots?* "Max, can't you see that to a disinterested observer your motive for wanting to meet a wealthy widow could be primarily to help get you through your financial problems with Gateway Orlando?  If a disinterested observer would assume this, you can be sure Larry Montgomery will spend much of your deposition trying to get admissions from you to make that point.  And once an admission is on the record, it's devilishly hard to undo it."

Max scowled.  "I think it's a stretch for him to make that argument, but what do you want me to do about it?  I can't change the facts or what's in the emails."

"That's correct, and I'm not suggesting you say anything other than the truth.  But you just told me how Greg and other friends had previously suggested you call Martha; I had never heard this before."

Max's eyes widened.  "Oh, I thought I had told you."

"That's the sort of information you should include in your answer at an appropriate time. Unless you go through these documents and try to remember the context in which they were written, you may leave out some vital information or give testimony that gives a different slant on the facts than what was intended at the time.  Can't you see that?"

*      *      *

Max sat still for a full minute to ponder David's statement.  He seldom assumed others would stoop to putting the worst possible construction on his motives, even though he often did so to others.  But now his own attorney was telling him that some of his statements, taken at face value, could be evidence of a scheme to take advantage of a widow to benefit his project.  David also warned him Montgomery would put an ungenerous spin on anything and everything he said or did with respect to Martha and her children.

137

It was a sobering realization for Max.  To make it in the world of real estate development, he always felt he had to be tough.  This often caused him to be brusque in his dealings with others.  His self-image, however, was that he had a soft heart beneath that tough exterior.  What David seemed to be telling him was that Martha's children and their attorney didn't see the soft heart; they only saw the tough persona.  They would do everything they could to ensure the judge saw only a greedy developer who exercised undue influence over a widow to complete his stalled project.

"I still think it's a stretch for Martha's children to say this email is evidence of a scheme to take advantage of Martha," Max finally said, "but I see your point.  I'll take the necessary time to go through the documents Maggie has selected for me to review."

The remainder of that day and the two additional days David and Maggie met with Max to prepare for his deposition made him feel like a mule plowing through crusted soil.  The process was not only tedious, but as he reviewed the documents in depth, the realization the record could arguably support a claim for undue influence gradually dawned on him.  Introspection had never been a prominent part of Max's character, and as he waded through the documents, an uneasy feeling about the case slowly rose up from his own words in letters and emails he had written months ago and settled deep in his gut.  The confluence of his growing unease, together with his sadness over Martha's death and his anger with her children for suing him, formed a noxious brew that soured his stomach and left Max irritated and depressed.

At the same time, he was grateful to review the documents in a new light, and he felt he would be as well prepared to testify as he could be.

# Chapter 11

David and Montgomery had agreed Max's deposition and those of Martha's children would be taken in their respective lawyer's offices.  Although Max's deposition was set for 9:30 in the morning, David had Max arrive forty-five minutes early for last minute preparation and a final review of the rules for the deposition.

"Max," David said, "remember that a deposition is testimony under oath, and the deposition of a party can be read directly into evidence at the trial—if the lawyer elects to do so. This seldom happens because most trial lawyers prefer to question a party at trial rather than read a cold transcript into evidence.  If Montgomery gets a helpful admission from you, he will ensure the jury hears the admission when he questions you at trial."

"Okay, I get it.  Remember, this isn't my first deposition.  What I have always wondered, though, is why we have depositions at all?  Why not just testify at trial?  I will be testifying at trial; so will Martha's children."

*Good question, Max.*  David had asked himself the same questions many times.  "Well, the original purpose of allowing pre-trial depositions was to avoid trials by ambush.  Depositions allow the lawyers to learn what the testimony of the witnesses will be at trial so there will be few surprises there."

Max shrugged. "Makes sense, I suppose."

"Over time, though, the primary purpose of depositions has morphed into lawyers getting as many admissions as possible from witnesses to bolster their client's chances of winning the case on a motion for summary judgment, which avoids a trial altogether. Getting admissions at depositions also enhances the client's chances of obtaining a favorable settlement."

"So, has the availability of pre-trial depositions improved the litigation process? It seems lengthy and expensive to me," Max said sourly.

"It depends on who you ask, Max. The combination of extensive pre-trial discovery, including depositions, and mandatory pre-trial mediation conferences, has resulted in far fewer trials, with the resolution of the suit frequently hinging on the testimony given at depositions. And you're right, having depositions—and other pretrial discovery methods—increases the time and expense to resolve cases. I, personally, would prefer less discovery and more trials."

"But back to today's deposition," David continued. "Remember to keep your answers short and to the point; don't go beyond the scope of the question in your response; and don't speculate in your answers."

David had gone over these rules previously with Max, and even conducted some simulated examination by Montgomery, which Max handled surprisingly well. David felt his client was well prepared.

Montgomery arrived at Jordan & McKenzie's office shortly before the scheduled time, unaccompanied by either of his clients. David was surprised because, as parties, the children had the right to attend the deposition—and he knew from prior experience that Montgomery usually had his clients attend the opposing party's deposition.

"Why aren't the children attending my deposition," asked Max. "I certainly intend to be present at theirs."

"I'm surprised they're not here, too, Max. Their absence may be an indication they prefer not to confront you if they don't have to—or perhaps both just had conflicting obligations today. But I doubt *neither* one was able to attend, especially for such an important deposition."

Karen Overton showed Montgomery into the conference room where the court reporter had already set up and was ready to begin. David and Max entered the conference room a few minutes later. After a civil but chilly introduction between Montgomery and Max, David and Max took their side of the conference table, with the court reporter at the head of the table and Montgomery across the table from Max.

As soon as he was sworn in by the court reporter, Montgomery had Max identify himself and then proceeded to go through an unnecessarily long preliminary set of questions about the rules for the deposition. Although David believed a long series of preliminary questions about deposition rules was unnecessary, he was not about to object. He and Montgomery had agreed the depositions of their respective clients would not exceed seven hours of actual testimony time for each of them. If Montgomery wanted to waste valuable time going over rules David had already covered with his client, this was fine with David.

Once Montgomery finally finished the preliminary questions, he turned to more substantive questions.

"Mr. Foster, Martha was your third wife, wasn't she?"

"Yes."

"Both of your previous wives filed for divorce against you, didn't they?"

"Yes, although I countersued for divorce against my second wife."

"In fact, in the petition for dissolution of marriage your second wife filed, she included allegations of adultery, didn't she?"

Max's jawline tightened.  David had warned him that Montgomery might include such questions, but under no circumstances should Max lose his composure.  Since Montgomery had only asked what was in the petition his former wife had filed, David did not object to this question.

After a long pause, Max calmly said, "Yes, and I made a similar allegation in my counterclaim for dissolution of marriage against her."

"Were the allegations by your former wife of your adultery true?"

"I object to this question," interjected David.  "It seeks information that is totally immaterial and irrelevant to this lawsuit.  If you insist on an answer to this question or otherwise pursue this line of inquiry, I will suspend this deposition until we can get a ruling from Judge Long on my objection."  David intended to stop any salacious questioning in the case immediately.  Under the rules governing depositions he couldn't instruct his client not to answer this question because it didn't involve a legal privilege, but he could suspend the deposition until the judge ruled on his objection.

As David suspected, Montgomery was just trying to embarrass Max.  He was not about to adjourn the deposition until they could schedule a hearing before Judge Long, which could be several weeks or more.  True to form, though, Montgomery didn't concede the point without a parting shot at Max.  "Oh, we'll have a hearing on this issue before Judge Long all right, but at a later date," Montgomery snarled.  "Mr. Foster isn't the only one who can testify as to the truth of these allegations." The implication that Montgomery might call the former wife or a former mistress to testify wasn't lost on David, or Max, but David would deal with that issue when and if it arose.

Montgomery then turned his inquiry to the Gateway Orlando project. In a thorough and efficient manner, he had Max describe the genesis, the scope, and the value of the project. Finally, Montgomery turned to problems Max was having with the project.

"As with most construction projects, you ran into some problems with the Gateway Orlando project, didn't you?"

"Yes. As you said, most construction projects have problems along the way."

"But this isn't just any project; it's the biggest development project you have ever handled, isn't it?"

"Yes."

"In fact, the scope of this project is more than fifty percent larger than any other development project you've ever had, correct?"

Max seemed surprised that Montgomery possessed so much information about his projects, especially this one. However, he maintained his composure and simply said, "Yes."

"In this, the biggest project of your career, you were having trouble getting all of the construction financing that you needed, weren't you?"

Based on his review of the documents with Max, David knew his client was prepared for this question. Max replied, "This project was being developed in phases and with different parcels. Our primary construction lender didn't want to be the lender on all phases and parcels, so we had to look for a second construction lender."

"All of the additional construction lenders you spoke to wanted you to invest more of your own capital into the project before they would consider becoming the second construction lender, correct?"

"Yes, that's correct."

"And one of the reasons that the potential lenders were insisting you invest more capital into the project is because some of your investors had not made the capital contributions they had promised to make?"

"Yes, that's true."

"Another problem you had to deal with was the City of Orlando's requirements on the project that increased the construction costs, right?"

"Yes."

Montgomery passed a document to Max. "Mr. Foster, I'm showing you a copy of an email which you sent to a Mr. Greg Oliver about a month before you actually met Martha. The court reporter has marked this document as Plaintiffs' Exhibit 1. Do you recognize this email?"

David was glad he'd prepared Max for the possibility Montgomery might inquire about this email. Max reviewed the email, then said. "Yes, that's an email I wrote to my friend Greg Oliver."

"Mr. Oliver was a close friend and confidant of yours?"

"Yes, we've been close friends since college."

"You were close enough that you shared confidential business information with him from time to time, true?"

"Yes."

"And you also shared confidential personal information?"

"Yes, sometimes."

"Now, Mr. Foster, directing your attention to Plaintiffs' Exhibit 1, immediately after discussing the development problems with your project for two pages, you requested that Mr. Oliver introduce you to Martha, didn't you?"

And there it was, the accusation David had anticipated.  Max was ready for it—or so David hoped.

"Yes, but my request that Greg introduce me to Martha had nothing to do with the problems with the project I mentioned to him."  Thankfully, Max remained calm.  "He and other friends of mine had told me about Martha and had urged me to call her and ask her out.  I didn't want to call her blindly, so I asked him to introduce me to her.  The fact this request comes right after I mentioned the problems with the project is coincidental.  One has nothing to do with the other."

"So, you deny that one of the reasons you wanted to meet Martha was to hopefully get her to become an investor in the project or be a lender to you for the project?"

Max's lips curled into a snarl as he said slowly and emphatically, "Yes, I deny that."

A sly, knowing smile crept across Montgomery's face as he picked up Plaintiffs' Exhibit 1, examined it for a long minute, then asked, "Do you see the response from Greg Oliver on Exhibit 1, stating that he would arrange a time and place for him to introduce you to Martha in person, as you requested?"

"Yes."

"Did such a meeting for the introduction take place?"

"Yes."

"After that introductory meeting did you subsequently go out with Martha?"

"Yes."

"And did you follow up with Greg Oliver after your first date with Martha?"

A cloud passed over Max's face, which quickly passed, as he said, "I don't remember, although I may have."

"Well, let me refresh your memory, Mr. Foster." Montgomery produced another document. "Here's an email from you to Mr. Oliver dated three weeks after your email requesting an introduction to Martha— apparently, after you had gone out with Martha. Do you recognize this document as an email you sent to Mr. Oliver?"

Montgomery handed the document to David to review before showing it to Max. It had the original email chain from Max to Greg, and Greg's reply email saying he would set up the introductory meeting. But all of this was on Plaintiffs' Exhibit 1, the email Max recognized and had produced. This document included those emails, but it also included a responsive email from Max to Greg. David did his best to hide his concerned surprise as he reviewed the text of Max's response:

*Greg, I just wanted to let you know that I had an enjoyable date with Martha last night. I may have found an answer to the problems with the project that we discussed.*

The last sentence of the email jumped off the page at David. These words solidified the connection between Max's request to meet Martha and Montgomery's allegation that Max viewed her as a source of capital for his project, the bedrock of the children's claim for undue influence. *How could I have missed this email in the documents Max produced? Why didn't Maggie bring it to my attention?*

As these thoughts swirled about in David's head, he noticed something else about this document. There were no Bates stamp numbers on the document.  Immediately, he turned to Montgomery and said, "I need to confer with my client about this document before we proceed further.  Let's take a short break."

With a sly nod, Montgomery said, "Of course, no problem."

As soon as David and Max were off by themselves, David said, "Max, there are no Bates stamp numbers on this document. . ."

"What are Bates stamp numbers?" asked Max, appearing totally confused.

"Bates stamps were hand-held devices we formerly used to put sequential numbers on documents being produced in lawsuits, so every page was separately identified, and a complete record was kept of all documents produced.  Those devices have long since been replaced by computer generated numbering systems, but the numbers are still referred to by lawyers and judges as Bates numbers.  We always put Bates numbers on documents we produce, and Montgomery usually does also.  So, where did this document come from, Max?"

"I have no idea," responded Max, apparently as mystified as David.

David didn't want to interrogate Max further about this issue then because it could rattle him for the rest of his deposition.

David and Max went back into the conference room, and David asked Montgomery,

"This document has no Bates stamp numbers it, so I assume this email was not part of the production of either party?"

Montgomery smirked.  "No, it has only come to our attention in the past few days.  Since it should have been part of Mr. Foster's production, I assumed he would be familiar with it."

David stifled his anger as he passed the document, now marked as Plaintiffs' Exhibit 2, to Max.  Had Max lied when he told David he was producing *all* relevant documents?  If Max had knowingly withheld the email, his action would constitute spoliation of evidence and could be fatal to his case.  David was curious as to how Max would explain why all of the emails between Greg and him were produced except this one.

"Mr. Foster, do you recognize Plaintiffs' Exhibit 2?" Montgomery inquired.

"I have no specific memory of it, but I can't say I didn't write it," responded Max.

"Do you know why this document was not included in the production of documents made by your counsel to me on your behalf?"

Max shifted in his chair.  "I don't.  It's my understanding that all relevant documents on our servers were provided to our counsel, and he produced them to you."

At this point David inserted, "Mr. Montgomery, I represent to you that we have withheld no documents from the production."

"Well, we will deal with the apparent spoliation of evidence later," commented Montgomery.  "For now, let's address how Martha was going to be the answer to your problems with the project, Mr. Foster.  When you went out with her, you were in need of capital to keep your project going, weren't you?"

Max had to admit he was in need of capital.

"When you went out with Martha, you were aware from media reports that her late husband had sold his business less than a year before he died, true?"

Through gritted teeth, Max said, "Yes." David sensed Max was boiling inside; thus far, he was controlling his temper—but barely.

"You were also aware that the sales price for his company was over $20 million, according to media reports?"

"Yes."

"So, when you went on your first date with Martha you were aware of her capability to make a significant investment or loan for your project, if she could be persuaded to do so?"

"I gave no thought to anything other than getting to know Martha on that date," Max hissed, clearly perturbed at this line of questions.

"When did you first discuss the possibility of a loan or investment by Martha for your project?"

"We didn't have that conversation until after we were married, when she was looking for stable and secure income without stock market risks."

"I see," said Montgomery, his annoying smile revealing his pleasure with how his little trap had obviously rattled Max.

"The next document I am showing you is a memo you wrote to Martha three weeks after you were married. It's marked as Plaintiffs' Exhibit 3. Do you recognize this memo?"

"Yes, it's a memo I wrote to Martha at her request."

"Well, the memo doesn't say it's being written at her request, does it?"

After Max admitted it did not, Montgomery took Max through the memo and got him to admit that he recommended Martha put her assets in a trust with Max as co-trustee, that Max would become the sole trustee if Martha pre-deceased him, and that all of this would be planned out by the lawyer that Max recommended, who also happened to be Max's estate planning lawyer.  From David's viewpoint, these admissions could have been minimized as the normal kind of asset planning husbands and wives do.  But with the unforeseen email Montgomery had sprung on them, Max's actions looked increasingly like the execution of a plan he had concocted before actually meeting Martha.

"Next, I am showing you a document marked as Plaintiffs' Exhibit 4, a memo you wrote to Martha shortly after all of her assets had been transferred into her revocable trust.  Do you recognize this document?"

"Yes … a memo I wrote.  Martha had asked my advice about her investment assets.  After we discussed my recommendations, she asked me to put them in a memo for her to consider.  She liked to see recommendations in writing in order to evaluate them."

"Now, Martha did have a financial advisor at the time, didn't she—one who had put her in a mix of stocks and bonds?"

"Yes, and she was not satisfied with the return she was getting, especially with the performance of the stock market over the previous two years.  She wanted a better, guaranteed return.  I offered to pay her eight percent interest on a loan for $10 million, far above what she could earn from a certificate of deposit or from bonds."

"But she sold stocks, not bonds, to come up with the $10 million she would lend you, didn't she?"

Max nodded.  "Yes, that is ultimately what she decided.  She wanted less risk and a guaranteed return."

"In fact, her stock market portfolio has generated better than a ten percent return since you obtained the loan from her, hasn't it?"

"That's true, but we didn't know the market would perform that well when the loan was made."

"You didn't recommend to her that she discuss your loan proposal with her investment advisor, did you?"

"Well, no, but Martha had consulted with him previously. If she felt the need to do so then, I assumed she would discuss the loan with him. I never suggested that she *not* consult with him."

Montgomery then took Max through a series of questions which cast serious doubt on whether the loan to him was *safer* than Martha's stock portfolio, despite Max giving Martha a first mortgage on two parcels in Gateway Orlando. Montgomery also had Max confirm he had received the $10 million and had invested the entire amount in the project so he could get the remaining construction loans he needed. Although he quibbled and tried not to answer the question, Max eventually had to admit that without the $10 million loan his project would have likely been in serious trouble.

Montgomery then turned to the issue of the amended trust and the amended will.

"Mr. Foster, Martha was diagnosed with stage four uterine cancer only four months after she made the loan to you, correct?"

"Yes."

"And only three months after she was diagnosed, you recommended some amendments to her trust, didn't you?"

Max sighed but remained calm. "Yes, but only after she asked for my recommendations."

"She had been undergoing three months of chemotherapy treatments for her cancer at the time you made the recommendations, right?"

"Yes."

"Would you agree that her mental acuity and energy were not as strong after three months of chemo as they had been previously?"

As David had suggested, Max chose his words carefully. "Well, she was tired after the chemo treatments, but her mind was sharp. We discussed in considerable detail the proposed changes, and she fully understood them."

"The changes you recommended were: first, that you be named the sole trustee; second, that in the event of her death you would receive one-third of the assets of the trust in order to be assured of completing the Gateway Orlando project. Correct?"

Max shook his head. "These were not my recommendations. They were the two changes we ultimately agreed upon after discussing the situation. I don't recall specifically who brought up the topic of my being the sole trustee, but I do recall that she brought up including me in her estate plan. Martha was doubtful she could continue to carry out her duties as trustee and wanted me to stay on as a trustee. I told her I wouldn't take any action she disapproved of. I also told her that if she wanted to include me in the distributions from her trust upon her death, I would, in return, include her children in my estate plan."

"Was it the same lawyer you recommended to her initially that made these changes to the will and trust?"

"Yes."

"Did you personally take her to the lawyer's office for the meetings with the lawyer?"

Max nodded and offered a weak, "Yes."

"You testified earlier that Martha asked you to put your recommendations to her in writing for her to consider. We haven't seen any memos from you regarding these two recommendations in the documents you have produced. Did you prepare any such memos for her?"

"No, these recommendations were straightforward, and Martha said she didn't need a memo to help her make a decision."

"So, to summarize, first you became the sole trustee of her trust. Second, you became a one-third beneficiary of her trust. You then had your lawyer prepare these changes to the trust, and you took Martha to his office to sign the documents making the changes. All of this was done without any memos explaining it to Martha, as you had done previously. Is all of that correct?"

Max paused, obviously working hard to control his temper. Finally, he said through clenched teeth, "My answer to each part of your question is the same as before."

"Mr. Foster, did you ever recommend to Martha that she inform her children of the changes to the trust and will you recommended?"

"In fact, I did, but Martha didn't want to mention the changes to the children. They weren't happy about Martha marrying me, especially since we didn't take them with us to Las Vegas for the wedding. As a result, Martha and her children were estranged, and she said she didn't want the situation to get worse in the short time she had left."

The rest of the deposition addressed more peripheral issues, none of which, in David's opinion, did any damage to Max's case—not that any additional damage was necessary.  Finally, Montgomery said, "I have no further questions for this witness."

David asked for a break before deciding whether he would ask Max any questions.  He seldom asked his own client any questions at their depositions.  After conferring briefly with Max in another room, they returned to the conference room, and David said, "I have no questions for Mr. Foster."

Normally, this would bring the deposition to an end, but Montgomery quickly responded, "I apologize to you, Mr. Foster, and to counsel, but I do have one more question.  Do you know what happened to Martha's diary?  It wasn't included in the documents you produced."

David glanced quickly at Max, who seemed puzzled by the question.  After a momentary pause, he said, "I didn't know Martha kept a diary.  If she did, I don't know where it is.  I've never seen it."

Max's response brought the deposition to an end after more than four hours of grueling examination.  In David's opinion, Montgomery had lived up to his reputation of being a capable lawyer, although one who clearly took pleasure in the pain of those he examined.  As one of David's lawyer friends who had often done battle with Montgomery aptly stated, "Montgomery revels in schadenfreude."

*      *      *

After Montgomery left, David asked Maggie to join them in the conference room to debrief the deposition.  David gave Maggie a brief summary of the deposition, highlighting the email from Max to Greg Oliver they had not seen previously.  He then turned to Max and posed the question that had been hovering over them since the email appeared.

"Max, did you send the email to Greg after you went out with Martha?"

"I answered truthfully—I don't remember. However, after thinking about it further, I'm pretty sure I did send such an email. But I didn't have some grand plan to get Martha's money. After our first date, during which we didn't discuss her finances, I just felt she might be able to help me get a loan from a bank or other lending source. It was just an off-hand comment."

"But your off-hand comment plays nicely into the story Montgomery is telling," Maggie responded.

"Yeah, I know," Max said sourly while shaking his head. "Is such a short email that harmful to my case, David?"

"We can try to explain away the comment, and we might be able to do so. However, the deletion of this particular email from your server makes the email look more sinister than it otherwise would be. That raises the next question—did you delete the email from your server?"

"David, I swear to you, I did *not* delete that email. Furthermore, even I know that just hitting the delete button doesn't permanently delete an email from the server. You warned me about preserving all records, and I gave strict instructions to preserve them."

"Well, if *you* didn't delete the email from the server, who did?"

"The only person in my company that has access or the knowledge to delete an email permanently would be our IT director, James Moss. But I can't imagine he would do such a thing or would even know the importance of that particular email."

"We're going to have to have a serious talk with Mr. Moss, and soon," David replied. "I expect Montgomery will file a motion for sanctions due to spoliation of evidence within the next week or two.  By the time of the hearing on his motion, we'll need to be able to explain to Judge Long what happened."

"There's another question regarding the email to Greg Oliver," Maggie noted.  "How did Montgomery get a copy of that email?  Even if James Moss did decide to permanently delete it for some reason, do you think he would first make a copy to give to Montgomery?"

"I can't imagine James would do that."  Max shook his head.  "We've always had a great relationship, and I trust him more than any other employee in my company."

Maggie looked up from the notes she was taking.  "The only other source from which Montgomery could get that email was Greg Oliver or someone he may have forwarded it to.  We need to talk to him as well."

"I'm even closer to Greg than to James," replied Max.  "I just don't understand how this could have happened."

Max did seem genuinely perplexed over how the email made its way into Montgomery's hands and why it wasn't on Max's server, but at this point, David wasn't sure about Max.  From the beginning, David's instincts told him Max would be a difficult client.  Just as David was beginning to feel more comfortable representing Max, the missing email turned up.  David clearly needed to get answers to these questions—and soon.  He was concerned there might be more surprises in store in this case, and Max couldn't afford many more surprises like he had today.

As Max was about to leave the office, David posed one last question.  "What did you make of the question about Martha's diary?  This is the first we've heard about a diary."

Max turned to face David. "I have no idea. If Martha kept a diary, I knew nothing about it, and I certainly have no idea where it may be. I've been in her study many times, and I've never seen one. If it's not in her study I don't even know where to begin to look."

Turning to Maggie, David said, "Maggie, take Rodrigo with you and go over Martha's study with a fine tooth comb to see if you can find a diary. We don't know if it's a paper diary or perhaps an electronic diary kept on a thumb drive. If there's a diary there somewhere we need to find it soon—preferably before the children's depositions."

Addressing Max again, David asked, "If there *is* a diary somewhere, Max, what do you think we'll find in it?"

By this time, the depressing effect of the deposition, and especially the unforeseen email, was plainly weighing on Max. There was no longer any cockiness or swagger in him; his shoulders drooped, and his demeanor was that of a defeated man. "I honestly don't know," he replied weakly.

"Go home, Max. Get a good night's sleep. We'll talk again soon," David said.

When Max had left, Maggie asked David, "How bad was it today? Do we still have a defense in this case?"

"It was pretty bad. The worst part is that it appears Max or someone working for or with him deleted a key email, which gives the deleted email more importance than it would otherwise have if it had not been deleted. A tough case has just gotten tougher for us. If Martha actually kept a diary, let's just hope there are no more unpleasant surprises in it."

## Chapter 12

The initial euphoria over Carol having few side effects from the chemo treatments wore off quickly.  After her first four infusions, Carol was nauseated, weak, and having difficulty focusing on anything for more than fifteen minutes.  When she tried to eat some of the spicier Italian dishes she loved, she wound up vomiting off and on throughout the night.  After the first week of chemo, she had two weeks off before starting another round, during which all of her side effects subsided, although the chemo treatments lowered her white blood cell count.  By the second week after the first round of chemo, she had developed a persistent cough that left her throat raw and her voice raspy.

What amazed David was the worse she felt the more determined she was to press on with her fundraising efforts.  She would pull herself out of bed after a fitful night's sleep, try to eat at least some breakfast without upchucking it, then dress and head out for another day of pursuing funding for WCC.  David and Jenna both repeatedly urged her to stay home and rest, particularly on her worst days, but Carol gave in to their request only once.  Even then, she spent most of the day on the telephone making calls from her bed between bouts of nausea.

After the second round of chemo treatments, Carol was more fatigued and thinner, although the nausea had ameliorated somewhat. When she and David visited Dr. Marks, they hoped for encouraging news the chemo treatments were effectively fighting the cancer.

Dr. Marks' firm glance told David the good news they hoped for was not coming. "It's still early in your treatment. Thus far, the tumor in your breast has not grown, but neither has it shrunk. Unfortunately, there is still cancer present in your liver, but it hasn't spread beyond the liver."

David's heart sank with this news. He had been optimistic, hoping the strong chemo treatments that made Carol so miserable were putting the cancer in remission. Dr. Marks' report poured cold water on those hopes. When David looked at Carol, however, she was as serene as she was on the first visit to Dr. Marks. She appeared to have accepted without reaction, and certainly without rancor, whatever news Dr. Marks provided. She seemed determined to be unflappable and not waste her limited energy on things she couldn't control.

"The fact that the tumor has neither shrunk nor grown … what does that tell you, Dr. Marks?" Carol asked, with no apparent urgency.

"Candidly, I hoped the tumor would have begun to shrink in size by now. However, the fact your tumor has not grown, and the cancer has not spread beyond your liver shows that the treatment is working, although not as well as we hoped, at least thus far. I think we need to complete the next two rounds of chemo and re-evaluate at that time."

Carol seemed to accept Dr. Marks' advice with little outward reaction. To David, however, the recommendation to just wait for the results after two more rounds of chemo treatments was underwhelming, to say the least. *Surely there are alternative treatments Dr. Marks could try.* David decided to discuss the situation further with Carol to see if she'd be receptive to asking Dr. Marks for other options.  Based on her understated reaction to Dr. Marks' comments, however, David was unsure whether she would be willing to consider alternative treatments, if there were any.

*      *      *

When Jenna got home from school, David and Carol had just returned from her appointment with Dr. Marks.  Jenna's first words to either of them were, "How did it go today, Mom?"

"Not bad," responded Carol, minimizing the disappointment that she knew David felt and not wanting to disappoint or frighten Jenna.  "Dr. Marks said my cancer hasn't spread and is no worse.  So the treatments have stopped the cancer's momentum.  He wants me to continue with the next two rounds of chemo, then see what progress I've made."

Jenna glanced at David.  From her expression, he knew she could tell her father wasn't thrilled with the news.  "Only no worse, Mom?  After all you've gone through with the two rounds of chemo, I thought the tumor would have shrunk at least a little by now."

David knew Carol sensed Jenna's disappointment but did not want her to be afraid or to have the same disappointment her parents felt.  There was still hope, and typical of Carol's thoughtfulness, she wanted to make sure Jenna would be hopeful as well.

Carol gave Jenna a big hug as she said, "Well, we all would have preferred to hear that the cancer was gone … or almost gone … but Dr. Marks said the chemo is working—just not as fast as we had hoped.  Let's pray for the treatment to work faster by the next visit."

With a skeptical expression, Jenna said, "Okay, Mom …"

Carol continued with a smile, "I actually feel better today, and I'm going to fix one of our favorites—black grouper—for dinner tonight. Go get your homework done. I'm going to run to Publix to get ingredients for a salad to have with dinner. I may pick up a surprise dessert there also."

With that, Carol grabbed her keys and purse, then headed for her car.

As soon as she left, Jenna cornered David. "Seriously, Dad? The best news today was that the cancer didn't get any worse. I'm worried. I assumed that with a good doctor like Dr. Marks and the latest chemo treatments, at least some progress would be made by now. Did Dr. Marks have any explanation?"

David knew better than to try to paint a false rosy picture for Jenna. He and Carol had tried that previously, with disastrous results. "I was disappointed, too, Jenna. I thought Mom would be making more progress. Now, Dr. Marks did say that the chemo was working, as was evident from no increase in the cancer. If there's no progress on our next visit, though, I'm going to push Dr. Marks hard to consider alternative treatments. I still believe he's the best oncologist to be found in Florida. But if he needs to consult with someone outside the state to get the best possible outcome, that's what we want him to do."

Carol returned in twenty minutes, and within thirty minutes thereafter she pulled together a dinner of fresh broiled black grouper, scalloped potatoes, and a citrus salad. The wonderful dinner lifted everyone's spirits, especially the Florida key lime pie for dessert. By the end of dinner, sincere hope had begun to creep back into everyone's comments.

After Jenna went to bed, David decided to discuss the possibility of asking Dr. Marks for alternative treatments. As he and Carol walked from the kitchen to their upstairs bedroom, he said as casually as he could, "I *am* thankful the cancer isn't spreading, but do you think we should press Dr. Marks for additional or alternative treatments for your cancer when we next visit him?"

Carol turned and gave David her knowing, loving look that usually told him he had already lost the argument he was trying to make. "David, you know I told Jenna we would ask Dr. Marks that very question at the next visit. What you're really asking is whether we ought to ask him *now*. No, we shouldn't. I have complete faith in Dr. Marks. We researched him thoroughly, and I truly believe I couldn't have a better oncologist. As I told you, I'm ready for whatever comes. I prefer to have complete remission, but we don't always get what we want in life." She squeezed his hand. "Please, just support me in this. I have a mission to complete, and I don't want to go out of state for treatment. Can you agree with me about this?"

"I'm certainly glad I never meet you in court," David said and kissed Carol's hand. "I never win an argument with you. Carol, you know I'm only asking that we check out every possible option for treatment because I love you so much. Okay, we'll wait until the next visit with Dr. Marks to ask about other treatment options. And I understand that you don't intend to go out of state for treatment. Let's just pray that isn't necessary."

"Thanks for understanding, David," Carol said with a sigh as she lay back on the bed, exhausted from an eventful day.

*          *          *

The following day, David was back in the office to meet with Maggie about the next steps to take in the Max Foster case. This was the first opportunity David had to meet with her since Max's deposition the previous week. They both had ridiculously full calendars.

David had been determined to cut back on his time in the office to be available to help his wife in any way he could. Since Carol had continued to charge ahead with her fundraising efforts for WCC, David's efforts to help her consisted primarily of taking her to doctor visits or chemo treatments and helping Jenna with kitchen duty at night. The anxiety he felt over Carol's illness and the worries of his heavy caseload—especially the troublesome issues associated with the Max Foster case—were beginning to weigh on him.

There seemed to be no area of his life free from stress or from which he could take a break. David's primary antidote for stress was exercise, and he now found himself having to start his morning run at 5:30 to get it in before his duties of the day began. He was holding up for now, but in his candid moments he admitted to himself he couldn't keep up this pace indefinitely.

When David met with Maggie in the conference room, the next big deadlines facing them were the depositions of Martha's children. Those depositions were scheduled for Thursday and Friday of the following week, and they weren't ready.

"Maggie, I have three items on my checklist for you to accomplish before the children's depositions next week. The first is to interview Greg Oliver about whether he sent Max's email to anyone else; the second is to interview James Moss about how that email got deleted from Max's server; and the third is to find Martha's diary, if there is one."

Maggie nodded. "Yep. Those are the three items I have on my checklist also. I've already called Greg Oliver, and we're currently playing telephone tag. I hope to speak to him before the day is over. James Moss hasn't returned my calls either, which is unusual. Until now, he's been very responsive. I fear the reason he hasn't responded is because he doesn't want to talk to me. I'm sure Max told him the deleted email was marked as an exhibit by Montgomery. If James did delete it, he probably assumed no one would ever become aware of its existence and doesn't know what to do now that it's been found."

"You're probably right, but we have to be sure. Let me know as soon as you find out what the story is with both Greg and James. When are you and Rodrigo going to Max's house to search for Martha's diary?"

Maggie tapped her notepad. "Friday afternoon. We've set aside two hours to thoroughly search Martha's office once more. I've already been through it once, but Rodrigo and I are going to go over it in detail this time. Honestly, though, David, I doubt we'll find anything. I don't believe there's any nook or cranny in her study that we haven't already searched. Max is going to give us access to a few other places in the house, but he's doubtful we'll find anything worthwhile in those places either."

"Understood, but we need to find the diary if there is one. In the meantime, I'll continue preparing for the children's depositions, which includes wading through a mass of documents."

*     *     *

Maggie returned to her office and within five minutes her phone rang. It was Greg Oliver. She grabbed her notepad.

"Mr. Oliver, thank you for returning my call. As I think you know, our firm represents Mr. Foster in the suit filed by Martha's children. When

166

Mr. Foster's deposition was taken last week, an email that he sent to you following his first date with Martha was produced by their counsel, Larry Montgomery. It was a follow-up to an email Mr. Foster sent you previously in which he discussed problems with his Gateway Orlando project. The email in question was sent after he had taken Martha out on their first date, and he stated in the email he might have found a solution to the problems with his project. Do you recall the email?"

"Yes, but to be candid, the only reason I remember is because Max called me after his deposition. He couldn't recall with certainty whether he had sent such an email. I checked my email files, and I found it."

"Well, we're puzzled about how Montgomery got a copy of it. Did you send it on to someone?"

There was a slight hesitation on Gregg Oliver's line. Then, "Yes, I followed up on that, too. I wasn't the only one urging Max to date Martha. Two other mutual friends of theirs had also been urging Max to take Martha out."

"I'm aware other friends had encouraged Max to date Martha. Please, go on, Mr. Oliver."

"After their first date, all three of us were anxious to know how it turned out. When Max sent the email to me saying he enjoyed his date with Martha, I just automatically forwarded it to our two mutual friends— one of whom was Marilyn Quarles. I didn't pay much attention to Max's comment about possibly finding a solution to his problems on his project, and I don't think Marilyn did then either. But after Martha died and the lawsuit was filed, Marilyn remembered the email. Apparently, she became incensed with Max."

Maggie paused from taking notes. "Why?"

"Martha's children and Marilyn's children were good friends growing up, and she immediately took Martha's children's view of what happened. Without letting Max know what she was doing, Marilyn sent Montgomery a copy of the email along with a cover note saying, 'I hope you nail the bastard.' I think it's safe to say Marilyn no longer considers Max a friend."

"Apparently not!" agreed Maggie. After a few follow up questions for Greg which failed to produce any other meaningful information, Maggie thanked him and ended the call. *That answers that portion of the puzzle, but why wasn't the email on Max's server? Did Max know it had been deleted?*

While Maggie was still pondering the answer to these questions, the phone rang again. This time it was James Moss. "Sorry for my delay in responding to your calls, Maggie. Max told me what happened at his deposition. I knew you would want to talk about the deleted email, and I had to do some research before returning your calls."

"Thank you for returning my call. I assume you're aware the email in question is one Max sent to Greg Oliver the day after his first date with Martha. The email said he had a good time and that he may have found a solution to his problems with the Gateway Orlando project."

"So this email is creating a problem for Max, then?" Oliver asked.

"Yes. The last part of the email is being treated like a smoking gun by the children's lawyer, Larry Montgomery. We now know how Montgomery got a copy of it, but what we don't know is why the email isn't on Max's server. Because the document wasn't on the server, it wasn't among the documents we produced to Montgomery. Therefore, Max was blindsided when Montgomery produced the email at Max's deposition. We expect Montgomery will soon file a motion for sanctions due to spoliation of evidence and failure to produce the e-mail."

"Yes, I think I understand the severity of the situation. That's why I wanted to do some research before speaking to you. I discovered our server crashed the day the email in question was sent. As a result of the crash, that email and a handful of other emails were lost."

Maggie paused from her note taking. "Aren't your servers backed up throughout the day to prevent data loss?"

"Maggie, although Max has some very large projects, we're still a relatively small office. All of our documents and data are on a single server. We usually back the server up on the weekend, not daily as, for example, your firm probably does. When this crash occurred, we tried to restore all of the data, but we were only able to get a partial data restoration. Unfortunately, the email in question was part of the data we lost."

"Did you have any discussions with Max at the time of the crash about what documents or data may have been lost?"

"I'm sure I mentioned the crash to him, but I don't recall discussing with him what specific data may have been lost."

"Don't take this the wrong way, James, but is there any way Max could have engineered this crash or taken any steps to ensure this particular email was lost? Sooner or later, Montgomery is going ask this same question, and he won't ask as nicely as I just did."

"No offense taken, Maggie. No, I can't conceive of any way Max could have caused the crash or permanently deleted the email in question. As you might suspect, he's old school. It took me a year to get him to replace his old flip-top cell phone with an iPhone. He can read

emails on his desktop computer and respond, and that's about it.  Even if
Max wanted to permanently delete a document, I don't think he would
know how to."

"The data loss you are referring to took place shortly after the
email in question was originally sent?"

"Yes, later that same day, in fact."

"And there was no data loss or computer crash after this lawsuit
was filed?"

"No. We've not had a crash or data loss in nearly a year.  I'm
rather proud of that record."

Maggie glanced at her notes before asking her next question.  "At
the time of the crash and data loss, did you have any idea Max had written
an email about his date with Martha?"

"No.  I didn't even know he had gone out with her until several
weeks later."

"So what you're telling me, James, is that the computer crash and
related loss of the key email from the server was a random event that
neither you nor Max caused?"

"That's correct, Maggie.  I know I didn't cause the crash, and Max
couldn't have pulled it off, even if he had wanted to."

Maggie thanked James, ended the call, and walked over to David's
office to bring him up to date on her telephone calls with Greg and with
James.  David was attentive as Maggie explained what she had learned, but
skepticism was written all over his face when she explained how the
deletion of the email was due to a server crash—one that had occurred
randomly at about the same time Max sent the incriminating email to Greg.

"So, in addition to trying to convince Judge Long the email really doesn't mean what it clearly implies, we also have to convince her that Max didn't have the email to produce because of fortuitous timing of a crash on his server?" David asked rhetorically.

"That's about it," Maggie replied. "I can't wait to hear for myself what our arguments are going to be."

David smiled ruefully, as if wondering how many more strange turns fate was going to throw at them in this case.

# Chapter 13

Maggie was awed by Max and Martha's house, the home where she and her late husband lived for twenty years before she married Max. The Spanish Colonial Revival house was carefully situated on a one and a half acre lot on Lake Virginia, part of the Winter Park chain of lakes, and only a few blocks from the Rollins College campus. The towering oak trees and sabal palms provided a lush, subtropical setting for the graceful home that was built in the mid-1930s. The downstairs family room, as well as the upstairs master bedroom, faced west toward the lake. On most days, Maggie imagined, Mother Nature painted a sunset for the view over the lake that no mere artist could ever match.

When Maggie and Rodrigo, the firm's paralegal, arrived at Max's house to look for a diary that Martha may have kept, Max welcomed them warmly. "I'm sorry about the setback at my deposition, Maggie. But I want you to know I have confidence in you and David. Any misgivings I had about you or David initially are gone. I especially appreciate your thoroughness in preparing me for my deposition. Except for unforeseen email, I felt pretty comfortable, and I can't blame that on you."

"Thanks, Max . . ." Maggie was surprised by Max's comments. In the short time she had known him he was seldom generous with compliments, which made her all the more appreciative.

"Other than her study, where could Martha have possibly kept a diary?" Maggie asked. "We want to look at those areas first before we begin our search of her study."

"As I told you and David previously, I don't know if Martha kept a diary. If she did, it's probably in her study. If it's not there, the only other areas it could possibly be are her main closet, our upstairs storage room, or our small storage room behind our garage. I've made a cursory search without finding anything, but you're welcome to go through those rooms again. Of course, if it's on a thumb drive, it could be almost anywhere. I've looked in every drawer in the house, and I have yet to find a thumb drive of any kind. You're welcome to look in all those places and any others you may want to see."

Maggie decided to start in Martha's main closet; she sent Rodrigo to search the upstairs storage room and the garage storage room. Martha's main closet was a revelation to Maggie. *Good Lord, this closet is nearly twice the size of my entire bedroom in my Mom's house.*

Maggie decided to keep this thought to herself. Now that she had gained Max's confidence, she didn't want to get crosswise with him. Most of Martha's clothes were still hanging in the closet, and Maggie quickly calculated that Martha had more clothes in her large closet than many boutique women's stores have on display. Likewise, Maggie had never seen so many shoes in one closet; there had to be well over 100 pairs of shoes. *It's true ... the rich really do live differently.*

The closet had many built-in drawers and bins, and Maggie meticulously combed each one. With each drawer she opened, it was readily apparent there was no book-type diary present. But she had to look carefully to insure there was no thumb drive inconspicuously mixed in with the other contents.  Because of the height of the shelves above the clothes

racks, Maggie had to climb the convenient ladder that was kept in the

closet for reaching the top shelves.  There, she found boxes of old

documents, old photos and some very old clothes, but no thumb drive or

diary.

Maggie even rapped on the walls and floors, looking for any kind

of hidden space where a diary could be hidden.  Still no results.  Finally,

after over forty-five minutes of carefully investigating every possible

hiding place, she concluded her search, confident that no diary, either in

book form or on a thumb drive, was to be found in Martha's closet.

Rodrigo finished his search of the two storage rooms only a few

minutes after Maggie finished her search of Martha's closet.  Each

admitted to the other they were blown away with all of the stuff they saw—

but none of it included a diary.

Accordingly, they moved their search on to Martha's study located

at the end of a very short hallway that peeled off from the main hallway

running from the front door back to the gargantuan family room.  Beautiful

French doors opened onto a spacious, well-landscaped pool, patio, and

deck.  The view from the family room or patio across Lake Virginia was

breathtaking. One could walk right by the door to the study without ever

noticing it because of the distracting view through the family room.  But

when Maggie opened the door to the study, she faced another impressive

room.

The study was large, twenty-five by twenty-five feet, by Maggie's

estimate.  The walls were lined with shelves and paneling, all

mahogany.  The décor would have given the study a heavy men's-club

ambiance if not for the windows high on the walls through which the afternoon sun provided a light, airy feeling. On the left side of the study were louvered doors, again made of mahogany, which covered almost the entire wall. When the doors were opened, they revealed nearly floor to ceiling filing cabinets, all of which were full of files and records going back decades.

In the center of the room was one of the largest traditional executive desks Maggie had ever seen. It, too, was mahogany colored, but the seat cushion on the executive chair was a pale blue and matched the blue in the tasteful Persian rug on which the desk, executive chair, and two guest chairs sat, and which lightened the feel of the room. Maggie was left with the impression this was a serious room where Martha and her late husband had made important decisions which led to their significant wealth. Maggie recalled Max's statement. "I never used the study myself. I preferred to conduct my business at my office since it's only a ten-minute drive from here."

Because nearly every inch of the shelves were full of books, Maggie and Rodrigo had to look through each book to be sure none of them was a diary in disguise. They each took half the shelves of books to examine, then went through in wearying detail every file in the filing cabinets to confirm none of them was actually a loose-paged diary or contained a thumb drive full of diary entries. When they were about two-thirds of the way through the filing cabinets, Maggie told Rodrigo to keep going while she began to search the main desk, which had drawers on both sides as well as a middle drawer.

After nearly two hours of tediously searching books, shelves, drawers and filing cabinets, Maggie and Rodrigo were exhausted and ready to wrap up their search as they plopped down on the guest chairs in front of the desk.  The rumor that Martha kept a diary was apparently false.  In fact, Maggie speculated to Rodrigo, "It may have just been a rumor that Montgomery concocted to keep us wasting our time."

"Might be," Rodrigo said.  "Sounds like something Montgomery would do."

"I don't see anywhere that we haven't carefully searched, do you?"  Maggie stood to stretch before leaving the room.

"Nor do I," echoed Rodrigo as he also slowly stood and turned toward the door to follow Maggie out.  As they reached the door, however, Rodrigo stopped, obviously deep in thought about something.

"What is it, Rodrigo?" Maggie asked, puzzled by the pensive look on his face.

"It's probably nothing, Maggie, but I just remembered an old detective series I used to watch on television.  I'm sure David's familiar with it; he likes old detective shows as much as I do.  Ever since we arrived at this house, I've had the feeling it's somehow familiar to me.  Now I remember why.  This house resembles a house on one of the episodes in which the main characters were searching for a document—just like we've been doing.  There was a desk about the size of Martha's, and the desk had a false bottom in one of the drawers.  That's where the key document was hidden.  As I said, it's probably nothing.  But, hey, we're here; it's worth one last look."

Maggie was skeptical, but said, "Well, you make a valid point.  We're here, so you go ahead and check the desk for a false bottom.  I'm going to find Max to see if he has any other suggestions as to where we should look."

*        *        *

As Maggie walked out the door, Rodrigo turned his attention to the desk.  Each side had two drawers; plus, there was one shallow drawer in the middle of the desk.  He quickly examined the middle drawer and determined there was no false bottom there.  He then carefully examined the two drawers on the right hand side of the desk, again confirming there was no hiding place in either of them.

Next, he carefully examined the two drawers on the left side of the desk.  From the outside of the drawers, nothing looked amiss.  However, when Rodrigo opened the bottom left drawer and removed the documents, he noticed how the bottom appeared to be slightly higher than it should be. *Is this just an optical illusion?*

To examine the drawer more closely, Rodrigo got down on his hands and knees to view the outside bottom of the drawer and compare it to where the interior bottom of the drawer appeared to be.  He ran his hand under the bottom of the drawer. To his surprise, his hand felt a button.

He pushed the button.

To his astonishment, he heard a very soft whirring sound as the interior bottom of the drawer began to rotate upward from the front. Rodrigo was so surprised he flinched backward. Then, still on his hands and knees, he peaked over the front edge of the drawer to see what was under the false bottom now rotating up.

A wide smile of delight spread across his face as he picked up a brown, leather-bound book about an inch thick, with the word *Diary* embossed on the front.

"Well, well, well . . ." Rodrigo muttered to himself.  "It's a good thing I like old detective mysteries."

*     *     *

David was working in his office when they returned.  Maggie seemed quite pleased as she entered his office and informed him about their discovery.

"I have to hand it to Rodrigo," Maggie said, shaking her head in disbelief.  "I searched that desk twice, and I never noticed there might be a false bottom in one of the drawers. Outstanding work by Rodrigo."

"Did you show Max the diary before leaving his house, and was he able to confirm it's in Martha's handwriting?" David asked.

"Yes, he has no doubt the diary is in Martha's handwriting.  But we may need to have a handwriting expert examine it to confirm this and enable us to get it into evidence at trial."

"Agreed," responded David.  "Did you have an opportunity to look over the diary to decide whether it helps us or hurts us?"

"I only had time to glance over it quickly on the way back from Max's house.  Martha started keeping the diary shortly after her first husband died, probably as a way to deal with her loss.  There are many entries about her conversations with her children.  I haven't had time to read them all, but this should give us a much better idea about the relationship between Martha and her adult children, and perhaps shed light on her estate planning decisions."

"Maggie, I'm going to continue to review documents for the depositions over the weekend.  I want you to review the diary in detail and be prepared on Monday to recommend the portions I should cover with the children during their depositions next week.  We need to get this accomplished this weekend so we can produce a copy to Montgomery early next week for his review before the depositions on Thursday and Friday."

Maggie smiled. "Yes, I anticipated you would want me to do that, and I've cleared my calendar for this weekend. With respect to giving Montgomery a copy of the diary before the deposition, though, I've reviewed all of the requests for production of documents that Montgomery has served on us."

David returned her smile. "And?"

"And, guess what? There are no requests for production of any documents authored by Martha. It's a significant oversight by Montgomery, but in the absence of a request for production of documents that would arguably include the diary, I don't see why we would be obligated to produce it to him in advance of the deposition."

"Really?" exclaimed David, surprised that Montgomery would make such a blunder. Although the man had his faults as a lawyer, lack of thoroughness was usually not one of them. "I agree with you, Maggie. In the absence of a request for production that encompasses the diary, we don't have to voluntarily give him a copy before the deposition."

David thought about this a minute longer, then with a sly smile said, "It looks like there's a little poetic justice at work here."

# Chapter 14

David, Maggie and Max arrived at Montgomery's office located on the twenty-first floor of Orlando's newest downtown office tower at 8:45 Thursday morning for the deposition of Richard Langley, Martha's son and one of the two plaintiffs in the lawsuit filed by Montgomery. David seldom had Maggie attend a deposition he was defending, but he almost always had her attend any deposition he was taking. Her job was to keep the exhibits organized and to ensure all documents they intended to introduce were, in fact, marked as exhibits. But more importantly, he wanted her evaluation of the witness and her suggestions for follow-up questions.

David was always thorough when questioning witnesses, but Maggie, who was not preoccupied with asking questions, could concentrate on evaluating the demeanor and credibility of the witness. Moreover, she usually had excellent suggestions on where David should press the witness for more details or challenge the witness with documents that conflicted with their testimony.

Montgomery's office décor was urban contemporary. The spacious reception area was separated from a large conference room only by a clear glass wall. The conference room, in turn, had a magnificent view of downtown Orlando and Lake Eola, including the iconic fountain shooting streams of water high in the air. Most of the furniture was in neutral colors, drawing attention to the bold, vivid colors of the abstract paintings adorning every wall in sight. The combination of the contemporary décor, bold colors, and breathtaking views of gleaming towers on the Orlando skyline whispered to anyone who entered, "Here is a lawyer of substance and success." David supposed this was exactly the image Montgomery wanted to convey to visitors, and it was undoubtedly a faithful representation of the image Montgomery had of himself.

Montgomery greeted David, Maggie, and Max, then ushered them into the conference room. Montgomery introduced them to Richard, who reluctantly shook hands with David and Maggie, but pointedly refused Max's extended hand. Since the court reporter had already set up for the deposition at the head of the conference table, David took the side facing the window, with the court reporter to his right, and across the table from Richard and Montgomery. Maggie was seated next to David, with Max further down the table.

Once Richard was sworn in by the court reporter, David had Richard identify himself, then very briefly covered the rules for the deposition. David placed the most emphasis on his charge to Richard to ask for clarification of any questions that might seem ambiguous. David didn't want Richard to be able to evade any admissions by claiming later he hadn't understood the question. David wrapped up this point by asking, "If you respond to a question I ask without asking me to clarify, I will assume you understood the question; fair enough?"

"Fair enough," Richard said.

David then directed his questions to Richard's background. Although his high school grades were good enough to get him admitted to Florida State University, Richard admitted he graduated from FSU only two years ago because it took him six years to complete his studies. David also confirmed Richard was very active in his fraternity, eventually becoming its president for the entire eighteen months it took him to complete his senior year. He blamed his mediocre grades at FSU on his heavy workload at the fraternity. Noticeably missing in his background was any mention of employment during summer breaks or at any other time during Richard's college career. David decided to press in on this issue.

"Mr. Langley, your father was still alive at the time you graduated from FSU, correct?"

"Yes."

"The fact you never had a job during summer breaks was a point of contention between you and your father while you were in college, wasn't it?"

Richard shifted in his seat. "Well, the subject came up several times while I was in college. But each time we discussed it, he eventually agreed travelling in Europe or South America over the summer gave me life experiences that surpassed any summer job I could get."

"How many summers did you travel abroad while in college?"

"I spent two summers travelling in Europe, and one travelling in South America."

"What did you do the remaining summers while in college?"

"I spent one summer working at the fraternity house getting ready for my term as president, and the only other summer I was still in college I was president and required to stay there over the summer."

"You said your father eventually agreed to your travelling abroad the three summers that you did so; did you ask your mother to intervene on your behalf to convince your father to let you travel rather than work over those three summers?"

"I wouldn't say I asked her to intervene. I did tell her I preferred to travel abroad rather than take a meaningless summer job. I believe she spoke to my father and supported my point of view. My father came around to my point of view and each time agreed to let me travel that summer."

"Well, your father had to do more than agree to let you go; he had to agree to pay for your travel, didn't he?"

"Yes, of course. I considered that part of my educational expenses."

"How much did your summer travels add to your educational expenses?"

Without hesitation, Richard answered, "I don't have an exact tally, but I think it was about twenty-five thousand dollars each summer abroad."

David handed Richard a note. "With respect to your summer travels, I show you a hand-written note, purportedly to you from your mother, which wishes you well on your trip to Europe for the summer before your junior year of college. The note also indicates your father wished you well on your travels. Do you recognize this handwriting?"

"Yes, I would recognize my mother's handwriting anywhere," Richard said as he returned the note to David. "This is a note that she sent me just before I left for London between my sophomore and junior years of college. And as you point out, my father was on board with my going."

David then had the handwritten note marked as an exhibit.  Though the note was unimportant in itself, Richard's ability to clearly identify his mother's handwriting would be critical to David's next series of questions.

"Mr. Langley, now that you've identified this note as being in your mother's handwriting, let me show you another document—also in your mother's handwriting.  Do you recognize this document?"

At this point, Maggie handed David the leather-bound diary Rodrigo had found in Martha's desk, and David placed it on the table between Montgomery and Richard.  Stunned to see the diary, Montgomery quickly grabbed it and began scanning its pages, which, as counsel, he had every right to do.

As Montgomery flipped through the diary, his face radiated concern.  Though remaining calm, he glared at David and demanded, "Why wasn't this diary produced to us before now? This gives us another ground to seek sanctions."

David ignored the threat.  "We found this diary hidden in a secret space in Martha's study after you asked about a diary.  Before then, we had no knowledge that a diary even existed.  But just as important, you haven't asked for any documents authored by Martha in any of your requests for production.  We were under no obligation to provide you a copy before today. However, we have brought an extra copy for you, as well as a copy to be marked as an exhibit in this deposition."

David slid a copy of the diary across the table to a noticeably frustrated Montgomery, who replied, "I request we take a short break so I can review the diary before we proceed with the deposition."

"Sure, Mr. Montgomery.  I'll be happy to take a break just as soon as Mr. Langley confirms he recognizes his mother's handwriting in the diary." Then turning to the witness, David asked, "Mr. Langley, do you recognize the handwriting in this diary to be the handwriting of your mother?"

Richard hesitated.

"I would remind you that you just testified you would recognize your mother's handwriting anywhere, and you are still under oath."

At the appearance of his mother's diary, Richard's outward confidence, so conspicuous thus far in the deposition, had melted away. He flipped through the first twenty pages or so, glanced quickly at Montgomery, who offered no help, and then muttered, "Yeah, I recognize the handwriting. It's my mother's."

The short break Montgomery requested took over thirty-five minutes. David noted that Richard's confident air did not return with him. The parties took their seats, and David resumed his interrogation.

"Mr. Langley, please look at your mother's entry dated March 2, 2016. This is only about two months after your father died, isn't it?"

"Yes."

"And you had just graduated from college about six months *before* your father died, right?"

"Yes."

"As of the March 2, 2016 diary entry you had still not taken a job following graduation, had you?"

"No, I was still considering my options."

David then read into the record the third paragraph of the March 2, 2016 entry.

> "I am worried about Richard. He still has not applied for a job despite graduating from FSU eight months ago. Charles

always wanted him to work during his summer breaks in college, and I'm beginning to regret my convincing Charles to allow Richard to travel abroad over the summers instead of working.  As Charles feared, Richard seems to have little desire to earn his own way in life and is content to continue to live off family money."

Richard was visibly irked by his parents' unflattering assessment of him, which David assumed was because it forced Richard to face an ugly truth about himself.

David continued, "According to your mother's statement, she did, in fact, convince your father to allow you to travel abroad during college rather than take a summer job.  You have no basis to deny this, do you?"

"I knew she talked to my father about my desire to travel; I didn't know she had to convince him," Richard said sourly.

"With respect to living off family money—you, in fact, lived rather well while in college, didn't you?"

"I don't know what you mean," Richard retorted.

"Well, let's talk about the automobile you drove while a student in college.  After your first year in college, you convinced your mother to buy you a new BMW, didn't you?"

Another reluctant, "Yes," from Richard.

"Your father was opposed to your driving such an expensive car while a student, wasn't he?"

"Yeah, my father was rather stingy with money.  He thought I should just have an old Honda or Volkswagen."

"Isn't it a fact, Mr. Langley, that throughout your college career, you and your father argued about whether you should work part time, as well as during summers?  And didn't you also argue about your high standard of living?"

"We had some discussions about those things.  I don't know that they could all be characterized as arguments."

"Isn't it also a fact that after your father died you and your mother frequently argued over money and your limited efforts to find a job?"

"We've had some arguments over those things, mostly after she met Max Foster."

David then had Richard read four additional entries from Martha's diary expressing her increasing concern about Richard's lackadaisical attitude about finding a job.  Three of these were dated *before* Martha met Max—the fourth, *after* Martha had begun dating Max.

Richard's face paled as he read the fourth entry.
"Max was so helpful to me today.  I told him how worried I was about Richard's spending habits and his lack of interest in finding a job.  I also told Max I haven't been very good about putting limits on Richard's spending.  Max pointed out the advantages of having a trust set up with independent trustees who can exercise some reasonable controls—controls parents may find hard to exercise.  Clearly something is going to have to change to limit Richard's spending and require him to get a job."

David let Martha's words from the diary linger in the air before continuing his questions.  "By the time of this entry, you had already asked your mother what would happen to the family money if something should happen to her.  Isn't that true?"

"Well, sure.  I was curious what the situation would be if my mother died at an early age, as my father did.  Our family had considerable wealth, and I wanted to know who would be in charge of it."

"You were not in favor of a non-family member being a trustee or having a bank or trust company acting as trustee, were you?"

Richard glared. "No, I didn't think that was necessary."

"You didn't want the arrangement because a non-family trustee or a corporate trustee would likely put limits on your spending and require more accountability from you regarding your spending. Isn't that true?"

"I just didn't think it was necessary and would cost a lot of money."

"Mr. Langley, please look at your mother's diary entry on December 15, 2017—shortly after your mother and Mr. Foster were married."

"Today, Max and I visited the lawyer who prepared the trust for me. All of my assets will be put in the trust, with both Max and me being the trustees. Although the consent of both of us is required for any decisions involving trust assets, I have the right to remove Max as a trustee at any time, as Max suggested. If I should die before Max, he will be the sole trustee, serving without pay; and the children will be the sole beneficiaries. I believe this arrangement will protect the assets for Richard and Laura and protect against Richard's profligate spending after I'm gone. Richard has been hounding me to appoint him as the trustee after I'm gone, but I'm convinced I've made the right decision for the children by appointing Max to be the trustee."

"Mr. Langley, it's true, as your mother states, that you were urging her to appoint you as the sole trustee after her death, isn't it?"

"Yes. I thought family money should stay in family hands."

"And when she denied your request to appoint you as sole trustee, you were angry with her, weren't you?"

"Yes."

"In fact, you told her to her face how angry you were with her for appointing Mr. Foster rather than yourself as trustee, didn't you?"

David assumed Richard had read this entry during the break. If so, he had no choice but to admit he told his mother he was angry with her.

"Yes, I told her I was angry," Richard admitted.

Next, David had Richard read entries written by Martha after learning about her cancer diagnosis. In this entry, Martha wrote about her fear of dying but more so about her disappointment with Richard and, to a lesser extent, with Laura. Martha's entry indicated, upon her informing the children of her cancer diagnosis, they both initially expressed shock and concern but then soon wanted to talk about how family assets would be controlled if Martha were no longer alive. Martha's disappointment with Richard and Laura was mentioned in each of her entries after the cancer diagnosis.

The entry following three months of chemotherapy was particularly poignant, and David had Richard read it into the record.

"My doctor told me yesterday that my chemo treatments have not been effective. My cancer has continued to grow and has spread to my bones as well as my liver and pancreas. It appears there are no other treatment options that might prolong my life. My doctor says I have no more than three months left at the most. When I told Richard and Laura, they showed concern but then wanted to talk about who would control the trust after I'm gone, arguing that Richard should be the sole trustee. Their attitude was like a gut punch to me and breaks my heart. Max, on the other hand, was even more supportive than he has been all along. He actually cried when I gave him the news. Max has been good to me, and I'm going to do something good for him.  He still has financial issues with his Gateway Orlando project.  I told him I want to amend the trust to give him one-third of the trust assets upon my death to insure he can finish the project.  Max actually said I shouldn't do that.  But after we discussed it, he said he would accept my offer.  In return, he promised to leave one-half of his estate to my children in his estate plan.  He has no children of his own, only a niece who has been through some tough times recently.  We are meeting with the attorney next week to make these changes to my trust."

David followed up this quote by asking, "Mr. Langley, in your complaint, you alleged that Mr. Foster asked for the bequest of one-third of Martha's estate.  What factual knowledge do you have that Mr. Foster initiated discussions about this bequest rather than your mother, as she stated in her diary?"

Richard stared at the table for what seemed like five minutes before finally responding, "I understand that, on several occasions, Max told my mother he had serious financial problems with his project.  But she never agreed to leave him a part of her estate until after she learned her cancer was terminal.  By that time, she was weak and wasn't thinking clearly.  It's pretty obvious Max finally got what he wanted from my mother."

"So, you don't believe that—in your mother's words—the gut punch you gave her after she learned her cancer was terminal had anything to do with her decision to leave a portion of her estate to Mr. Foster?"

Richard twitched a shoulder as if uncertain how to respond.  "I don't know how she arrived at that decision, but I believe Max encouraged it."

David saw no need to push this point further since Martha's rationale for a testamentary gift to Max was clear and compelling.  His last question had been rhetorical, and Richard would never actually admit he had given his mother good cause for all of the actions she had taken.

David wrapped up his examination of the witness by exploring every effort Richard had made since graduating from college to actually obtain employment. This didn't take very long because, as David suspected, Richard had done very little to find a job of any type. By the time David completed the employment questions, it was undisputed that Richard had held no job at any time during college; and he had taken no serious steps to find employment since graduating. Richard's own testimony validated his father's fears that Richard had little desire to earn his own way in life and was content to live on family money. Furthermore, Martha's diary confirmed she had belatedly arrived at a similar opinion of Richard and had taken reasonable steps to insure he would not blow through all of the family money after she was gone.

Following a late lunch break, Montgomery commenced his cross examination. Montgomery may have been down after the damaging evidence in Martha's diary, but he was not out. He skillfully went through multiple questions about the $10 million loan Max had convinced Martha to make to him, emphasizing the fact the children were never told the loan was made; they only learned of it after Martha died. Montgomery also asked Richard a series of questions about how risky the loan was—a topic about which Richard was not qualified to opine—but he gamely quoted from some of his business classes about the importance of assessing risk in making *any* financial decision, much less a decision about a loan of $10 million, close to half of his mother's assets.

David wasn't concerned about what Richard had to say because Judge Long would never allow Richard to opine on how risky the loan was, but it was a preview of the questions a properly qualified expert witness would be able to address.  Any expert would be able to plausibly call this a risky loan.

Montgomery also asked Richard numerous questions about his mother's mental and physical health before and after her cancer diagnosis.  He generally described her as lethargic once her chemo started and gave numerous examples of her mind being muddled, especially once she learned her cancer was terminal.  Montgomery was building a record he would probably later use as the basis for a psychiatrist's opinion that Martha lacked testamentary capacity by the time the amended trust was signed appointing Max sole trustee and including him as a beneficiary of Martha's trust.

Finally, Montgomery addressed the issue of who prepared the wills and trusts for Martha. "Mr. Langley, do you know who the family attorney was when your father was still alive?"

"Yes, it was Frank Bennett.  He represented my parents for over twenty years, and he prepared their wills before my father died.  Frank Bennett also prepared the will my mother signed before she met Max."

"Was Mr. Bennett the attorney who prepared the will and trust your mother signed after she married Mr. Foster?"

Richard shook his head.  "No, that will and trust was prepared by Matthew Silverton who is also Max's estate planning attorney."

"How about the amended will and trust your mother signed shortly before her death?  Do you know who prepared those documents?"

"Yes, again that was Mr. Silverton."

"Do you know how your mother was introduced to Mr. Silverton?"

"She was introduced to him by Max." By now, Richard began to regain some confidence and sat up straighter in his chair.

"How did your mother get to her meetings with Mr. Silverton?"

"Each time she visited Mr. Silverton's office she was taken there by Max."

"Before your mother signed the first will and trust Mr. Silverton prepared for your mother, was she open with you about her estate plan?"

"Yes, she even gave me a copy of the will she had Mr. Bennett prepare after my father died."

"How were her assets to be distributed upon her death under that will?"

"My sister and I would each get half of her estate."

"Did your mother ever tell you that she decided to give Mr. Foster one-third of her estate?

"No."

"Did your mother ever tell you she made a $10 million loan to Max?"

"No."

"Did you mother ever give you a copy of the trust or amended trust, or her new will or amended will?

"No."

"Did your mother ever tell you she decided to appoint Max as the sole personal representative of her estate?"

"No."

With that, Montgomery concluded his examination of his own witness. There were other areas he would likely address with Richard at trial, but David perceived Montgomery didn't want to tip his hand on all of his strategy at this time.

Though David couldn't do much on re-direct examination with most of the questions Montgomery had asked, he wanted to address Richard's testimony that his mother's thinking was *muddled*.

"Mr. Langley, are your mother's diary entries evidence of her muddled thinking you testified to?"  David wasn't too concerned about Richard's answer to this question.  A *yes* answer would hurt his credibility because Martha's diary entries were clear and precise.  There was nothing muddled about them.  A *no* answer would be an admission her thinking wasn't always muddled; therefore, David had a good argument that Martha's thinking was clear when she signed the documents in question creating her estate plan.

Perhaps because he had no good answer, Richard stared blankly at David for a few minutes before finally mumbling, "I don't know," whereupon the deposition came to a close.

# Chapter 15

Laura Langley's deposition was held the following day, also at Montgomery's office. Despite his extensive deposition preparation, David was unsure about what to expect from Laura. In most of Martha's diary entries she had expressed disappointment with both Richard and Laura, but David speculated Laura may have just been following her older brother's lead in asking Martha to appoint Richard rather than Max as the trustee of her mother's trust.

Significantly, there were no diary entries in which Martha expressed concerns that Laura appeared content to live off family money.  The diary entries were also silent about whether Laura held summer jobs, and there was no mention of Laura travelling abroad during summer breaks.

David was also puzzled by Laura's absence during Richard's deposition the day before. As a party to the lawsuit, she had the right to be present at any deposition; and attending Richard's deposition would help prepare Laura for hers.  Furthermore, from his previous cases with Montgomery, David knew Montgomery strongly preferred that his clients attend all significant depositions because he believed their presence gave him the opportunity to impress his clients with what a great lawyer he was.

Thus, the normal anticipation David felt before any significant deposition was heightened as he, Maggie, and Max arrived for Laura's deposition.

Montgomery and Laura were already in the conference room, along with the court reporter when David, Maggie, and Max entered.  Montgomery made the introductions.  Unlike Richard, Laura didn't refuse to shake Max's hand.  Though her greeting to Max wasn't warm, she didn't show the same antipathy that Richard had.  David also noticed Laura was soft spoken and didn't hold eye contact when the introductions were made, even with Maggie, whom David assumed might be less threatening to Laura than he or Max might be.

Laura was about five feet two inches tall, slim and tastefully but conservatively dressed. She seemed to be a somewhat shy, confrontation-adverse young woman who may have become involved in the lawsuit more out of family loyalty than out of a conviction that a wrong had been perpetrated against her and her brother.  This initial impression, if correct, would help explain her absence from her brother's deposition.  David also recognized, however, that shy, reserved people who prefer to avoid confrontations can still be strong, effective witnesses—especially if they're convinced, they are in the right, or if they feel they are being bullied by the opposing lawyer.  David decided he would initially take a softer approach with Laura than he had with Richard.

Once Laura was sworn in as a witness and David covered the preliminaries, he asked about her background.  He established that Laura was two years younger than Richard; and after graduating with honors from high school, she also attended FSU.  Because she was a more diligent student than her brother, she graduated in four years—the same year her brother graduated.  She was an elementary education major and graduated with honors.  Unlike her brother, she had a part time job every year, although an unpaid one.  She worked as a volunteer with the Boys and Girls Club of Tallahassee two afternoons a week throughout her college years. This experience helped convince her to major in elementary education.  Also, unlike her brother, who was heavily involved in fraternity life throughout college, she never pledged a sorority.  She preferred to live in the dorms for the first two years, and she shared an off-campus apartment with two other girls the last two years.

"Ms. Langley, what jobs, if any, did you hold during your summer breaks while in college?" David asked.

"The summers after my freshman and sophomore years, I worked for one of the Boys and Girls Clubs here in the Orlando area.  The summer after my junior year, I was able to get a teaching internship at Lake Sybelia Elementary School in Maitland for a special summer program for disadvantaged children."

"Did you ever travel abroad during the years you were in college?"

"The only trip abroad I have ever taken was a ten-day mission trip two years ago with my church to Belize to help build a clinic to provide very basic medical care to a remote village."

David was quickly revising his opinion of Laura.  This was a young woman of substance who could scarcely be more different from her brother.  Whether this would be helpful or not remained to be seen.  David first had to know more about Laura's relationships with her mother and brother.

"Ms. Langley, how would you characterize your relationship with your mother prior to your going to college?"

"We were very close while I was growing up. My dad worked very hard to build up his business, and often didn't get home from work until late at night. So, I spent much more time with my mother than with my dad."

"How about while you were in college? Did your relationship change then?"

"Well, I was home far less, and we didn't see as much of each other as we had previously. After my father died, Mom wanted me to come home more often than I did. She was disappointed I seldom came home, but between my studies and my job with the Boys and Girls Club in Tallahassee, I couldn't get home very often during the school year."

Laura was proving to be a credible witness. David hoped her innate honesty might result is his obtaining helpful admissions from her. It was time to find out.

"Did you and your mother ever have conversations about money—more specifically, family money?"

"No, Mom and I never talked about money … at least until after Daddy died."

"After your father died, what discussions did you have with your mother about money?"

"Well, even then, I didn't have many conversations about money with Mom. But when Mom decided to put all the family assets into a trust, with Max and her as the trustees, I got dragged into the discussions between Mom and Richard."

*Suspicions confirmed.* "Describe those discussions for me."

"Richard was opposed to anyone outside the family being the trustee of a trust holding family assets. When he learned Mom was putting all of the family assets in a trust and that Max would be a co-trustee initially—and sole trustee if Mom were to die—he was very disappointed and angry."

"Why was he disappointed and angry?"

"Two reasons, really. First, he was disappointed Mom didn't want him to be the trustee." Laura paused. "Second, he didn't trust Max because he thought Max was after Mom's money."

How did you feel about Max being a co-trustee of the trust and later, the sole trustee after your mother died?"

"I didn't feel nearly as strongly about it as Richard did, but at the same time, I had questions about Max myself. And … I was loyal to my brother. I knew I didn't want the responsibility of being a trustee."

"How would you describe your relationship with your brother, Richard?"

Laura remained composed but seemed to be choosing her words carefully. "Richard and I were very close growing up. He was my big brother, and I idolized him. By the time we got to college, though, I would say we were close but not as close as we had been as kids. Our interests diverged. Richard was more into fraternity life. He also liked travelling abroad during the summers, which I had no real interest in doing, unless it was something like the mission trip I went on."

"Is it a fair statement to say when it came to financial issues and family assets you deferred to Richard on how they should be handled?"

"Yes, I think that's a fair statement. My interest was in elementary education; I had very little interest in or knowledge about financial matters."

David decided to press Laura. "You do know your father and Richard argued about money at times, right?"

"Yes, I am generally aware, although I know no specifics."

"And you are also aware your mother and Richard have had arguments over money since your father died?"

"Again, I am generally aware, but I know no specifics," she said as if coached to respond this way.

"Your mother also pushed Richard to get a job after he graduated, didn't she?"

"Yes, I think that's a fair statement."

"Have you had any discussions with Richard about either of those topics?"

"Nothing substantive," Laura said, with a slight shake of her head. "Richard mentioned that Mom is beginning to sound like Dad about money. Richard also said he's tired of Mom harping about a job. He doesn't want to take a job he knows he'll be unhappy with after a month or so. He said when he finds an opportunity that moves him, he'll jump on it."

"I take it he hasn't yet revealed to you what kind of job it is that might 'move him?'"

"No, not yet . . ."

By now, David had a clear picture of who was the moving force behind this lawsuit—and it wasn't Laura. He decided to move into the substance of the allegations of the complaint.

"Ms. Langley, do you understand the complaint your attorney filed alleges my client, Mr. Foster, exercised undue influence over your mother to get her to sign the initial trust and will, as well as the amended will and trust, and that she lacked the capacity to know what she was doing when she signed the amended will and trust?"

"Yes, I understand that."

"What facts do you have knowledge of to support the allegation your mother lacked the capacity to know what she was doing when she signed the amended trust and amended will?"

Laura paused before responding, apparently undecided on how to answer the question. Finally, she said, "I can't point to any specific facts. I was just surprised she appointed Max as the sole trustee—and even more surprised she left him an equal share of her estate."

"You've read her diary entries by now, I assume."

"Yes. . ."

"Do you agree with me that the entry in her diary the day after she learned her cancer was terminal is clear with respect to why she wanted to leave one-third of her estate to Mr. Foster?"

Laura paused once more. Tears formed in her eyes as she said in a near whisper, "It seems clear to me."

"This same entry also states that when your mother told you and Richard she only had three months left to live at the most, you and your brother expressed concern but then wanted to discuss who would be the trustee after she was gone. Am I correct that Richard initiated those discussions?"

Laura's lower lip was now trembling, but she nodded her head and softly said, "Yes."

As gently as he could, David asked, "Did you say anything during that discussion, or did Richard do all the talking?"

Laura straightened, still trying to avoid full blown tears, and said, barely above a whisper, "Richard did all the talking."

David nodded his head in agreement, and then softly asked, "But you stood there silently by his side as Richard made his pitch to your mother to be the sole trustee?"

This time Laura just nodded, stifling tears obviously on the brink of flowing.

Montgomery finally asked for a break before continuing the deposition.  After fifteen minutes, he and Laura returned to the conference room.

"Just a few more questions, Ms. Langley.  What facts are you aware of that indicate Mr. Foster exercised undue influence over your mother to get her to make the loan, or to change her estate plan?"

"The main facts are that her estate plan changed once Mr. Foster showed up.  My mother created a trust; she made him a co-trustee; she made a very large loan to him; and then she gave him one-third of her estate as part of her estate plan.  It's all very confusing to me."

"You've read your mother's diary.  Isn't a reasonable explanation for all of those actions she took set forth in her diary entries?"

A pained, bewildered look settled on Laura's face.  She paused for a long moment before she shook her head, and said, "I don't know.  After the way my mother stood up for Richard with our dad, I can't understand why she did what she did when Max came along."

"But aren't her own words in her diary the best explanation of why she did what she did?"

Again, Laura just shook her head and whispered, "I don't know."

After a few less important questions, David announced, "I have no other questions for Ms. Langley."

With the time approaching the noon hour, all parties agreed to take a lunch break.

*       *       *

Montgomery began questioning Laura when they returned from the break.  He was more understated than he had been the previous day with Richard, perhaps because he was not as sure what her responses would be to some of his questions.  He asked the same questions about the loan that he had asked Richard, with mostly similar answers.  Montgomery also went through in exhaustive detail every document or bit of information Laura's mother had *not* given her once Max came along and contrasted her answers with how open her mother had been before her relationship with Max.  Montgomery also asked Laura questions about how risky the loan was, but her loyalty to her brother didn't go so far as to answer questions on a topic she knew absolutely nothing about.

Montgomery then asked Laura a series of questions about whether her mother's thinking was muddled, as Richard had testified the day before.  Since Laura's responses were far less helpful than Richard's had been, Montgomery pivoted to the same series of questions he had asked Richard regarding their family attorney and how Martha found her new estate planning attorney, Matthew Silverton.  Laura's answers to all of these questions, as anticipated, were the same as Richard's.

Montgomery wrapped up his questioning after just over an hour.  David had no further questions for Laura.  He believed he had obtained all of the favorable testimony he was likely to get, and he didn't

204

want to give her an opportunity to backtrack on any of the admissions she'd made under David's questioning.

*          *          *

David asked Max to return to the Jordan & McKenzie offices with him and Maggie. When they arrived, the three of them gathered in the conference room to debrief the two days of depositions. Max was euphoric about how the depositions had gone. He even wondered whether Richard and Laura would continue with the lawsuit. David quickly decided he needed to tamp down Max's expectations that his case had already been won.

"Max, the good fortune we had to find Martha's diary, and her very helpful statements in the diary, puts us in a much stronger position than we were after your deposition. But this case is far from won. Martha's children still have a story to tell, and as you know from your deposition, Montgomery will tell it well. We still have much work to do to be ready for trial. While we can be thankful for the progress we've made these last two days, let's all recognize we still have a tough road ahead."

Max nodded in agreement. "But given how low I felt after my deposition, I want to enjoy this moment for a bit."

Max paused, then looked David directly in the eye. "I confess I had misgivings at our initial meeting whether you could get the job done. But I want you to know how much I appreciate your efforts to date. I'm also glad you are representing *me* instead of Martha's children."

"Thanks, Max. I appreciate your confidence in us," David said as Max left the conference room.

David and Maggie remained behind to go over their to-do list for the next week. As they left the conference room, they were greeted by

Karen Overton. "I'm amazed. Mr. Foster was one big sourpuss on his first visit to our office. As he left just now, he greeted me with a pleasant smile—obviously happy. You must be doing something right with his case to bring about such a metamorphosis in him."

**Chapter 16**

The weekend following Richard and Laura's depositions was a quiet one at David's house. He was worn out from the pace he had been keeping at work over the past few weeks—culminating in the two depositions, which were successful but exhausting. Feeling as though he had no energy reserves, David wanted to do nothing but sleep and hang out at home.

Carol had finished her fourth round of chemo on Friday and was more tired after this round than after any of the three previous rounds. Her fatigue wasn't solely due to the chemo, however. She had made absolutely no progress in raising money for WCC over the past few weeks and felt helpless as the available time in which to raise the necessary funds was slowly ebbing away. "Without a minor miracle, David," she'd said, "we're not going to raise the funds we need." That admission seemed to add to the fatigue and hopelessness already overwhelming her.

Jenna had a sleepover at a friend's house for the weekend, so there was no reason for David and Carol to get up early on Saturday. Nevertheless, they were both surprised neither of them woke up until 10:00, the latest either could remember sleeping in years. David crawled out of bed first and offered to brew the coffee and cook his breakfast specialty—cheese omelets. While David was preparing breakfast,

207

Carol joined him in the kitchen, poured a cup of coffee for each of them, and set the table. David blamed the frustrations of the past weeks of fundraising and chemo treatments for her pensive mood.

"You know, most people would say we're living the dream," Carol said. "We both have interesting jobs that pay us enough to live comfortably in a nice home. We have a great marriage and a wonderful daughter. Until I came down with cancer, we had no problems other than the ordinary problems most people face. So, why do we so often feel like we're drinking from the firehose of life? We seldom have time to actually enjoy this wonderful life we have; instead, we so often seem to just watch as it whisks by."

David met Carol's pensive gaze. "That's a good question, Carol. The only answer I have is that a meaningful life is usually one that places meaningful demands on us." He took her hands in his. "What creates meaning in life is not our possessions, but rather our relationships—especially those relationships that require us to give of ourselves, often sacrificially. Your creating and running WCC is a good example. It has brought great meaning to your life and hope to many women and children, but it has also made great demands on you. Would you expect it to be any other way?"

"No, but along the way I would like to find time to rest—not in the sense of sleeping or doing nothing—but rather in the sense of having time to contemplate what our lives are and have been, and finding satisfaction in what and who we have given ourselves to. Does that make sense?"

"It does, and I share your desire to slow down before life totally rushes past us. I promise you, once your cancer treatments are over and I finish the Max Foster case, we're going to find time to have the kind of rest you're talking about."

Once they had finished their breakfast, including two cups of coffee each, they had the energy to discuss what lay ahead during the coming week. "We go see Dr. Marks again on Wednesday afternoon at 2:00," Carol said. "Now that I've completed all four rounds of chemo over the last three months, he should have a report on how I'm doing and give us recommendations for further treatments. I must say, I hope we get something more definitive than his statement at our last visit—something more positive than, 'the cancer isn't getting worse.'"

"Yeah, me too. Remember, if there hasn't been significant improvement at this visit, I'm going to push him for some alternative treatment recommendations."

"I know. At this point, I wouldn't mind some alternative treatments myself … if they won't make me feel so bad. What's going on with you over the next week?"

David rose and began clearing the breakfast dishes as he spoke. "We have a busy schedule in the Max Foster case from now until trial, which is only six weeks away. The mediation conference in only four weeks off. This case isn't heading to trial at a good time, especially if you begin a new regime of treatments. But somehow we'll get it all done."

"Max Foster," Carol mused. "You've mentioned him several times now. Every time you do, I feel like I know the name, but I can't place him or remember why his name is familiar."

"Well, he's a prominent developer in town, and his Gateway Orlando project is frequently mentioned in the news."

"Yes, but I seldom remember names I just hear in the news. There's some other reason his name's familiar. I just can't remember why. In any event, I hope his case goes well for you."

"So, do I," David muttered to himself. "So do I."

*       *       *

David decided to try working from home on Wednesday morning before taking Carol to Dr. Marks' office for her afternoon appointment. David had never been particularly efficient working from home, but he was still tired, even after a restful weekend at home. Driving to the office for a half-day of work feeling so fatigued would, he felt, deplete what little energy he had left. Sleeping an extra hour and avoiding the drive on construction-clogged I-4, would, in his opinion, improve his mood, if not his energy.

Besides, he wanted a little more time to prepare himself for whatever news Dr. Marks might have. Outwardly at least, Carol had shown no improvement over the last visit when Dr. Marks said the cancer was no worse but also no better. David didn't know what to expect this time, although he was praying for better news while preparing for worse.

Neither said much as he parked the car and they walked toward Dr. Marks' office building. The lack of any warmth or appeal in the "office modern" building hit David once more, and he feared it portended unhappy news for their visit. He immediately tried to put this thought out of his mind, but try as he might, the thought lingered in the back of his mind, silently tamping down his hopes for this visit.

They only had to wait five minutes in the reception area before Dr. Marks' nurse invited them back to the examination room where she took Carol's blood pressure and other vitals, reviewing her symptoms and

210

medications. After making a few notes, she said, "Dr. Marks will be with you shortly." True to her word, Dr. Marks came in almost immediately.

He greeted them with his usual friendly handshake, then quickly glanced over Carol's records. David couldn't read any signals from Dr. Marks' demeanor; his tired, weathered face gave no hint of what was to come.

He looked up from Carol's records to face them. "I suppose I should get right to the point. Carol, I wish I had better news to give you today. When we met after the second round of chemo, I said your cancer was no better, but also no worse. Despite these last two rounds of chemo, the tumor is now slightly larger. But more significantly, we've detected the presence of cancer cells in your lungs as well as your liver. In short, although the chemo treatments have slowed the advancement of the cancer, they haven't been efficacious enough to stop the growth or put you in remission."

As she was during her previous visits with Dr. Marks, Carol was serene, calmly accepting the information Dr. Marks just gave her, without comment. Even David, who was bitterly disappointed upon hearing Dr. Marks' assessment, was not shocked. The lack of progress after the first two rounds of chemo treatments had hardened him to the possibility a full recovery might not materialize. Neither Carol nor David said anything for nearly two minutes while Dr. Marks allowed time for his comments to sink in.

Finally, Dr. Marks said, "I want you to know that from the outset all of your cancer markers indicated the course of treatment I prescribed was the most suitable one, and it held the most promise. All of my experience in treating metastatic breast cancer also pointed toward the treatment prescribed.  Unfortunately, your body just didn't respond to the treatment as well as I thought it would.

"What options do we have, Dr. Marks?" David asked.

"We can tweak the treatments in another round of chemo to see if a different combination of chemotherapy drugs might be more efficacious, but I think the better plan is to identify one or more experimental clinical trials—including some immunotherapy treatments.  I've already begun searching for some appropriate experimental clinical trials and have identified several, all of which are out of state.  I will be happy to go over some of them with you to give you a better idea of what's involved."

Carol remained calm, but David sensed Dr. Marks' comments about experimental clinical trials outside of Florida had caused her more concern than even the cancer.  "Dr. Marks," Carol responded quickly, "you've given me a lot to think about.  I don't think I'm up to hearing the details of the clinical trials today.  If you have any written materials about the clinical trials, even if they're just summaries, I'd like to review them and then ask you any questions I may have."

David met her gaze as she added with a soft, loving smile, "My husband has wanted to ask about experimental clinical trials for several weeks, so I'm sure he will help me evaluate any information on clinical trials you send me."

David nodded.  What could he say?  His grief was too great to ask the questions he had wanted to ask.  For the moment, all he could think of was Carol's earlier statement that she didn't want to go out of state for clinical trials.  Based upon what Dr. Marks seemed to be saying, a clinical trial looked like Carol's only chance of prolonging her life for any significant period of time.  If she wouldn't pursue what seemed to be her only hope, then David was out of hope also, and he could focus on nothing at this moment other than his sense of loss.

"Sure, I'll be happy to e-mail you articles about the clinical trials I've identified," said Dr. Marks. "I'll rank them in my order of preference for you, Carol. After you and David have reviewed them, let's talk further about how to proceed. I'll make time available for you next week so we can decide on a course of treatment right away."

Carol and David were both somewhat dazed as they left Dr. Marks' office. Although they had separately tried to prepare themselves for the very news they received, actually hearing the words spoken by a doctor they trusted was a shock. They both tried to get their thoughts around what the path forward might be as they headed home.

*        *        *

Jenna was already home when they arrived. "I couldn't focus at soccer practice today, so I told Coach I wasn't feeling well and got his permission to skip practice."

Carol scowled. "You lied to your coach? Jenna . . ."

"I didn't actually lie, Mom. I've been so worried about you that my stomach is upset, my body aches as if I have the flu, and I've had a throbbing headache all day. I needed to find out the results of your doctor's appointment. . ." Jenna paused, looking desperately from her mother to her father for good news.

When neither David nor Carol responded immediately, Jenna burst into tears and ran into her mother's arms. Carol pulled Jenna tight to her chest and wept with her. David joined his wife and daughter, and the emotional weight of the past several months finally took over as they all

213

released their pent-up fears in deep, anguished sobs, desperately clinging to one another.

*           *           *

After ten minutes, their sobs finally subsided. As they all sat down on the living room couch, Jenna asked. "Mom, how bad is it? What did Dr. Marks say?"

Both Carol and David knew they couldn't sugarcoat the news—not after the emotional honesty of the last few minutes. David was in awe as Carol pressed through her own pain to respond to Jenna with a reassuring calm. "The chemo treatments aren't working, Jenna. Or at least they aren't working well enough to put the cancer in remission. They've only slowed down the spread of the cancer. It's now in my lungs as well as my liver."

"What does he recommend, Mom?"

"He thinks I should get involved in a clinical trial, and he's recommended several for me to consider. Unfortunately, all of them are out of state."

Jenna's gaze seemed far too adult, her pragmatic comments beyond her years. "But, Mom, if a clinical trial will cure the cancer, you need to do it."

"I don't know, Jenna. It's just experimental; it may do no good."

Jenna glanced at David, seeking his support. "You don't know unless you try."

"If I go out of state for the treatments, there is no way I can continue with the fundraising for WCC, and it will likely go under. That would just destroy me. Besides, I don't want to be separated from you and your father, even for short periods of time."

214

"Mom, you have to do what's best for your own health … and what's best for your own family."

"I know, Jenna. We're going to look at all the options carefully. I promise."

David and Jenna just looked at each other. He was bewildered over how Carol could consider any alternative to a clinical trial, given the recommendation from Dr. Marks. At the same time, David realized—and Jenna was beginning to suspect—Carol may be unwilling to spend the remainder of what little time she may have left getting experimental treatments that may make her feel miserable, with little chance of a cure. She might prefer to spend her remaining time with family and pursuing WCC's goals.

*      *      *

Later that night, after Jenna had gone to bed, David and Carol retrieved the email Dr. Marks sent Carol outlining the three clinical trials he recommended. Carol had wanted to read them first so she could state out loud the key points for them to consider.

"The first one Dr. Marks recommends looks promising, but with some big drawbacks. It's a clinical trial for an experimental immunotherapy drug that has had some success in animals, but this is the first clinical trial in humans. The success rate in animals has approached twenty-five percent, although they are quick to disavow any expectation of a success rate that high in humans. Here's the kicker—it's at a hospital in Seattle, Washington, will last four months, and they want the patient there the entire time. David, I can't be separated from you and Jenna for that long, and you can't just drop everything here for four months."

David said nothing. Any hope that a clinical trial of some experimental drug or course of treatment could be the answer for Carol didn't look promising so far. He asked, "What are the other clinical trials, and where are they?"

"The second one he recommends is a combination of immunotherapy and a new, much stronger, chemotherapy regime. There's a warning that the combination may make patients feel even worse than they normally do with more traditional chemotherapy treatments. The current drugs given to ameliorate the adverse side effects of chemotherapy have shown little benefit in the only previous clinical trial of this treatment regime. The location of this one isn't much better; it's at a hospital in San Francisco. There are three six-week sessions with a two-week break between sessions, during which time the patient can come home—if they are strong enough to travel. That doesn't sound very encouraging to me."

Again, David offered no comment. He was so mentally tired and emotionally exhausted he couldn't think clearly, much less offer an opinion on such an important issue. Whatever thoughts he had for Carol to consider would have to come later.

Carol continued, "The third one is in Boston. At least, we would be in the same time zone. This clinical trial has been conducted previously, with about fifteen percent of the patients showing significant improvement and twenty percent more showing some improvement. It also consists of a combination of immunotherapy and chemotherapy treatments, but with combinations that haven't been tried previously. The combinations for this clinical trial are even slightly different from those used in the previous clinical trial with these drugs. This one will include four rounds of two weeks of treatment followed by one week off.  Again, however, they want the patient to stay at the hospital even during the week off."

David and Carol just looked at each other, overwhelmed by the day, overwhelmed by the decisions facing them, and overwhelmed by the turn their lives had taken.  Obviously, they would have to discuss these options further with Dr. Marks, but at the moment they were too exhausted to think about anything further and went to bed.

# Chapter 17

David was unusually subdued as the lawyers gathered in the conference room for the Monday meeting the following week.  Only Jesse knew the latest about Carol's cancer.  By the look on Steve, Maggie, and Sarah Garcia's faces, David recognized their concern and suspected they knew he was wrestling with more than his caseload.  He realized he shouldn't keep them in the dark with respect to the decisions he and Carol would have to make—decisions which would affect them as well.

"Let me begin our meeting by bringing you up to date on Carol's condition.  Regrettably, she hasn't responded to the chemotherapy as well as we had hoped."  Their worried looks deepened as David paused, struggling to control his emotions before continuing.

"Dr. Marks recommends Carol participate in a clinical trial, and we are considering several different ones.  Unfortunately, all of them are out of state, which raises a whole separate list of issues as compared to receiving treatment here in Orlando.  We haven't decided which clinical trial, if any, Carol will participate in.  We just ask for your continued prayers as we decide how to proceed."

The somber announcement cast a pall over the meeting, the surprise and disappointment evident on everyone as each offered words of support.  "Times like these remind me why having people in the firm who are like family is so important," David responded.  He knew their words of disappointment and encouragement were not just perfunctory.  Each knew and loved Carol, and each felt his pain.

After a few minutes, David continued, "Thank you again for your concern.  This is an extraordinarily difficult time for our family; I can't tell you how meaningful your support is for Carol and me.  But we still have client needs to address.  Maggie, please bring everyone up to date on the Max Foster case."

"As you know, Richard and Laura Langley's depositions were helpful primarily because of Martha's diary which we found shortly before the depositions.  This morning we received a motion for sanctions that Montgomery has filed asserting Max is guilty of spoliation of evidence. He asks the court to prohibit us from introducing Martha's diary into evidence at trial and to prohibit any reference to it in the children's deposition testimony or in any testimony offered at trial."

"I'm not surprised," Steve snorted.  "This is just Montgomery being himself."

David nodded.  "I'm not surprised either."

"Additionally," Maggie continued, "in a separate motion, despite both children identifying Martha's handwriting in the diary, Montgomery asks the court to prohibit any use of the diary because, he contends, it's a forgery.  Finally, Montgomery has filed a motion for summary judgment.  It's rather convoluted.  Essentially, he asserts that once the diary is excluded, Max has no evidence constituting a reasonable explanation for his acts—and those acts amount to undue influence.  He further argues Max actively procured the amended will and trust, and in the absence of the diary there is no evidence to the contrary."

"Wow! That's quite a combination of motions," Steve said. "Do you think he has a chance of prevailing on any of the motions or getting the judge to strike the diary?"

"Let me respond to your question about the motion for sanctions due to spoliation of evidence. David can respond regarding the summary judgment motion," replied Maggie. "The primary ground for the spoliation motion is the fact Max failed to produce an email he sent to a close friend and confidant after his first date with Martha. In it, he said he may have found an answer to the problems with his project. That statement by Max is not at all helpful to his defense. But the reason the email wasn't produced is because it wasn't on Max's company's server."

"Why not?" Jesse asked.

"Unlikely as it may seem, there was a server crash shortly after the email was sent, and the company's IT director was unable to recover the lost documents, among which was the email in question. Montgomery got the email from a former friend of Max's and surprised him with it at his deposition. Fortunately, Max has a good, credible IT director who will testify that a server crash occurred about the time the email was sent, and it was lost from the server. I'm reasonably certain Judge Long will believe the IT director and deny the motion for sanctions, although it's no slam dunk for us. Even if she were to grant the motion for sanctions, I don't believe she will prohibit our use of the diary. Both children identified their mother's handwriting, and we have an expert witness ready to testify the diary is in Martha's handwriting."

"What about the summary judgment motion, David?" Jesse asked. "Do you think Montgomery has any chance of prevailing on that motion?"

"Well, as Maggie pointed out, unless the court prohibits our use of Martha's diary, Montgomery has no chance of winning the motion. Even if he were to prevail on keeping the diary out of evidence, I believe Max's deposition testimony raises an issue of fact that would preclude the judge granting summary judgment. As you know, if *any* material fact is in dispute, the judge can't grant summary judgment. I'm confident Judge Long will conclude she must hear the evidence at trial rather than grant the summary judgment motion. I think the true purpose of Montgomery's motion is to attempt to pre-condition the judge for the evidence she will hear at trial. He's also trying to create enough fear in Max to motivate him toward a reasonable settlement offer at the mediation conference."

Jesse took a sip of coffee, then asked, "Speaking of mediation, what do you think the chances are of settling at mediation?"

"Not very good," David responded. "The biggest problem is the current state of development of Gateway Orlando. First of all, the relief the children have demanded includes an order finding Max exercised undue influence, and as a result the judge should set aside the amended will and amended trust. Second, due to the undue influence, the children demand that Max be removed as personal representative of the estate and as trustee of the trust. If Max is removed as trustee and one of the children—likely Richard—is appointed trustee, he will undoubtedly demand the promissory note for $10 million be repaid immediately. Max can't afford to repay the promissory note in full at this time, and probably won't be able to repay it for a year or more, even if his development is successful. Finally, the complaint asks that Max be required to pay the plaintiffs' attorney fees. He can't do that at this time, either. I doubt the children will be willing to settle for much less than what they will obtain if they win the case, and

Max can't give them what they want … absent a miracle.  So, I'm not optimistic we'll settle at the mediation conference."

"When is your hearing on the motions Montgomery filed?" Steve inquired.

David smiled.  "Ah, I'm glad you asked.  Montgomery must have reserved some hearing time weeks ago because these motions are set to be heard the Friday before the Monday mediation conference.  Obviously, Montgomery would like nothing better than to have the judge exclude the diary from evidence.  Obtaining such a ruling on the eve of the mediation conference would give him a much better bargaining position at mediation, and it would strengthen his hand for trial.  On the other hand, if we prevail on the motions and Judge Long refuses to disallow use of the diary, we will be in a stronger bargaining position at mediation and at trial."

David then asked Jesse to cover several of the cases she was working on, after which Sarah Garcia brought up several administrative issues to wind up the meeting.  Jesse lingered behind to talk to David as the others left the conference room.  "How are you holding up, David? Trying to deal with Carol's health issues at the same time you're getting ready for trial and the mediation conference in the Max Foster case has to be taking a toll on you."

"I won't lie to you, Jesse.  It's been tough, and it doesn't look like life is going to get easier anytime soon.  In addition to dealing with Carol's issues, seeing how Carol's cancer is affecting Jenna is tearing me up inside.  I'm so grateful to you for taking Jenna out for ice cream last weekend to talk to her.  I've been so focused on trying to help Carol I haven't given Jenna all the support she needs now."

"I'm thankful I can help. Jenna is one amazing young woman. She's hurting inside, but she's also strong, mature beyond her years. I think she'll be fine, but she's struggling with the question why this happened to her mom."

"Yeah, I'm dealing with the same question, and I think I know exactly who I need to talk to about it."

*        *        *

David recalled how Father John, as he was known, became both his friend and priest. The family had attended his church for nearly ten years. When they first visited All Souls Episcopal Church, David and Carol were so impressed with the rector, Father John Williams, they soon became members—and considered him a friend.

They had also been close friends of his wife, Sonya, before she died four years ago of a heart attack. Sonya was only fifty-five at the time, two years younger than Father John. David remembered how excruciatingly difficult her death was for his friend. David was as shocked as Father John and the church members had been by Sonya's sudden death, and David did all he could to offer support and comfort. Part of those efforts included meeting Father John for breakfast every Wednesday morning for over a year. The breakfast meetings deepened their relationship and offered David an insight as to how this man of great faith had dealt with personal tragedy that had come upon his family without warning.

They talked often about Father John and Sonya's life together and how much Sonya had meant to the church, their friends, and anyone who had known her. Yet, as far as David could remember, they never discussed the question now raging within him and demanding an answer. *How could*

*God allow something so bad to happen to a good person like Sonya or Carol?*

Because he was seeking a counselling session with Father John, David asked to meet at the church rather than at a restaurant. Father John had time available Friday of that same week, and David showed up at the church office promptly at three o'clock.

Father John was a tall, slender man with slumped shoulders, a slight potbelly, and a forward tilt of his head that made him appear to always be leaning forward. His angular face was kind and expressive, with deep lines around his eyes that had a tinge of sorrow to them, and thin lips which easily broadened into a warm smile. The combination of expressive, sorrowful eyes and a warm smile somehow enabled Father John to exude both weariness and joy simultaneously. His voice, however, was firm, deep, and melodious, and held the attention of anyone engaged in a conversation with him or listening to his sermons. His strong voice, combined with his quick mind and sense of humor, gave the impression of someone younger than his sixty-one years, despite his poor posture.

As soon as David arrived at the church, Father John came out of his office to greet him. "David, it's been too long since we last met for breakfast. I'd hoped we'd have a time to chat ever since I learned of Carol's illness. But as busy as I know you are, I thought I should wait until you called me. As you know, I've spoken with Carol a few times."

As they settled into chairs around a small conference table, David began, "I appreciate your meeting with me today. I've been thinking about making an appointment with you for at least two months, because there's no one else who would understand what I'm going through better than you."

"How is Carol doing?"

David sighed. "Carol's treatments have been ineffective, and the cancer is continuing to spread. That pushed me to call you. Thank you for seeing me so quickly."

Father John just nodded, so David continued, "John, how do you deal with the possibility of losing your wife, and of your daughter losing her mother? This has been almost more than I can bear. Whenever I begin to think maybe I can find my way through this, my thoughts turn to Jenna. Then I feel overwhelmed again and feel guilty for not being strong enough to be able to provide the emotional support both Carol and Jenna deserve."

As he said this, David struggled to control his emotions and the tears about to fall.

Father John met David's pleading gaze. "I know how difficult this is for you, David. Let me first set your mind at ease about one thing. Each time I've spoken to Carol she's mentioned how supportive and understanding you've been to her. She also commented glowingly about how you've comforted Jenna and been there for her. So, don't be too hard on yourself. You're doing better in those areas than you realize."

David just nodded, unable to express his gratitude for Father John's reassurance.

"As to how you deal with the possibility of losing your wife, I didn't have to face my loss in the same way you have. Sonya died unexpectedly of a heart attack before we even knew she had heart problems. I didn't have to face a drawn out period of time in which all sorts of unpleasant outcomes were constantly running around in my mind. Of course, losing her so abruptly was indeed a shock. But I suspect that was easier to deal with than the strung-out process you're going through where death is always a possibility—yet, at the same time, you hope for a good outcome … if not a miracle."

"Yes. I do pray for a miracle."

John's tender eyes reflected his empathy for his friend. "Whether death comes quickly or threatens over a long period of time, it's normal to feel undone and perhaps even to have anger toward God. Is that how you're feeling?"

"Yes, that's part of what I want to talk about. Carol is such a good person. She has dedicated her life to supporting the women and children at WCC, even to the detriment of her own health. Why would God allow this to happen to Carol, especially at such a young age? It would be bad enough if this happened after Jenna were grown. Dealing with this when she is only twelve makes it that much harder to deal with."

David raised his head as if asking heaven itself, "Is God punishing us? Certainly, he could make all this go away if he wanted to, couldn't he? And, if so, why doesn't he?"

"David, you are asking questions that have been asked by some of the best philosophers and theologians for centuries. I've asked these very same questions myself. I still don't have perfect answers. There are still mysteries in life I can't explain, but I can offer you a few thoughts that will hopefully help strengthen your faith and enable you to get through these trying times.

"Do you remember the class I taught a few years back on the parables of Jesus?" Father John continued.

David nodded.

"One of the reasons Jesus told the parables was to help people understand what God is like."

"Yes, I remember discussing this."

"Outside the Jewish faith, people believed the gods should be appeased so they would leave you alone. If you angered the gods—and it didn't take much to anger them—they would punish you. Even within the Jewish faith, many believed that if bad things happened to people it was punishment from God. And those who prospered did so because God had blessed them. The parables Jesus taught, however, paint a somewhat different picture of what God is like. Do you remember the parable of the prodigal son?"

"Yes. I remember we studied it, but I haven't read the story in quite a while."

"This parable is all about what God is like. The story is about a wealthy man who had two sons. The younger son went to his father and asked for his portion of the inheritance now, instead of waiting until the father died. Asking for his inheritance while his father was still alive was a terrible thing for the son to do. Under Jewish law and culture at the time, the younger son was saying to his father, in effect, 'I wish you were dead so I can have my inheritance now.' Rather than punish the son or deny his request—as the father had every right to do—he gave the son what he asked for. Then the son gathered all his newly acquired wealth and left to live in a distant country. There he squandered his wealth in dissolute living. After a famine hit, he was so destitute he was forced to get a job, and the only one he could find was feeding pigs—a job no self-respecting Jew would take. After nearly starving to death, the son came to his senses and decided to return home, confess his sin against his father, and ask to be treated as a hired hand rather than a son.  So, the son set out to return to his father, but while the son was still a long way off, the father spotted him and rushed out to meet him.  Before the son could utter his speech humbly asking to be treated as a hired hand, the father embraced him, instructed his servants to clothe him with the finest robe, put a ring on his finger, and put sandals on his feet.  He then instructed his servants to kill a fatted calf and prepare a banquet to celebrate the son's return.

"So, David, what does this parable tell you about God?"

David paused, thinking deeply about his response for a long moment, then said, "It tells me God is far more forgiving than I am.  Even before the son could apologize, the father generously took back a son who had wished his own father was dead.  This isn't a father looking to punish his children, but rather one who loves them unconditionally."

David paused again, pondering what he was about to say.  "I find it interesting how the son is considered the prodigal in this story because of his lavish living that exhausted his wealth. It seems to me the father was at least as lavish in the way he loved his son.  He forgave a son who didn't deserve mercy and restored him, without penalty, to the status of a son once again—something the son had not even asked or hoped for.

"That's right.  This story tells us God is for us, not against us.  There is another story about Jesus that shows how tragedies don't necessarily mean someone is being punished. In the thirteenth chapter of Luke, Jesus is asked by certain Jews from Galilee about some of their fellow Galileans who were slaughtered by Pontius Pilate, the Roman procurator, as they were in the act of offering sacrifices.  They asked Jesus what terrible sin their fellow Jews must have committed to have something so horrible happen to them."

David had wondered about this himself. "What answer did Jesus give?"

"Jesus's response was that they were no worse sinners than anyone else. He then gave another example of a tragedy—a tower at Siloam which fell, randomly killing eighteen people. Again, Jesus said they were no more guilty of offending God than anyone else. Just because a tragedy occurs, we shouldn't assume the people affected are being punished by God. Can you accept this?"

"I can accept it at an intellectual level, but emotionally I'm still having trouble accepting that my wife may die, and God, who has the power to prevent it, may not intervene to prevent Carol from dying at a relatively young age."

"I get that, David. I had some of the same feelings myself when Sonya died. I asked God why he didn't prevent her heart attack. Questioning these situations is perfectly normal, especially when these bad things happen to someone we love. In fact, Sonya's death caused me to search for answers just as you're doing."

David sighed. "Then how did you come to acceptance?"

John reached for his Bible and found the passage he wanted. "One of the scriptures I found most helpful was Psalm 116, verse 15. 'Precious in the sight of the Lord is the death of his faithful ones.' I take this verse to mean the Lord was no happier about Sonya's heart attack than I was—or about Carol's cancer than you are. But he welcomed Sonya to himself because he loved her even more than I did. And he loves Carol, whatever the outcome of her cancer."[2]

"But why does it have to be this way, John? Why do we have to endure so much suffering, pain, and death?"

Father John's eyes seemed more kind than sorrowful, and his smile was that of a teacher who had longed to see his student grasp concepts the teacher had so often tried to explain. "Again, David, I have no perfect answers.  But it's obvious we live in a troubled world.  This world is not the way God intended it to be, but it is the way it is because of decisions we, mankind, have made—not because of decisions God has made.  God gave us free will, and we have abused that free will to go our own way rather than be obedient to God.  We rebelled against God's way and rejected him.  The whole purpose of Jesus's incarnation was to restore the relationship between mankind and God.  The Bible even tells us that nature itself has been affected by our rebellion and disobedience.  As a result, bad things are going to happen—to good people as well as to people who are not so good.  The Bible, both the Hebrew scriptures and the New Testament, give many examples of this."

"Such as?" David asked.

"The book of Job is perhaps the best example.  Job had many of the same questions you have, but not all of his questions were fully answered either."

"So, are you saying I'm probably not going to fully understand why these bad things happen—at least not in this life?"

"David, millions, perhaps billions, of words have been written about why bad things happen to good people, and why there is pain and suffering in the world.  Not surprisingly, the authors frequently don't agree.  I believe the biblical version I have just briefly summarized provides the best explanation, and I think you believe that, too.  If you accept, in faith, that God loves Carol, you, and Jenna and that he will be with you throughout this ordeal, he will give you the strength to get through it.  He won't take away all of your pain, but you will find comfort and strength to carry on."

David sat there without responding, considering what Father John had said.  As a lawyer, David didn't like having to deal with situations or issues over which he had no control or over which he did not, at least, have an opportunity to *try* to exercise control.  Based on what Father John said, however, this situation was one over which David would not have control or even understand fully.  But he could control his own response to the situation and respond in faith to the one who did have control.

"You've given me a lot to think about, John, and you've brought some degree of clarity. Thank you."

David and John reminisced for a while about their times together while Sonya was still alive.  When David rose to leave, Father John said, "David, I'm here to talk further with you at any time.  Please don't hesitate to call me."

"Don't worry; I won't hesitate to call," David responded with sincerity.

He left Father John's office with his pain still intact, and with some questions still unanswered, but with a newfound strength to see his family struggle through to the end—
whatever the end might be.

# Chapter 18

Two weeks later, the lawyers at Jordan & McKenzie gathered for their Monday meeting. Before they began discussing their pending cases, Maggie asked David how Carol was doing. "We've been considering the clinical trials Dr. Marks found and have decided on the one in Boston.  Unfortunately, we just learned the trial has been delayed for a month.  Dr. Marks has recommended Carol go through another round of chemo to keep the cancer at bay until she can participate in the clinical trial.  This means Carol will start it about the time the Max Foster trial wraps up."

By their expressions, David could tell the other lawyers recognized his emotional reserves would be diminished, if not depleted, following a difficult trial—as the Max Foster trial promised to be—but no one mentioned this aloud.  Instead, Maggie asked, "What can we do to help, David?"

"You're going to help me get ready for the trial.  Jesse has agreed to help with Jenna, and you and Steve may have to entertain Jenna occasionally.  Think you can handle all that?" David asked with a smile.

They quickly said they could, although the expressions on their faces belied their assurances they could manage to entertain a twelve-year-old.

"Speaking of the trial, David, what's the schedule between now and then?" asked Jesse.

"The trial begins four weeks from today. Montgomery and I have agreed to have our meeting to prepare the pre-trial statement two days after the mediation conference, which will take place two weeks from today, the Monday after the Friday hearing on the pending motions. By then, we should have a good idea of the issues that are actually going to be tried. We have the pre-trial conference with Judge Long the Friday before the trial starts. Obviously, there's a lot of work to be done. Maggie and I will be devoting most of our time between now and then to trial preparation, although we also have to prepare for and attend the mediation conference. We may need some assistance with trial preparation from you and Steve. Do you have time to assist us, if necessary?"

"Sure," both Jesse and Steve said in unison.

"Is there anything we can do to assist you in getting ready for the mediation conference?" Steve added.

"No, I think we will be well prepared," David responded. "We have Bruce Mankin as our mediator, and he is as good as they come. If there is any chance for us to settle, Bruce will find it. But, as I've told you previously, I'm not very optimistic. We're meeting with Max next Monday to discuss the mediation conference and how we want to approach it. Of course, how we approach the mediation conference will be governed to some extent by how Judge Long rules on the pending motions."

*        *        *

The following Monday, Max arrived at the Jordan & McKenzie offices promptly at two o'clock, as scheduled, and Karen Overton showed him into the conference room. David and Maggie were waiting on Max—

having long ago observed Max didn't like waiting on anyone for any reason. "Thanks for coming today, Max," David began. "We want to discuss the mediation conference and also the hearing scheduled the Friday before. Obviously, how Judge Long rules on the pending motions may have an impact on our approach at the mediation conference."

Max interrupted David before he could go any further; something was clearly on his mind. "David, you don't need to spend a lot of time going over what takes place at a mediation conference. I reviewed my records regarding the number of mediation conferences I've attended, and I calculated I've attended at least a dozen. Mediation conferences and the associated lawsuits are an unfortunate part of the real estate development business. However, before we discuss the mediation conference, there's something I need to tell you."

David suddenly felt apprehensive. He hoped Max hadn't held back something important to his case. "Go on, Max."

"I knew my project was drawing attention from some of the largest real estate investors in the country. They weren't sure Orlando was ready for such a large mixed-use development. Well, they apparently are now convinced that it is. Late last week, I received a telephone call from a publicly held real estate investment trust—a REIT—that owns malls, apartments, and mixed-use developments all over the country. They said they intend to make an offer to buy my Gateway Orlando project, and they want to keep me on as the contractor to finish the construction. I seriously doubt they'll make a good enough offer to tempt me to sell, given the financial projections we have for the project once it is built out. But if the case goes badly at trial, it would be nice to have an acceptable offer in my back pocket to enable me to pay off the $10 million loan."

"That *is* good news for you, Max," David responded, "but I'm unsure how the offer affects the approach you will take at the mediation conference."

"David, this is the largest project I've ever attempted—the crown jewel of my career as a real estate developer. If it's anywhere nearly as successful as I think it will be, based upon our financial projections, it will secure my financial future, even if I never develop another project. I don't want to sell; I want to complete the construction and then manage the project for the foreseeable future. So, if the offer from the REIT is at least reasonable, I will have insurance against a bad result at trial. That makes me less likely to agree to settle at mediation. I would rather take my chances at trial."

"I see your point," David replied. "I don't disagree with your reasoning, assuming the offer from the REIT is acceptable. Candidly, I've assumed all along we would be going to trial, given the positions the plaintiffs have taken in this case. When will you receive the offer?"

"They told me they would have the offer to me, in writing, by Wednesday of this week."

"That's just two days before the hearing on the pending motions."

"Friday of this week, right?"

"Yes."

"And the mediation conference will take place next Monday? Just wanted to be sure."

"Yes. It will be a busy few days. Please keep me informed about the offer."

David then carefully went over the rules and procedures governing mediation conferences with Max, despite his poorly concealed irritation at having to sit through something he felt sufficiently informed about.  They then went over several items in the pre-trial statement David would jointly prepare with Montgomery to submit to the court the following week, followed by a discussion about the pending motions to be heard on Friday.  Finally, after nearly two hours, David wrapped up the meeting.

Maggie and Max rose to leave the conference room as the door opened, and Jesse walked into the room.

"David, I apologize for interrupting your meeting, but I'm off to WCC to meet Carol and attend the board meeting.  Before I go, I need a brief meeting with you about a firm management issue.  Could I speak to you privately for just a minute?"

"Yes, of course," replied David, who then turned to Max.  "Excuse me for a minute, Max. I just remembered another item I need to discuss with you briefly before you leave."

Max sat back down, looking surprised, almost shocked.  David found Max's reaction puzzling, but stepped outside the conference room to discuss the firm management issue with Jesse and then returned to the conference room.

Before David could address the additional issue he wanted to discuss, Max asked, "Did she say she was going to a meeting at WCC?  Is that the Women's Crisis Center?"

"Yes, why?" asked David.

"Two years ago, my niece, Megan Barkley, lived at WCC for eight months and received help to recover from a debilitating drug problem.  I have no children of my own, but Megan is my sister's daughter.  After my sister and her husband divorced, Megan's father was absent from her life.  He provided child support but little else.  Once her father essentially abandoned her emotionally, Megan went into a downward spiral that eventually resulted in drug addiction. At that point I got involved in her life, and we got her into WCC. David, WCC literally saved her life. We had tried therapists and drug rehab programs. Nothing worked until she went to WCC. Megan is like a daughter to me, so I'm delighted that one of your partners is on the board of WCC. Who is the Carol she's meeting there?"

"Carol Jordan—my wife, the founder and president of WCC."

"My God!" exclaimed Max. "Your wife is *that* Carol Jordan?" It was clear from Max's expression he could not have been more impressed if David had said he was related to Mother Teresa. "David, Carol is more responsible than anyone for Megan being alive today. Carol helped bring Megan back from the precipice she was about to go over due to drug use. Please tell your wife Megan is doing well now. She has held a steady job for the past year and has enrolled in college again."

"I will, Max. Carol will be glad to hear some good news. She's had precious little good news lately."

"I'm sorry, David. Is Carol not doing well? She was the most energetic woman I've ever met the last time I saw her."

David paused, considering how much to tell Max. Yet, given how strongly Carol had affected his life and Megan's, David decided Max was entitled to the truth. "Carol has stage IV breast cancer. The chemotherapy treatments have been mostly ineffective, and we're now trying to get her into a clinical trial to hopefully get better results."

Max shook his head as if thunderstruck. "Oh, no. I had no idea. How has WCC managed to get along without her?"

David repressed the sudden emotion wanting to surface. "They haven't had to get along without her. Because WCC is in the middle of a capital campaign to raise $3.5 million to build a new facility, Carol has continued working at WCC to try to raise the funds."

"While going through chemo?" Max asked.

"Yes. Frankly, I don't see how she manages, but she has refused to stop working."

Max's expression was now beyond thunderstruck. "Why would she risk her health to raise money for a building? Is the building that important?"

"WCC's financial supporters have all told Carol they need evidence it has staying power before they will commit significant additional monies. They want to see a permanent building that will enable them to carry on their mission to help drug addicted or battered women and their children. Without the new building, WCC will be hard pressed to make it another six months without going under."

Max's mouth literally fell open as if he were unable to comprehend what he was hearing. "Are you telling me WCC's financial supporters won't provide further support without a building but without the financial support WCC can't build the building? That's a catch-22 if I ever heard one."

"Unfortunately, that pretty much sums up the situation they're in. If you have any thoughts about how WCC might navigate this conundrum, Carol would certainly like to hear them."

"I have no solutions to propose now, but I will certainly give it some thought … David, how are you dealing with all of this while handling my case as well as the rest of your case load?"

"Max, I'm just doing the best I can. Fortunately, I have Maggie assisting me, as well as the other lawyers in the firm. It helps to occasionally get my thoughts off my problems by dealing with someone else's problems—like yours."

"Well, you've certainly put my problems in perspective," Max said quietly. "If there's anything I can do to help, please call me. After all Carol has done for Megan and our family, I would really like to help."

"Thanks, Max. If any ideas come to me, I'll certainly let you know. In the meantime, let's do all we can to win your case for you."

"I agree. I'm more determined now than ever to see this case through."

*       *       *

David was always impressed by The Orange County Courthouse in downtown Orlando, a massive twenty-four-story, postmodern building containing over 965,000 square feet of interior space, with a separate building on each side housing the State Attorney's office and the Public Defender's office. He recalled how public support for such a massive and expensive structure solidified after the former 1920s era courthouse had to be shut down due to unsafe levels of asbestos. A converted former hotel had served as the courthouse in the interim until the new courthouse was completed in 1997 at a cost of $100 million.

David and Maggie met Max in the spacious multi-floor atrium of the courthouse just as Max came through the airport-like security line that all visitors must pass through. They then took the smart elevator directly to the eighteenth floor where Judge Long's courtroom was located, arriving fifteen minutes before the hearing was to begin. Judge Long's previous hearing was wrapping up just as they entered the courtroom. As soon as counsel from the previous hearing exited, David, Maggie, and Max took the counsel table on the right, the table nearest the jury box.  Directly across the courtroom from the counsel tables was the elevated bench from which the judge commanded the courtroom.

Judge Long left the courtroom for a quick break before Max's hearing began as David and Maggie spread their hearing materials on the counsel table.  Five minutes later, Montgomery, together with Richard and Laura Langley, entered the courtroom and took their places at the counsel table on the left.  Finally, the court reporter entered and set up her recording machine in front of the bench.

Promptly at ten o'clock, the bailiff called the proceeding to order.  Judge Long entered from behind the bench and took her seat.  "We're here today on several motions filed by Plaintiffs," Judge Long announced.  "Would counsel for the parties please identify themselves for the record."

After Montgomery and David did so, Judge Long opened the file before her, reviewed the notes she had written to herself and then addressed the courtroom.  "I've reviewed the motions and memoranda filed by Plaintiffs and the responses by Defendant.  I want to take up the motion for sanctions first.  Mr. Montgomery, it's your motion; let me hear from you first."

Montgomery rose and went to the podium.  "Yes, Your Honor.  The basis for my motion is simple.  We filed a broad request for documents that included any communications by Mr. Foster with anyone regarding his introduction to or relationship with his now-deceased wife, Martha Langley Foster.  This request was made because we believed Mr. Foster solicited an introduction to Martha mainly because she was a wealthy widow, and he was desperate for money for his Gateway Orlando project. Any such evidence is relevant because it would show a clear intent by Mr. Foster from the beginning of the relationship to unduly influence Martha to use her assets to help finance his massive project.

"In response to our request, Mr. Foster, through counsel, produced a large volume of documents but withheld the one email that clearly confirmed our suspicions. This email was written to a close friend and confidant of Mr. Foster, with whom he had discussed in detail all of his financial problems with the project. This friend is the same man who introduced Mr. Foster to Martha, at his request. The email said, 'I had an enjoyable date with Martha last night. I may have found an answer to the problems with the project we discussed.' That statement confirms, in Mr. Foster's own words, that he viewed Martha as the solution to his significant financial problems with the biggest project of his life and intended to unduly influence her to use her assets to solve those problems.

"Mr. Foster's subsequent behavior during their short marriage, particularly after Martha was diagnosed with cancer, is consistent with the intent this email reveals. Obviously, Mr. Foster realized how damaging this email was to his defense in the case, and he withheld it from his own counsel and from us, apparently in the hope it would never see the light of day. Fortunately, a mutual friend of Martha and Mr. Foster was sent a copy of the email at the time. She recently realized its critical importance and provided me with a copy. This is how I happened to obtain a copy of this critical document despite Mr. Foster's unlawful attempt to hide it.

"Mr. Foster's behavior is a clear violation of the Florida Rules of Civil Procedure, the orders of this court, and the basic honesty we expect of litigants in this court. We respectfully ask you to grant our motion and to sanction Mr. Foster as we have requested."

Judge Long turned her attention to David. "Mr. Jordan, these are serious allegations. What's your response?"

"Your Honor," responded David, "we recognize these are serious allegations, and we assure the court that neither Mr. Foster nor I was aware we had failed to produce any document within the scope of Mr. Montgomery's request for production. We have filed the affidavit of James Moss in response to this motion, and it clearly states the email in question was not produced because it was not on Max Foster Enterprises' server. Mr. Moss also confirms in his affidavit it was not on the server due to a computer crash that occurred the same day the email was sent. Once Mr. Moss saw the email for the first time after Mr. Foster's deposition, he noticed the date and time it was sent, and he was able to confirm this email was among about thirty other documents he was unable to recover after the crash. Mr. Moss is an experienced IT professional, and he worked for a law firm before going to work for Max Foster Enterprises.

"As he states in his affidavit, he's well aware of the consequences of failing to produce relevant documents. However, the email in question was no longer available for Max Foster Enterprises to produce. Furthermore, Mr. Foster had no independent recollection of the email. There was never any attempt to hide any document from Plaintiffs. Had this document still been on the server, it would have been produced.

"Furthermore, the affidavits we submitted from Mr. Moss and Mr. Foster refute any contention Mr. Foster intentionally or knowingly withheld from his production any document, including the email in question.  If the court has any doubt at all concerning whether Mr. Foster was guilty of spoliation of evidence, the court should hear the live testimony of Mr. Moss and Mr. Foster.  This hearing was not noticed as an evidentiary hearing, so I assume the court is not prepared to hear live testimony today.

"Finally, Your Honor, Mr. Montgomery has made no argument that his clients have been harmed by not receiving the email during the normal production schedule.  He not only had the email by the time of Mr. Foster's deposition, he also examined him in detail about it.  Since Mr. Foster was surprised by the appearance of an email he did not remember, this worked to Plaintiffs' advantage."

David restrained himself from adding that surprising Mr. Foster was exactly what Montgomery intended to do, but David felt he had made his point by saying Mr. Foster was surprised by the email's appearance at his deposition.

"Any response, Mr. Montgomery?" Judge Long asked.

Montgomery was immediately on his feet, and in a voice dripping with sarcasm, replied, "Yes, briefly, Your Honor.  I only want to point out it is extraordinarily convenient that the key piece of evidence in this case mysteriously disappeared due to a computer crash which occurred at precisely the only time a computer crash could make this key piece of evidence disappear.  The affidavits of Mr. Moss and Mr. Foster are not plausible and should be disregarded."

"I agree with you that the crash came at a conveniently critical time," Judge Long commented, glancing at David and Max as she spoke, "but I do have two facially sufficient affidavits that prevent me from granting the motion.  Here is what I'm going to do.  I'm denying your motion, Mr. Montgomery, but without prejudice to your right to renew your motion once the evidence has been presented at trial on this issue. If you still believe you have good grounds for sanctions, you can renew your motion then. However, if the testimony on this issue is consistent with the affidavits of Mr. Moss and Mr. Foster, there are no sufficient grounds for sanctions."

David wished the judge had denied the motion outright. However, the ruling was fair, and it was highly unlikely Montgomery would be able to successfully resurrect the spoliation issue at trial.

"Next is your motion to strike any use of the diary Martha apparently kept," Judge Long continued. "Please explain how you can contend the diary is a forgery when both of your clients—Martha's children—testified under oath during their depositions the handwriting in the diary was their mother's."

"Your Honor, Richard Langley was surprised by the diary. To his knowledge, his mother never kept a diary. Admittedly, at first glance the writing appears to be hers. But after the deposition, Richard noted some letters are different from other examples of his mother's handwriting in his possession. We asked a qualified documents examiner to review the diary and the other handwriting samples, then provide an opinion. As you can see from our expert's affidavit attached to my motion, his opinion is that the diary is not in Martha's handwriting."

"But Mr. Jordan has submitted an affidavit from his expert documents examiner that opines the handwriting *is* Martha Foster's," Judge Long responded. "So … we appear to have a battle of the experts. What about Laura Langley? Did she also change her mind about whether the diary contains her mother's handwriting?"

"Your Honor, Laura Langley just assumed it was her mother's handwriting because her brother had testified to that fact the day before her deposition. At this point, she isn't sure and will defer to the expert."

As Montgomery said this, David glanced at Laura who was frowning and seemed most unhappy to be in the courtroom listening to the arguments being made. Her brother, on the other hand, was smugly listening to every word Montgomery said. Richard appeared to have regained some of the cockiness he lost during his deposition under David's questioning.

Judge Long turned to David and asked, "Mr. Jordan, do you have anything to say in response to Mr. Montgomery's comments?"

"Judge, I would only add that Mr. Foster testified in his deposition and in his affidavit that he had no knowledge Martha was keeping a diary. And the diary was found in a hidden space in Martha's desk he didn't know existed. So, who, then, could have possibly forged the diary? Mr. Montgomery hasn't addressed this issue. Furthermore, as you have pointed out, where the experts have offered conflicting opinions, there is no legal basis on which the court can grant a motion to strike the diary— a critical piece of evidence in this trial."

"I agree, Mr. Jordan." Judge Long said. "However, Mr. Montgomery, you can address this issue with testimony from your expert at trial if you wish to do so. I will reserve ruling on your motion until that time."

Based on Montgomery's sour expression, he wasn't happy with Judge Long's ruling, although David was confident the ruling was not unexpected. He assumed Montgomery was hoping for at least some comment from the judge to engender concern in David and Max over how the judge might ultimately rule at trial, thereby giving Montgomery more leverage at the mediation conference.

"The final motion to be heard today," Judge Long continued, "is your motion for summary judgment. Is that correct, Mr. Montgomery?"

"It is, Your Honor."

Before Montgomery could begin his argument on the summary judgment motion, Judge Long said, "Given my ruling on your motion to strike the diary, I don't see how I can rule on your summary judgment motion today. Your motion appears to be contingent on my granting the motion to strike, which I have already declined to do. Do you disagree, Mr. Montgomery?"

Clearly sensing that any argument with what the judge just said would be futile, Montgomery wisely responded, "No, I don't disagree, Judge."

"Well, then, I think we are finished for today. I will see counsel at the pre-trial conference next week." With that comment, Judge Long rose and exited the courtroom by the door behind her bench.

David motioned for Max and Maggie to wait for Montgomery and his clients to leave before stepping into the waiting area outside the courtroom. "This hearing could not have gone any better today, Max," David commented once they were alone. "Although Montgomery can still raise his motion for sanctions and his motion to strike any use of the diary at trial, he's not going to get very far with Judge Long on those motions."

"So, what does all this mean for our mediation conference on Monday?" Max asked.

"First, it means we're in good shape for trial; therefore, we're in good shape for the mediation conference. There is still some risk the judge will find that you exercised undue influence over Martha with respect to the loan and the amended will and trust, but I feel better about our chances of winning at trial than I have at any other point in this case.  Second, you don't have to compromise at the mediation conference if you're willing to take the risks inherent in a trial."

"That's good to hear," Max responded.  "The person from the REIT who contacted me didn't make the offer earlier this week as promised.  They are calling me tomorrow morning.  I have a lot to think about over the weekend."

As Max spoke, he had a faraway look in his eye as if he were considering the position he was in for the first time.  His gaze puzzled David because earlier in the week Max seemed more determined than ever to win the case at trial, and David expected today's result would only strengthen Max's determination.

*What a strange client I have,* David thought while he, Max, and Maggie walked to the elevators.  As they were leaving the building, David reminded Max they were to meet at the Orange County Bar Association building on Orange Avenue at 8:45 Monday morning for the mediation conference.  Max just nodded his agreement and left for his car.

After he left, Maggie commented to David, "This is one strange man; I expected a very different response given the results of the hearing today."

"My thoughts exactly," said David.

# Chapter 19

On Monday morning David pulled into the parking lot of the Orange County Bar Association building located on Orange Avenue in a neighborhood known as the North Quarter District.  When he first began practicing law in Orlando, he was surprised to learn the Orange County Bar Association was one of the first bar associations in Florida to have its own building.  His older lawyer friends told him how the neighborhood had consisted mostly of one or two-story buildings housing small businesses when the two-story Bar building was completed in 1982.  Now, as he looked around, there were numerous mid-rise luxury apartment buildings with roof-top pools and upscale amenities providing the burgeoning downtown workforce with suitable housing and a short commute to work.  As the neighborhood became more upscale, so did the Bar building.  In the early 2000s the building was renovated to include a large meeting hall and conference rooms on the second floor, providing a neutral site for mediation conferences or other meetings.

David and Maggie met Max at the Bar building, and they were ushered into the larger of the two conference rooms reserved for the day.  The receptionist told them Montgomery and the Langley siblings had already arrived and were in the smaller of the two conference rooms.  Shortly thereafter, the mediator, Bruce Mankin, entered the conference room to introduce himself to Max.

David had already informed Max about Mankin's background. Sporting a full head of gray hair, the sixty-five-year-old lawyer's legal practice had been limited to mediation conferences over the last twenty-five years. He had an active litigation practice for the first part of his legal career. But when mediation conferences became mandatory in most cases in Florida, he recognized an opportunity that suited his talents even better than being a trial lawyer. He converted his entire practice from litigation to mediation. His success at getting even recalcitrant litigants and lawyers to settle their cases rather than have a judge or jury resolve them brought him all the business he could handle at ever increasing hourly rates. His current rate of $800 per hour, split between the two sides, was $300 higher than David's current hourly rate. Although quite expensive, Mankin was viewed by most Orlando lawyers as being a good value because he settled so many cases. They reasoned that it is far preferable for the parties to pay the high hourly rate for a mediator who would likely get the case settled than pay less per hour for one who would probably not get it settled.

As Mankin shook Max's hand, he said, "Mr. Foster, I've admired your developments for years. I'm especially looking forward to seeing how your Gateway Orlando project turns out."

David could tell Max was flattered by Mankin's comments. He was skilled at building rapport with the parties in litigation, and the trust he engendered by carefully building rapport was one of the key reasons he was so successful at getting parties to settle—even when the parties themselves believed there was little chance of settlement. David could easily imagine the degree of flattery Mankin would use with Richard to build rapport and trust, and he had little doubt such flattery would be effective.

"I'm going to chat with the plaintiffs and their counsel for a few minutes," Mankin continued, "and then I'll bring them into this conference room for our opening session. I know you've been involved in a number of mediation conferences, Mr. Foster. However, the plaintiffs have not. I'm required by the rules governing mediations to go over certain issues with the parties, so don't be surprised if my comments last a little longer than you might think is necessary. The extra time explaining the process for the plaintiffs' benefit will pay off before the day is over."

Five minutes later, he returned with Montgomery and his clients. The parties all shook hands and took their places at the conference table. Mankin directed his initial comments to the parties rather than their lawyers. In his folksy way, he reminded them everything discussed during the mediation conference was to remain confidential, that no party would be compelled to enter into an agreement they didn't consent to, and that any agreement reached would be reduced to writing. Otherwise, the agreement would not be enforceable.

Finally, he commented, "The judge will not be told what the parties said at this mediation conference, only whether the parties settled or not. Therefore, you can be candid in your discussions. I told you this proceeding is confidential. However, I'll feel free to discuss anything you tell me with the other side, unless you instruct me to keep any particular information confidential. In that case, I won't discuss it with the other side. Hopefully, there won't be a lot of information you want me to keep confidential. In my experience, the more information is shared, the better the chances of reaching a settlement."

After covering a few housekeeping items and explaining he would caucus with the parties separately, along with their attorneys, Mankin asked the lawyers to make any opening statements they wished to make, with Montgomery going first.

"This is a straightforward case, Mr. Mankin," Montgomery began. "The evidence we have uncovered shows Mr. Foster's primary reason for seeking an introduction to Martha Langley was to get access to the significant wealth left to her by her deceased husband—my clients' father—to enable Mr. Foster to complete his Gateway Orlando project, the largest private mixed-use development ever in central Florida. In fact, we have an e-mail from him informing his best friend and confidant that she was the solution to the problems they had discussed with the project, which problems were financial and were described in detail in an earlier e-mail to the same friend."

Montgomery glanced quickly toward Max, then back at Mankin before continuing. "Mr. Foster married Martha after a relatively short courtship. Soon after they were married, he unduly influenced her to put all of her assets into a trust. He also convinced her to appoint him as a co-trustee of the trust and the personal representative of her estate. Then he convinced her to make a $10 million loan to him to keep his project going. Shortly after Martha was diagnosed with cancer, Mr. Foster convinced her to make him the sole trustee of her trust, as well as a one-third beneficiary of her estate and trust. There is no doubt Mr. Foster was the procuring cause of the changes to Martha's estate plan. He suggested all the changes from her prior will, convinced her to use his estate planning attorney, and took her to all her appointments with the lawyer. This is a classic case of undue influence.  The relief we are seeking includes the following:

"First, the amended trust and the amended will should be declared null and void.  Second, Mr. Foster should be removed as trustee and as personal representative.  Third, the loan of ten-million dollars should be repaid immediately.  And fourth, Mr. Foster should be responsible for paying the plaintiffs' fees and costs and reimburse the trust for any fees and costs he charged to the trust.

"We are confident the judge will award us all of the relief we are seeking, but we are here in good faith to see if a settlement is possible."

"Thank you, Mr. Montgomery."  Mankin motioned toward David.  "Any response, Mr. Jordan?"

"Yes, and I will be brief.  As Mr. Montgomery knows, the real reasons for all of the changes to Martha's estate plan are set forth in a detailed diary Martha kept from soon after her first husband's death until shortly before her own death.  In it, Martha discussed in detail the reasons for all of the changes to her estate plan and for the loan.  She had good reasons for every decision she made.  The presumption of undue influence does not apply as between husband and wife.  With the explanations for her decisions set forth in her diary, we believe the plaintiffs cannot prevail in this action.  If necessary, we will be happy to explain in caucus the reasons for any and all of the decisions Martha made.  The discovery in this case has uncovered the reasons for *all* of Martha's actions.  Plaintiffs are well aware of what they are.

"We, too, are here in good faith to see whether a reasonable settlement can be reached, but we are confident we will prevail at trial."

David decided to intentionally keep his comments short, and to avoid commenting upon Richard's lack of desire or effort to find a job. Doing so would only inflame Richard and make it much harder to bargain with him. At trial, however, David planned to focus much of his examination of Richard on his meager efforts to find a job—as David had at Richard's deposition—because this helped explain why Martha made the changes to her estate plan.

Mankin addressed the advantages of the parties reaching a negotiated settlement, then added. "I will first meet with the plaintiffs." He left the room with Montgomery, Richard and Laura to caucus in their separate conference room.

Once they left, David commented to Max, "I suspect their initial offer will be to settle for everything they could possibly be awarded at trial. Have you given any thought to what your initial counter-offer will be?"

"Yes, I've thought about it, and I agree they will initially ask for everything they've demanded in the lawsuit. However, before discussing with you what my counter-offer will be, I want to hear what their initial offer is."

Max's reluctance to inform his own lawyer what his initial counter-offer would be was disappointing, but unsurprising, to David. He understood his client preferred to keep his decisions close to his vest until he had to disclose them, and it would do no good to press Max about what his counter-offer would be.

After only ten minutes, Mankin returned to meet with David, Maggie, and Max. "As I'm sure you expected, the plaintiffs' initial offer is what they demanded in their complaint, and as Montgomery outlined in his opening statement. I pointed out this would hardly be a compromise, but Montgomery was insistent. He thinks he has a good shot of getting Martha's diary excluded from evidence at trial."

"Well," responded David, "this will be a very short mediation conference if that's the approach they intend to take all day. It's highly unlikely Judge Long will exclude the diary from evidence when both of the plaintiffs—Martha's children—testified the diary was in their mother's handwriting. If the diary goes into evidence, as we are confident it will, Judge Long will have a clear explanation for every decision Martha made that was in question. And the explanations are all in Martha's own handwriting."

"Yes, I understand that, and I pointed out as much to them, but they were insistent on making the offer they made. Do you have a counter-offer to make?"

"Yes, I do have a counter-offer to make," Max interjected. "It's the only offer I will make all day, and the offer will only be available today. If my offer is rejected, there will be no further settlement offers from my side. I want you to make this point very clear to Martha's children and their lawyer."

"I'm listening," Mankin said.

"This is my offer. First, I will resign as trustee of Martha's amended trust and as personal representative of her estate once this settlement agreement is approved by Judge Long.

"Second, the successor trustee and personal representative must be a trust company or bank having a trust department. It cannot be Richard or Laura Langley, or anyone designated by them.

"Third, I will repay the $10 million loan within thirty days of this settlement agreement being approved by Judge Long.

"Fourth, I will disclaim any interest in the trust or in Martha's estate, except I will have a life estate in Martha's house, which means I can live there until I die or until I move out; in either of those events the life estate would end.

"Fifth, the children must release me from my oral promise to leave them a portion of my estate. I realize that promise may be legally unenforceable, but I want a written release from them.

"And finally, each party will bear his or her own attorneys' fees and costs, but the children can pay their attorneys from the trust assets—with Judge Long to decide the reasonableness of Mr. Montgomery's fees. I will pay my own fees and costs."

As Max went through the terms of the settlement offer, both David and Maggie were increasingly puzzled. Max had consistently said he was not going to give the children what they were demanding in the lawsuit, but this offer included almost everything they had demanded—except for Richard being the trustee.

Before Mankin could comment on the offer, David said, "Bruce, would you please give me a few minutes alone with my client before you relay his offer to the other side. There are a few points I need to confirm with him before the offer is officially made."

"Sure," replied Mankin, who appeared as surprised as David by the offer. "Let me know when you're ready for me to take the offer to the other side."

As soon as Mankin left the room, David turned to Max. "Why are you making such a generous offer? These terms are better than what they are likely to get on their best day at trial. I thought you were ready to fight to the end in this case. If this is what you want to do, of course it's your call. But as your lawyers, we need to be sure you know what you're doing. If they accept, you will have an agreement and your offer will be binding. I have no doubt Judge Long will approve the settlement, and then you'll have to comply with its terms. Are you sure you're in a position to do all you're promising to do in this offer?"

Max nodded, his jaw set with determination. "Yes, David, I'm sure I will be able to comply with the terms. I prefer not to tell you my reasons for making such a generous offer until we know whether Martha's children accept or reject it.

David paused, slightly irritated, and held Max's gaze before responding. "Max, you don't have to give us any explanation if you don't want to. We just need to know you can fulfill what you are promising to do."

"Good. Now let me bring you up to date on why I'm able to make this offer. On Saturday, I finally received the offer from the REIT I mentioned to you previously. They have offered me $35 million for ninety percent of my interest in Gateway Orlando; I will retain a ten percent interest."

"That's great news, Max, but I didn't think you wanted to sell." David said.

"I didn't originally, but this helped change my mind. They want me to continue overseeing the construction of the project for a $1 million fee. On top of that, my firm will be the leasing agent for Gateway Orlando for the next ten years, with an option to renew for another ten years if certain performance criteria are met. So, yes, I know what I'm doing. I know it's a generous offer, but I will definitely be able to fulfill my obligations in the settlement agreement."

David tried to tamp down the disappointment rising within him. He was looking forward to trying the case—which had seemed almost unwinnable earlier—and delivering a victory to his client. Nevertheless, he had to honor his client's wishes regardless of his personal opinions. "Okay . . . if that's what you want to do. I'll bring Mankin back in and spell out the terms of the offer for him to convey to Montgomery."

Once Mankin was back in the room, David covered the details of the offer, then added, "I want you to convey two additional points to Montgomery. First, this generous offer is being made for reasons other than my opinion about the risks Mr. Foster would face at trial. Don't assume we believe we would lose; to the contrary, I believe we would win. Second, Mr. Foster is dead serious when he says this offer is only available today. If rejected, the offer is rescinded, and Mr. Foster will make no further offers; we will proceed to trial."

"Got it," Mankin said, obviously pleased he would be able to convey such a generous settlement offer, though evidently surprised Max would make so good an offer—particularly as his first—and only— counter-offer.

*            *            *

When he entered the conference room with Montgomery, Richard, and Laura, Mankin could easily recognize tension on the faces of Richard and Laura. Even Montgomery seemed anxious about what the counter-offer would be. Mankin assumed that Montgomery had explained in some detail to the siblings the impact that Martha's diary would have on the outcome of the case.  He had probably also advised them it was likely the diary would be admitted into evidence by Judge Long.

Nevertheless, Montgomery had agreed—probably at Richard's insistence—to initially demand all the plaintiffs were seeking in the lawsuit.  From his previous experience with Montgomery, Mankin guessed Montgomery had preferred to make a lower initial offer to signal a willingness to compromise, but Richard and Laura apparently wouldn't agree.

Mankin took his seat at the head of the conference table, then looked at them with a reassuring smile.  "I have some good news. Mr. Foster has made a more generous offer than I anticipated from him.  However, there are two comments I have been instructed to convey with the offer.  The first is that you should not assume the terms of this offer reflect Mr. Foster and his legal team's opinion as to the likely outcome of the case. Mr. Jordan, and I believe Mr. Foster, are both confident they will prevail at trial.  The second comment is that this offer is only good today; if rejected, the offer is withdrawn.  There will be no further offers, and the case will go to trial.  I must say, I believe Mr. Foster is serious, so keep that in mind as I go over the terms of the offer."

Mankin then carefully went over each term.  As he did so, he could see the tension draining from the faces of Montgomery, Richard and Laura.  The tension in the faces of Montgomery and Laura appeared to be replaced by relief and joy that the case may soon end on favorable terms.  When Mankin glanced at Richard, however, the tension in his face had morphed into a defiant and determined sneer.  Obviously, he was more interested in being a *winner* than accepting a favorable settlement.

As soon as Mankin finished explaining the terms of Max's offer, Richard declared, "They're convinced we're going to win this lawsuit. They're scared to death to go to trial. I think they're bluffing, and we should reject this offer. You watch, they'll come forward with a better offer once we reject this one. I can tell you this—I'm not going to agree to the appointment of a bank or trust company to be the trustee. The assets of the trust are family assets, and I should be the trustee."

*       *       *

Montgomery was more than a little surprised and alarmed at Richard's response, especially since it would put Montgomery's fee at risk. If the plaintiffs didn't prevail at trial—which seemed a real possibility to him—he wouldn't be paid at all due to his contingent fee agreement. He was to be paid a percentage of whatever he recovered in the lawsuit. If the plaintiffs lost the case, he would get nothing.

From his many chats with Laura, Montgomery knew she adored her mother. Martha's candid diary comments about Richard had caused Laura to re-evaluate her opinion of her brother. She had admired him all her life, overlooking his shortcomings and never admitting he had any faults. But when she read for herself her mother's comment that she agreed with their father Richard had little desire to earn his own way in life and was content to just live off family money, Laura began to look at him more realistically.

Richard's contrasting reaction to this generous offer from Max Foster seemed to confirm in Laura's mind her parents' worst fears about her brother. The main thing he was concerned about was that someone other than himself might be the trustee of the trust, controlling the family assets.

261

As he considered how to respond to Richard's demand to be appointed trustee, Montgomery glanced at Laura. He could tell from her expression she wasn't happy about Richard's demand. Perhaps she now finally realized if Richard had control of the trust, he would deal with it as his own piggy bank—never achieving anything in life, much less become self-reliant, which could be the worst thing that could happen to Richard.

Before Laura could voice her disagreement with her brother, Montgomery asked Mankin to give him an opportunity to discuss the offer with his clients in private. As soon as Mankin left, Montgomery said, "Richard, you heard the statement by Mr. Mankin that if you reject this offer, it's off the table and no further offers will be made. I've had many disagreements with David Jordan over the years, but he has always been true to his word—and he seldom bluffs. He would never have instructed the mediator to convey these comments unless Jordan meant what he said. I strongly urge you to accept this proposal. It's too good to pass up."

Richard scowled. "Look, Mr. Montgomery, I meant what I said. I won't agree to anyone other than me being appointed as trustee. I don't want some pointy-head banker having control over our family assets. You watch; if we make a counter-offer with the same terms, except with me being the sole trustee, Max Foster will accept it. Why wouldn't he? Once he's no longer the trustee and a beneficiary of the trust, what difference does it make to him?"

Finally, Laura spoke up. "Richard, you're not the only one who gets a vote on whether to accept this offer. After reading our mother's diary entries, I can see why she made the decisions she made. I've now come to believe those were wise decisions. Furthermore, you know the diary is in her handwriting.  If necessary, I will testify at trial it's her handwriting and that you admitted as much to me after your deposition."

Richard sat in surprised, but rigid, defiance.

Laura continued, "Why would Mr. Foster insist upon the trust having an independent trustee?  It's probably because our mother feared you would act exactly as you're acting now—putting our financial future at risk so you could do whatever you want to do with the family assets.  Your ego has gotten in the way of making sound decisions.  I vote to accept the offer Mr. Foster has made."

Richard looked at Laura, obviously stunned that his younger sister, who had always gone along with whatever he wanted, would stand up to him.  "You do know you could put the entire lawsuit at risk with your testimony, don't you?"

Montgomery intervened.  "Richard, you should also know if you and Laura can't agree on whether to accept the offer, I will have to ask Mr. Jordan to keep the offer open long enough for us to retain separate counsel for either you or Laura.  I can't represent two clients in a case where their interests and instructions are not in agreement.  Based upon what the mediator has told us, the offer is only on the table today; Mr. Foster may not agree to an extension of time for another lawyer to be retained.  Again, my advice is to accept the offer.  It's more than I anticipated they would put on the table today and more than we are likely to get at trial."

The cocky look on Richard's face had finally disappeared.  The shock of his own little sister standing up to him, when she had gone along with anything he wanted for their entire lives, must have rattled him.  He stared at Montgomery as if incredulous his attorney was telling him he couldn't accept or reject the offer without Laura and him being in agreement—something he had never contemplated.

Montgomery felt almost sorry for Richard. The mediation conference wasn't going the way he thought it would go. Obviously, Richard couldn't understand why anyone would want someone other than him to be the trustee—especially his little sister—and now his lawyer was urging him to agree to the counter-offer.

"You can't mean that, Laura—my own sister testifying against me and voting against my being the trustee?" Richard finally responded. "We have always been in agreement. Can't you see the wisdom of me being the sole trustee? Can't you see Foster is just bluffing?"

Laura glowered. "Oh, I meant what I said. As your younger sister, I *have* always gone along with whatever you wanted, but I now understand doing so wasn't always good for you or for me. This time, you better agree with me before we lose a settlement offer better than we are likely to get from a ruling by the judge. Frankly, the money doesn't matter much to me, but I'm not going to support you in the self-destructive course of action you want to take."

As Laura's words washed over him, Richard slumped as all of the fight left him. "My parents didn't always go along with what I wanted, but you have always supported me. Now you're giving me the same criticism as Mom and Dad. This is a bitter pill to swallow; I feel as rejected as I've ever felt in my life." Richard paused for a long moment before continuing. "Give me five minutes to think this over," he said, then left the conference room.

Mankin entered the conference room. "I just saw Richard leave. Have you decided to accept the offer?"

"No, not yet," Montgomery said. "Laura wanted to accept the offer, but Richard didn't. However, he's reconsidering in light of Laura's demands."

"How can you represent both Laura and Richard if one wants to accept the offer and the other doesn't?" Mankin asked.

"I can't," responded Montgomery, irritated that Richard might foolishly jeopardize the most generous offer they could hope to get.

"Would it help for me to talk to him?" Mankin responded.

"I don't think so, at least not yet. Let's let him think this through for himself. If he still won't agree to accept the offer when he returns, then we'll all take a turn at trying to bring him to reality. Laura has been quite clear she wants to accept the offer. One of the primary reasons is she doesn't want her brother to be the sole trustee of the trust." Montgomery looked at Laura who just nodded her head in agreement.

After a long five minutes, Richard returned to the conference room, looked at Montgomery—but not at Laura—and said, "Okay, I'll agree to the offer. I'm going downstairs to the reception room until the settlement agreement is ready to be signed."

Mankin and Montgomery went to inform David the offer was accepted.

*       *       *

David had taken advantage of the time Mankin spent with Montgomery and his clients by preparing a draft of the settlement agreement which Maggie typed on her laptop. David went over the terms with Montgomery, and they quickly reached agreement on all points. Given Richard's attitude, Mankin went to have Richard sign the document first.  When he returned, Laura signed.  Then Mankin gave the document to Max for his signature.

As he signed and handed the settlement agreement back to Mankin, Max asked him, "Would you please inform Laura I would like to speak to her briefly before she leaves?"

"Of course, but her lawyer will have to agree."

When Max exited, he'd left the conference room door ajar.  David had not meant to eavesdrop but could overhear the conversation between Max and Laura as they talked just outside the room where David and Maggie waited.

"Max? Mr. Mankin said you wanted to talk to me, and Mr. Montgomery said I should. What do you want?"

Laura, I just want you to know that I truly loved your mother," Max said, his tone respectful.  "I realize Richard can't accept that yet, but hopefully someday he will."

"Thank you.  Your words mean a lot to me.  I'm pleased this suit is behind us."

"Me, too.  More than you know."

When Max returned to the conference room, Mankin was gathering his notes and his copy of the settlement agreement into his briefcase.  Before leaving, he shook Max's hand, and said, "Mr. Foster, it has been a privilege to be your mediator.  I anticipated a much longer and more contentious mediation conference.  You made my work much easier today."

Max returned the handshake.  "I had my reasons."

As soon as Mankin left the room, Maggie declared, "Max, David and I aren't going anywhere until you tell us why you made this offer to settle.  We don't understand why you were so generous, especially when the case finally began to turn in your favor.  And why wouldn't you tell us what your reasons were unless they accepted your offer?"

Max smiled, his expression one of peace.  "Yes, I can understand your questioning my motives, but I did have my reasons, which I will explain in a minute.  First, however, let me tell you something about myself.  I've failed to take advantage of opportunities to help other people in need many times in my life, sometimes even people who were important to me.  I was too wrapped up in my own busy life—my own business and my own priorities.  In retrospect, my selfishness was the main reason my first two marriages failed."

These admissions seemed so uncharacteristic of the man who'd hired Jordan & McKenzie to represent him.  "Max, you don't know for sure . . ."

"I think I do know, David.  The one exception to my selfishness was when I helped my niece, Megan Barkley, overcome her drug addiction.  Even then, her recovery would not have been possible without someone else making a much bigger sacrifice than I did by forming and running WCC.  Without WCC and your wife's personal efforts, I don't think my niece would have survived her addiction."

David knew Carol helped a lot of people, but hearing Max credit Carol with saving his niece's life drove home to David—more than anything else could—the importance of Carol's work.

"When the offer by the REIT came through on Saturday, I realized I had an opportunity to do something better than anything I've done previously in my entire life.  It meant selling most of my interest in

Gateway Orlando but that's a small price to pay, especially given the generous terms of the REIT's offer."

"What in the world are you going to do, Max?" David asked, genuinely puzzled.

"I 'm going to give $3.5 million to WCC for their building.  The only conditions I am placing on the gift are that the building be named The Carol Jordan Women's Crisis Center and that one of the rooms in the building be named The Martha Langley Foster Dining Hall, or something similar.  Also, I plan to make a gift of an additional $1.5 million to be used to solicit matching gifts from public and private sources to create an endowment for WCC to help cover its operating expenses and to insure its financial stability well into the future."

David was flabbergasted by Max's generosity, realizing Carol's prayer for WCC had been answered.  "I don't have the words …"

"I realized you would feel like you had a conflict of interest in advising me regarding the settlement.  This was why I couldn't tell you my reasons for making the offer.  I didn't want to put you in a compromising position.  I was afraid you would tell me I couldn't make the offer without consulting with independent counsel first.  Time was of the essence here, in my opinion. Please don't be angry with me for concealing my motives.  What I am doing brings me more happiness than anything I've ever done.  However, for the present, let's keep the gift anonymous, although you can tell Carol and the board."

David was so shocked and overcome with emotion he literally could say nothing.  His eyes filled with tears, and his lips trembled as he unsuccessfully tried to blurt out how grateful he was.  Telling Carol about

Max's gift would bring more joy to both Carol and him at this time in their lives than anything he could imagine.

Maggie, on the other hand, was not similarly constrained in her response. She leaped out of her chair, exclaiming in almost a shriek, "Max, this is the best news ever!" She gave Max a huge hug. "I am so proud of you, and Carol will be thrilled."

David finally gave up trying to say anything and brought Max into a bear hug, refusing to let go. Finally, he released his hold and mumbled, "Max, I can't thank you enough. You have no idea how much joy this will bring to Carol."

"Carol will have no more joy in receiving this gift than I will have in giving it, I assure you. You've accomplished a lot today. Why don't you go home and give Carol the good news now?"

# Chapter 20

Carol had just completed another chemo infusion on Monday morning before returning home to bed.  Each infusion was taking an increasing toll on her; she couldn't remember ever feeling so drained physically and emotionally.  Shortly after she lay down, she heard David arrive home and head upstairs to their bedroom.  As he entered the room she rolled over and with effort gave him a small smile.

"Hi, I'm afraid I'm not too chipper today, David.  What are you doing home so early?"

"We settled the Max Foster case today at mediation, Carol.  And I have the most wonderful news for you."

Carol couldn't imagine what good news David could have for her, other than settling his case, but she slowly managed to sit up in bed as David sat beside her.  Despite being in a fog of weariness, Carol's eyes reflected the curiosity that stirred within her in response to his statement.  After a moment to focus, she said, barely above a whisper, "That *is* wonderful news.  I'm so glad the case settled. I know how much you've worried about the case . . . and now it's over."

David took Carol's hands in his as he snuggled closer to her.  "Yes, I'm glad the case is over.  But that's not the good news."

A puzzled expression passed over Carol's face before David continued.

"Do you remember I mentioned to you that Max is the uncle of Megan Barkley who lived at WCC for about eight months?  Max wanted me to relay to you how well Megan is doing now.  She has her life back together and is again enrolled in college."

Carol nodded.  "Yes.  I remember.  I'm so pleased to hear she's doing well," Carol responded quietly with a sincere but small, tired smile.

David squeezed Carol's hands.  "Well, Max is more grateful than you can imagine for what you did for Megan."

"I'm glad to hear that," Carol said with a bigger smile that managed to show her pleasure through the weariness that still controlled her face.

"He's so grateful that he has just committed to giving $3.5 million to completely fund the new WCC building.  And he wants the building to be named 'The Carol Jordan Women's Crisis Center.'"

Through the foggy haze of Carol's weariness David's words seemed like something from a distant voice she couldn't quite understand.  His words were not indistinct, but their meaning swirled about in her mind as in a dream without coalescing into thoughts that she could understand.  She just stared blankly back at him and said, "What?"

David's face lit up as he continued.  "Carol, it's wonderful.  Max was able to settle the case because a real estate investment trust made him an amazing offer to buy his Gateway Orlando development.  He will retain a ten percent interest, and they will pay him to supervise the remaining construction.  He will also be appointed as the property manager for the entire development.  The offer enabled him to settle the case."

Carol continued to stare back at David, trying to make sense of what he was telling her.  Again, she said, "What?  I don't understand."

"Don't you see?  The primary reason Max decided to settle the case was to make this gift to WCC, and the real estate deal gave him the means to do so.  Not only does he want to fund the building, he's going to give WCC an additional $1.5 million to use as challenge funds to get matching gifts from your supporters.  This should solve WCC's financial problems for the foreseeable future."

Finally, the fog began to lift, and the enormity of what David was telling her gradually transitioned from a remote, hazy dream to a realization the project that had consumed her for most of the past several years might finally come to pass.

"Are you telling me Max Foster has committed to the *entire* $3.5 million for the building?"

"Yes, that's exactly what I'm telling you."

"And he wants to give us an *additional* $1.5 million as challenge funds to get other donors to match him?"

"Yes!" David exclaimed.

Carol leaned back on the pillow on her bed, as the fatigue and pain on her face gradually faded away, replaced by an angelic expression of gratitude and joy.  This was the fulfillment of Carol's dream for WCC since its founding, and she was overwhelmed by the realization her dream had finally come true.  As this realization continued to sink in, she began to shed tears of pure joy and rose up to embrace David, who was beginning to shed tears of his own.

*         *         *

The celebratory dinner at the Jordan household that night was a memorable and joyous occasion.  Because Jesse was so involved with the effort to raise money for WCC, David and Carol invited her to dinner to share in the celebration.  Carol wasn't physically up to having *company* for dinner, but Jesse wasn't company.  She was family, and Carol wanted all her family with her to celebrate.

"David," Carol said, "you should have heard Jesse when I called to invite her to dinner.  I think they could hear her screeches of happiness over Max's gift all the way to New York City!"

Jesse laughed.  "Well, maybe not that far.  But I must admit, I think I was as overwhelmed as both of you must have been when Maggie told Steve and me the news about Max's gift."

David had ordered the Jordan family's favorite dinner—Antonio's lasagna, Caesar salad, and tiramisu.  As the family sat down to celebrate their good fortune, Carol insisted upon offering the blessing—a prayer of gratitude not just for the food, but also for Max and his gift to WCC.

*            *            *

"You know, I can't remember when I've seen you guys so happy," Jenna said. "I'm glad I have this memory of all of you."

The joy of accomplishing something that was so important to all of them created an atmosphere that Jenna would never forget.  Her mother's cancer had been difficult for her to deal with, but for tonight, at least, the cancer was forgotten.  The reassuring comfort and joy of being with her family, including Jesse, calmed the fear that had lurked in the back of her mind since she had learned of her mother's cancer.  She felt the love of her parents and of her Aunt Jesse wash over her throughout the evening, and she reminded herself repeatedly how blessed she was to have the family she had.

*            *            *

David, too, could not recall ever feeling the combination of relief and joy he felt tonight. The end of a contentious case always brought a sense of relief, even more so if a win helped his client find justice. But tonight was different. The settlement could hardly be called a victory from a legal standpoint because the plaintiffs got almost everything they asked for, despite David and Maggie putting up an excellent defense. The fact Max voluntarily decided to be generous with his adversaries when he had the power to defeat them seemed somehow even more satisfying than a legal victory. *Okay. Perhaps the fact the settlement benefitted Carol and WCC, while also enabling Max to find some sense of redemption, is why I'm so happy.* He couldn't remember another case that brought him so much personal satisfaction, and it was bliss to enjoy that feeling with the people he loved most.

*         *         *

Jesse was also filled with the spirit of the evening. She had been almost as involved as Carol in seeking funding for the new building while taking on increased management duties at Jordan & McKenzie to relieve David, who was preoccupied with caring for Carol and defending Max. Only when the case finally settled, and they learned funding for the building had been secured, did Jesse realize how much stress she had been under. She felt that a huge weight had lifted from her shoulders. And the joy of seeing Carol and David so happy increased her own joy. She felt privileged to be part of the celebration that night with David, Carol and Jenna—something she knew she would long treasure.

*         *         *

But for Carol the evening meant even more than it did for the others. Tonight felt like the culmination of everything her life was meant to be.  She loved her husband even more tonight than she had before—and she didn't think that was possible.  She also realized tonight what she had known subconsciously before but without that subconscious thought ever migrating into her conscious mind.  Jenna—her daughter—was quickly growing into a most remarkable young woman who was caring, smart, sophisticated and innocent, all at the same time.  She was proud, but humbled, to be Jenna's mother.  Finally, although Carol and Jesse had been close before, she felt tonight that no sisters could possibly be closer than she and Jesse.  It was a bond she treasured, and she knew that few people ever experienced such a bond.

*      *      *

When they had devoured the lasagna and delighted in the tiramisu, David went to the refrigerator and took out a bottle of sparkling grape juice, rather than wine, for a toast since Carol couldn't have alcohol due to chemo and Jenna was too young to drink.  After pouring the juice into champagne glasses, David raised his glass.  "To Max Foster and to WCC."

They tapped one another's glasses with a hearty, "Here! Here!" and took a sip.

Carol then clinked her glass to get their attention.  "I have a toast to make also."  She looked deeply into the eyes of each of them, beginning with Jesse and ending with David, and then offered the toast:

"To family ...."  They all looked at each other for a long moment, tipped their glasses to each other, and then they drank.

*      *      *

David arose with the early morning sun the next day and completed his usual run around half past six.  While taking a long shower, he realized he had nothing pressing on his schedule because he had cleared his entire week for trial preparation. He decided to take the day off, giving himself time to recover from the hectic pace of the last few weeks.

Once he was dressed, he went downstairs to the kitchen for coffee and breakfast. Carol had just sent Jenna off to catch the bus for Maitland Middle School and was heading back upstairs to bed. Fatigue was once again written all over her face. "Let's talk when I get up," Carol mumbled to David as they passed in the hallway.

David cooked his cheese omelet specialty, toast and bacon, and enjoyed a second cup of coffee as he ate and read the Orlando Sentinel to catch up on local and national news. After devouring the Sentinel, he found the novel he started three months ago but had set aside when Max's case heated up. He'd read a third of the book but had to start from the beginning because he'd forgotten most of what he'd read before.

When David next checked the time, it was almost noon. Since Carol was still in bed, David decided to check on her. The lights were out in the bedroom, and the shutters were closed. Carol rolled over in bed and opened her eyes, but only halfway as she groggily came awake. "How are you doing, honey?" David asked. He'd been concerned since Carol was not recovering quickly from yesterday's infusion and was obviously in pain.

"Not well, David. We need to talk."

"Sure. What can I do for you?" David tried to sound chipper, but he had never heard such fatigue—or despair—in Carol's voice until now.

"David, you have done as much as any husband possibly could, but now I have to ask you for even more understanding than you have already given me."

"What do you want, Carol?" David asked, wary and afraid of the answer he might get.

"David, I can't do any more chemo; I just can't.  I feel like it's killing me more than the cancer, and my body just can't take any more.  The clinical trial in Boston will have even more chemo."

David steeled himself, fearfully aware of what Carol might say next.

"I'm not going to do the clinical trial."

He knew Carol wanted him to say something, but he couldn't speak.

"David, please try to understand.  If you were in my situation, you would make the same decision."

David didn't know how to respond.  He wasn't totally surprised by Carol's statement, given what she had said from the beginning of her cancer treatments.  But now the full impact of a decision to cease any curative treatment hit him with an emotional impact that took his breath away.  When he could finally speak, all he could say was, "Carol, what will you do?"

"I'll get palliative care.  Hopefully, I'll be able to enjoy whatever time I have left with you and Jenna.  David, I don't want your last memories of me, or Jenna's last memories of me, to be me throwing up all over you and being so sick from chemo I can't even function as a human being."

David still had no words to offer.

"I know this is my decision to make, but please give me your consent.  I would do it for you if you were the one having to make this decision."

As Carol said this, David took her in his arms and held her, unable to speak.  He laid his head on her shoulder, and the entire arc of their life together flashed through his mind:  their meeting and dating in Tallahassee … the early days of their marriage at Moody Air Force Base … her support and encouragement while he was in law school at the University of Florida in Gainesville … their move to Orlando when David took the job with Smith & Bridges … Jenna's birth … Carol's delight and encouragement when David and Jesse formed Jordan & McKenzie … Carol's founding and running WCC … the daily routine of their life together.  These memories might seem unexceptional and even common to others, but to him they were rich and deeply satisfying, fulfilling his every hope and desire for marriage with this good woman.

When David could finally speak again, he pulled back slightly, looked her in the eye and through tears said, "You have my consent."

# Chapter 21

The end came quickly for Carol.  Only four weeks after she made her decision to have only palliative care, Carol passed away in her sleep one early November morning.  Although her time was short after giving up hope of a cure, her last days were full and satisfying.  The palliative drugs Dr. Marks prescribed relieved most of the pain and nausea.  She had renewed energy—not to the level she had known previously but enough to allow her to visit with and say goodbye to all her friends and family.

Carol's last days were bittersweet for David and Jenna—sad because the reality of these being the last days, they would be with her hit them anew every morning as they awoke.  Yet, the joy of being with Carol without her having overwhelming pain at the end was a gift they treasured, giving them a final opportunity to say things they had often thought but seldom verbalized to one another.  *Why do we wait to tell someone our deepest feelings for that person until the very last?*  David had no good answer, but he was grateful for this final opportunity to make up for all the unused opportunities he had wasted previously.

The funeral was set for the following Wednesday morning at All Souls Episcopal Church, with the interment of Carol's ashes to take place immediately afterward in the memorial garden on the church property.  Even the weather reflected the sadness of the occasion.  The skies were gray and overcast, with a chilly northeast wind blowing in overnight, bringing an end to the Indian summer central Florida had been enjoying for the past several weeks.

David and Jenna arrived thirty minutes before the service was to begin to meet with Father John and go over the service arrangements they had discussed. The most pressing issue was the number of people who would likely be attending. Although none of the local governments or philanthropists had been willing to commit significant funds to WCC until a new building was built, WCC remained a well-respected and highly visible local institution. As the founder and president of WCC, Carol was a well-known public figure in her own right, and she and David were widely regarded as one of the more prominent power couples in central Florida. Therefore, the high and the mighty, as well as personal friends and acquaintances, planned to pay their last respects to Carol.

"David, given the number of inquiries we've received about the service, we may have 500 people or more in attendance," explained Father John. "Our church sanctuary will only hold 250. To accommodate the overflow, we've set up a closed circuit television feed in our parish hall. As you requested, we've reserved two rows of pews for family members and your law firm. We've also reserved two rows for residents and staff of WCC in the church sanctuary. Given how well known Carol was, we hope this will be sufficient. We don't want to turn anyone away for lack of room, but you know how strict the Maitland fire marshal is."

David just nodded his approval, and Father John continued, "Have you decided whether you want to give a eulogy?" David and Jenna had discussed among themselves whether one or both of them would speak at the funeral, and they quickly decided neither of them would likely get through a eulogy without breaking down.

"Yes, Jenna and I have decided there will just be a homily by you.  We know you would include this without our asking, but please emphasize how important WCC was to Carol and especially how pleased she was that its mission will continue."

"Of course, David.  I anticipated you wouldn't be up to delivering a eulogy, so I've included some remarks about WCC and its recent funding.  I understand this information has not yet been made public, so the news will be welcomed by all who knew Carol."

Father John then turned his attention to last minute preparations for the service.  From where they currently stood, David and Jenna held each other's hand and watched the church sanctuary fill up.  David was delighted to see Max and his niece, Megan, enter the church and find a seat immediately behind the pews reserved for family.  From a distance, Megan gave no hint of a young woman who had ever had a drug problem.  She appeared confident and strong, although somewhat overwhelmed by the enormity of attending the funeral of a woman who had meant so much to her.

A few minutes later, Jesse entered the church, accompanied by Dr. Faulk.  The usher took them to the family section where they took their seats next to the spaces reserved for David and Jenna.  David found the strength to smile as he softly muttered to Jenna, "Well, well, this relationship has gone farther than I realized."

Jenna returned David's smile.  "I like him, Dad. The last time Jesse took me out for ice cream, he was with her and I got to know him a little.  I think they're good for each other."

To David, this was high praise. Jenna was young, but her assessments of people were usually spot on.

Over the next few minutes all of the other employees of Jordan & McKenzie filed into the church. Steve and Maggie came in together, followed by Sarah Garcia and Karen Overton. The office was closed today with only a voice recording advising callers the office was closed for Carol's funeral. A few minutes later, Rodrigo Alvarez and the secretaries entered together, and all were seated in the family section as David had requested.

With only five minutes left before the service was to begin, a group of mostly young women in their twenties and thirties entered the church. David immediately identified them as residents of WCC and was delighted nearly twenty of them had been able to attend the service.

Whereas the rest of the crowd was dressed in their Sunday finery, these women were dressed in somewhat tattered and out-of-style dresses. Some still had bruises on their face or neck, visible even through the attempted camouflage of heavy makeup. Although they were not stylishly dressed, there was a dignity to them. They were clean, reasonably well groomed, and carried themselves as women with newfound self-respect who were gaining confidence they could make it in this world. Their past history of drug addiction or physical abuse by a husband or other family member would no longer define who they were as women, and their carriage reflected this newfound self-knowledge. As they sat down in the pews reserved for them, David told himself, *These women are a testament to Carol's life work. There's no finer evidence she accomplished what she set out to do.*

When the time came for the service to begin, Father John led David and Jenna to the family section of pews.  Once they were seated, he took his place at the pulpit and began the liturgy for the burial of the dead, Rite Two, from the Book of Common Prayer.  Following the initial liturgy and scripture readings, Father John led a prayer that Carol's family and friends would find comfort:

"Most merciful God, whose wisdom is beyond our understanding, deal graciously with the family and friends of Carol in their grief."[4]

"Surround them with your love, that they may not be overwhelmed by their loss, but have confidence in your goodness, and strength to meet the days to come; through Jesus Christ our Lord. Amen." [5]

Despite the plea for the congregation not to be overwhelmed by their loss, a heaviness settled over the congregation as the magnitude of their loss became almost tangible.  Perhaps feeling the heaviness, Father John stepped down from the pulpit, moving closer to the congregation as he began his homily.

"Dear family and friends of Carol Jordan, we're gathered here today to celebrate her life and to commend her to Almighty God.  In my entire ministry, I don't recall meeting anyone who has had a greater impact on so many people or who has served more people in need.  Her compassion for those she served has directly impacted them, but it has also inspired others to make our community a better place by following her example of unselfish service.  So, in spite of the sadness of losing her, we are here to celebrate her life and offer our gratitude to God for the time we were privileged to know her.

"Carol was well known as the founder of the Women's Crisis Center and she shepherded it from its founding until her death.  She was its president, its head fundraiser, and its lead cheerleader.  Her load was often heavy because WCC has seldom had the necessary funds to fully carry out its mission.  Indeed, for the last six months WCC has been engaged in a fundraising campaign for a new building, without which the organization might not be able to keep its doors open."

As Father John said this, David could feel the heaviness increase, but he didn't despair. He knew what was coming next.

"I am pleased to be able to report to you today," Father John continued, "what Carol learned shortly before her death and what made her departure from this life a little easier.  A generous donor, who has asked to remain anonymous for the present, has committed to give $3.5 million— the entire construction cost—for the new building."

David anticipated that when Father John made this announcement there would be applause or some verbal reaction from the congregation.  But for nearly five seconds there was nothing but silence as the meaning of Father John's unanticipated words began to sink in.  Then, the whole congregation, as one, erupted with applause, led by the WCC women, with a few "Thank God" and "Hallelujahs" thrown in.  The applause went on for over a minute as Father John patiently waited to make his next announcement.

"One of the few conditions the donor placed on the gift is the building must be named "The Carol Jordan Women's Crisis Center."

As he completed this statement the applause erupted again, and nearly half the congregation leapt to their feet, clapping their approval.  This time the applause went on for minute and a half.

When the congregation finally settled back in their seats and calm returned, Father John continued.  "Oh, there's one more thing.  The anonymous donor has also committed $1.5 million to be used as challenge funds to encourage local governments and other donors to make matching gifts.  This should assure WCC will have sufficient funds for the foreseeable future."

At this, the entire congregation in the church and in the parish hall stood in applause, led by the high and the mighty and the other donors to WCC, who were perhaps feeling sheepish that they had refused to give generously to this worthy cause until the anonymous donor had done the heavy lifting.  Now, there were not only "Thank God" and "Hallelujahs" but foot stomping and an occasional shout or two.  The clapping, shouts of gratitude, and celebration lasted over two minutes this time.  The heaviness had lifted, replaced by the joy of renewed life and purpose, inspired by the life of the person whom they were there to celebrate.  The fact this happened in a rather staid Episcopal church better known for proceeding decently and in good order made the atmosphere even more unusual—and profound.

In the midst of the celebration, David scanned the congregation, and saw on the faces of those celebrating how much Carol had meant to them.  The WCC women were hugging each other amidst tears of happiness.  Even formerly hard-hearted Max was wiping his eyes, while Megan stood beside him, bawling with pride over what her uncle had wrought.

When things finally settled down, Father John continued his homily, speaking now to a far different congregation than the one to which he began.  Hope and the joy of life had returned, even in the midst of a celebration of the dead.

"As one philosopher once observed, 'It is not necessarily a tragedy for an old man to die at the end of his long life.' But when one so young, so full of life and so good as Carol Jordan dies, it's natural for us—we who remain—to view death as a tragedy. We ask ourselves why this has to be, why one so young, so accomplished and so beloved would have to leave us now?" It's a legitimate question and one that pricks our souls and troubles our minds.

"I have to tell you up front I don't have a completely satisfactory answer. No matter what answers I come up with, I have to acknowledge we will still feel the pain of Carol's death. Great love must bear great pain at times, no more so than when the loved one is taken by death. But I do have a few thoughts about Carol's untimely death, and its meaning. I hope these thoughts will not only bring you comfort, but also challenge you.

"First, we should acknowledge that Carol's death is a tragedy to us, not to Carol. She has gone on to a better place where she has rejoined her mother and father and waits in God's presence to see again her husband, her daughter, and her friends gathered here today. No, the tragedy is to us because we must go forward in life with a hole in our hearts where she resided. She was a wife, a mother, a good and faithful friend, a servant to those she helped, an inspiration to those whose lives she redeemed, and an example to all of us of a life well lived.

"So, why would God let such a person die so young? Again, I don't know, but I am reassured by the Psalmist who says in Psalm 116, verse fifteen, 'Precious in the sight of the Lord is the death of his faithful ones.' Carol was, without question, one of God's faithful ones. Jesus said, 'If you have done it unto one of the least of these, you have done it unto me.'[3] Carol dedicated her whole life to serving others, particularly at

WCC.  Her lifetime of service has and will continue to result in life and happiness for those she touched by her service.  Clearly, her death is precious in the sight of God.

"Second, we should realize Carol's death is a challenge to those of us who remain.  By her example, Carol has shown us what is possible if we are willing to dedicate our lives to serving others.  There are many ways to serve others, and Carol would never claim her way was the only way.  But I can think of no one else I've known who better exemplifies a true servant's heart.  She showed compassion to women and children going through perhaps the darkest days of their lives.  By her actions, she gave them hope and a way forward to regain their lives that circumstances, or their abusers, had nearly destroyed.  If we are inspired by Carol's example to do even a tenth of what she did, lives will be changed and our community will be immeasurably better.

"So, I suggest you view Carol's death, not as a tragedy, but as a challenge.  Every time you have an opportunity to help someone in need, to encourage someone suffering through a difficult time, or to make a sacrifice for the public good, think of Carol.  Imagine her challenging you to make someone's life a little better, to bind up the wounds—whether physical or emotional—life has dealt that person.  If we who remain will do this, we will honor Carol's memory in the best way possible.  And we will make this troubled world a better place.

"No, following her example won't totally take away the sting of Carol's death; we will still have to live with the emptiness in our heart her death leaves.  But there is a lesson for us even in the emptiness.  Over the past few days, I've thought about that, and I've come to a realization that should have been obvious to me before but wasn't.  I've been a minister for thirty-five years.  I've performed funeral services for the very young, the very old, and all ages in between.  What I've noticed is there are usually far fewer people at the funeral of someone who died at the end of a long full life than the number at the funeral of someone who died much younger, like Carol, at full flower of her abilities, influence, and example.  Those who die after a long life have usually outlived most of their friends, and even their most significant achievements have dimmed in the memory of those left behind.  But look around this church and the parish hall.  Both areas are full to capacity because Carol's impact on every one of us has been so great, amplified by our knowing her in the midst of our own busy lives which are so full of all the joys and challenges of life.  Therefore, her inspiration to us, and her challenge to us, is much greater now than it would be if she died peacefully at ninety-seven years old, when most of us would no longer be around.

"So, if we accept Carol's untimely death as a challenge to us to imitate her generous and unselfish spirit and to inspire us to listen to our better angels as we live out our lives, then we will truly honor her memory and bring some of the joy Carol had into our own lives. Amen."

Father John then informed the congregation the interment of Carol's ashes would take place immediately thereafter in the church's memorial garden, with only family present.  All other guests were invited to a reception at a local hotel where the guests could pay their respects to David and Jenna, and other family members, who would join them after the interment.  Father John then led those in the family section and those in the WCC section—for they also were considered family—to the memorial garden where Carol's ashes would be interred and her name added to the plaque listing all whose remains were there.

As they were gathering before Father John commenced the interment liturgy, David looked around the memorial garden.  All members of Jordan & McKenzie were there, as David requested, because they were his extended family.  All of the WCC women and staff were there because they were Carol's legacy.  Max and Megan were also there because of their connection to both David and Carol.  The presence of each of the people there brought comfort to David. The heaviness of the day had lifted, and a sense of peace came over him now that was unimaginable even earlier that same day.

Father John had David and Jenna pour Carol's ashes into the area prepared for them and then offered the prayer of commendation from the Book of Common Prayer:

"Into your hands, O merciful Savior, we commend your servant Carol.

Acknowledge, we humbly beseech you, a sheep of your own fold, a lamb of your own flock, a sinner of your own redeeming.

Receive her into the arms of your mercy, into the blessed rest of everlasting peace, and into the glorious company of the saints in light.

Amen."[6]

# Epilogue

Two weeks later, at the end of a bright, cool November Sunday, David and Jenna took a walk around the lake in front of their house. There was a brilliant sunset in progress as they headed out for the one-mile walk, and the brisk air encouraged them to keep up their pace to complete their walk before darkness fell.

"How did it feel to be back in school last week, Jenna?" David asked as they started out. He had been so occupied with other issues after Carol's funeral that he had failed to ask Jenna about school. It reminded him, once again, how difficult being a single parent would be. He'd relied on Carol for so many things that were now his sole responsibility.

"It went better than I thought it would, Dad. My classmates were very nice to me, even some of them I haven't been close to. I was afraid I would be way behind in my schoolwork, but the only class I haven't caught up with already is my Spanish class. I should be caught up in it by the end of next week. My Spanish teacher allowed me additional time before taking the latest exam, so I should be all right."

"Sounds good. When is your next outing with Jesse? She told me she plans to do something with you at least once every week, and more when her schedule permits."

"We're going to a movie next Friday … if it's okay with you. I don't want to leave you alone, but Jesse promised me it would just be us girls. After all, if she's going to give up seeing Dr. Faulk for movie night, I don't see how I can bring you along as my date," Jenna said with a smile.

"Yeah, I can see how that would be awkward," David responded with a chuckle. "Don't worry about me. I'll find a good mystery to watch on TV." David thought he would never laugh again, but Jenna's good humor was contagious.

They walked in silence for another few moments. Then Jenna stopped, turned to face David, and asked in a voice that sounded far too mature for her age, "How are you doing without Mom? I know this has been hard for you."

"It *has* been hard. But you remind me so much of your mother it's almost like she's still with us. I know that sounds silly, but it's how I feel. We'll get through this together, Jenna."

They walked a little farther in silence before Jenna stopped again. "Can I ask you something, Dad?"

"Sure, what is it?"

"You don't have to give me an answer right away, but please consider it, okay?"

"Of course, I'll consider it, Jenna." Warily, David asked again, "What is it you want me to consider?"

"Do you think we could get a dog?"

*         *         *

The next morning David returned to the office for the first time since Carol's funeral. He hadn't told Jesse or anyone else in the office when he would return, so they were understandably surprised and seemed delighted to see him when they gathered for their usual Monday noon meeting. Jesse offered to have David lead the meeting, but he declined.

"I'd like to ease back in, if you don't mind. It's going to take me at least a week to get *caught up*, as Jenna would say."

Jesse led the discussion on the new cases. "I received a telephone call this morning from a lawyer in Atlanta who wants us to represent an individual defendant in a lawsuit filed in federal court here in Orlando. I haven't seen the complaint yet, but the Atlanta attorney says it alleges our client left a company that has had an exclusive contract with the Army for the past ten years to provide virtual training environments for the Army's special forces units. Our client allegedly took certain trade secrets and proprietary software to his new employer—who was also sued—which enabled the new employer to win the competitive bidding for the contract. The plaintiff is seeking millions in damages and an injunction to prevent our client from working for the new employer. The case should keep Steve and me busy for months to come."

Since the settlement of the Max Foster case, David had felt no desire to jump back into a major case. He was so consumed with Carol's illness, death, and funeral that all thoughts of legal battles had receded almost to irrelevance in his mind. As David heard Jesse discuss her new, interesting case, however, he felt unexpected pangs of envy. *What I wouldn't give to get involved in a new, exciting case like this one. Maybe Jesse will let me help her with that case.*

As Jesse was about to wrap up the meeting, she turned to David. "Oh, I almost forgot. We received a phone call on Friday from a man who wants to meet with you as soon as possible. He's what is called a 'bird dog' in the citrus business. He arranges contracts between citrus fruit growers and processing plants for citrus concentrate. He said he represents a group of major citrus growers who are in a contract dispute with the public company that owns the processing plant where they deliver their fruit. Apparently, the dispute is over millions of dollars. Your assistant has his name and number; we told him you would call him to set up an appointment as soon as you were back in the office."

As David listened to Jesse, he felt the competitive juices begin to flow once again. Suddenly, he couldn't wait to meet the client and get immersed in what promised to be another interesting new case.

David returned to his office following the meeting and began going through the piles of mail that had accumulated during his absence. What had often seemed dull and a chore was now an enjoyable task. He was back among his extended family, and he realized this was exactly where he should be.

# ENDNOTES

1.  Pg 88  Psalm 6: 6-7   Used with permission Revised Standard Version Bible, copyright © 1989 by the Division of Christian Education of the National Council of the Churches of Christ in the United States of America.

2.  Pg 230  Psalm 115: 15 Used with permission Revised Standard Version Bible, copyright © 1989 by the Division of Christian Education of the National Council of the Churches of Christ in the United States of America.

3.  Pg 287 Psalm 116:15 Used with permission Revised Standard Version Bible, copyright © 1989 by the Division of Christian Education of the National Council of the Churches of Christ in the United States of America.

4.  Pg 283 Used with permission The Book of Common Prayer Rite II, The Book of Common Prayer and Administration of the Sacraments and Other Rites and Ceremonies of the Church:  together with the Psalter or Psalms of David According to the Use of the Episcopal Church.  New York:  Seabury Press, 1979.

5.  Pg 283 Used with permission The Book of Common Prayer Rite II, The Book of Common Prayer and Administration of the Sacraments and Other Rites and Ceremonies of the Church:  together with the Psalter or Psalms of David According to the Use of the Episcopal Church.  New York:  Seabury Press, 1979.

6.  Pg 289 Used with permission The Book of Common Prayer Rite II, The Book of Common Prayer and Administration of the Sacraments and Other Rites and Ceremonies of the Church:  together with the Psalter or Psalms of David According to the Use of the Episcopal Church.  New York:  Seabury Press, 1979.

# ABOUT THE AUTHOR

Darryl Bloodworth is a graduate of the United States Air Force Academy where he excelled academically and as an athlete.  He lettered three years in football and in baseball and was captain of the baseball team his senior year.  He served in the Air Force as a pilot and instructor pilot.  He graduated with High Honors from the University of Florida Law School and has been a trial lawyer for over 47 years.  He is a Fellow in the American College of Trial Lawyers and a former president of the Central Florida Chapter of the American Board of Trial Advocates.  He is also a former president of The Florida Bar Foundation.

www.DarrylBloodworth.com